THE LION AT BAY

THE LION AT BAY

SAM HOUSTON
BOOK THREE

ROBERT WISEHART

WOLFPACK
PUBLISHING
— EST 2013 —

The Lion at Bay
Paperback Edition
Copyright © 2025 (As Revised) by Robert Wisehart

Wolfpack Publishing
1707 E. Diana Street
Tampa, FL 33610

www.wolfpackpublishing.com

Paperback ISBN 979-8-89567-236-5
Ebook ISBN 979-8-89567-235-8

THE LION AT BAY

1

SAM HOUSTON STEPPED onto the bustling Nashville dock, took a deep breath, and inhaled the old familiar scents. It felt good to be back in Tennessee after so many years.

He hoisted his son in one arm and extended his other to Margaret as she made her way off the steamboat Victory. Escorting his wife safely to the dock, he turned to see a boy dressed in the blue-and-white livery of the Hermitage standing at his side, holding a sealed letter in one hand.

"Are you Mistah Houston?"

Houston nodded and the boy held out the letter.

"This here's for you."

He set little Sam down, gave youngster a gentle push toward Margaret, and broke the letter's wax seal:

> Sam,
>
> We hope this reaches you in time. Please come quickly. The general is dying.
>
> My regards to you and your family,

Marian Adams.

He remembered Marian well. A distant relative of the Jackson family, she'd lived at the Hermitage off and on ever since her husband's death more than fifteen years ago.

"Margaret, watch little Sam!" he ordered. "I'll be right back!"

Alarmed at the sudden change in her husband, Margaret gathered the child in her arms.

"Sam, what is it?"

Ignoring her for the moment, Houston sprinted toward a livery stable he remembered a short distance away on a side street, dodging people on the crowded street as he ran. If he hired a carriage and laid a heavy lash on the horses, he calculated that they could just make it to the Hermitage before dark.

Hearing Houston's call, a stable hand slowly rose out of the dim light of an empty stall, sour straw clinging to his filthy hair, beard, and clothes. Judging by the stink, the man was sleeping off a bad drunk.

With an indifferent shrug, the hand said there was nothing available. "Maybe in the mornin'. Cain't say fer sure, though. You'll have to take yer chances."

Scratching his behind, he turned to shuffle back into the stall. But before he could take another step, Houston grabbed his shoulder and jerked him around so they were face to face. Seizing two fistfuls of filthy shirt, Houston pulled him up close so that the man was on his toes.

"My name is Sam Houston!" he snarled into the stable hand's red face. "I am here to see Andrew Jackson, and by God you *will* find me a carriage!"

His insolence shattered like broken glass, the hand blubbered that there just might be something out back after all, now that he thought about it. It was the owner's personal carriage but Governor Houston was welcome to it. Not only that, he'd hitch up two good horses at a bargain rate. They'd be ready in no time at all.

Seeing her husband disappear into the stable, Margaret came up with little Sam just as the arrangement was consummated. Assessing the hand's red face and cowed manner, she whispered, "Oh, Sam, what have you done now?"

"It's nothing to worry about, my dear," Houston replied. "Just a little negotiation, that's all."

He told Margaret about the contents of the note and within ten minutes they were careening through the narrow Nashville streets on their way out of town.

"What about our luggage?" shouted Margaret, trying to keep from looking as terrified as she felt at her husband's hell-for-leather driving.

"The boat's purser will keep it until we send someone," he replied, bellowing over the clatter of the carriage and the delighted yelps of little Sam, who was gleeful at this new adventure after so many days of being cooped up on the steamboat.

By the time they clattered to a stop in front of the great columns of the Hermitage, the lathered horses were wheezing in agony and red froth bubbled from their mouths and nostrils. The horseman in Houston subconsciously noted that they'd be worthless for weeks.

Houston vaulted out of the carriage and ran up the verandah to the wide double doors, where a house slave opened the doors. The old man wordlessly nodded toward a downstairs bedroom, his furrowed black cheeks wet with tears.

Houston handed his broad-brimmed hat to the slave and walked past the old sofa of woven horsehair in the entry hall where he remembered that Jackson liked to take his post-dinner naps. He eased through the bedroom doorway,

3

suddenly conscious of the sweat and dust from the wild ride. A silent cluster of people hovered around a big feather bed. He probably knew most of them but none of the faces registered. All he saw was Andrew Jackson, his friend and mentor for more than thirty years. Jackson's eyes were closed and he was in a half-sitting position, his upper body supported by thick pillows and his shock of white hair spread out around his long leathery face. The outline of his body under the blankets was shockingly small.

Someone, Houston didn't know who, said, "It's over, less than an hour ago."

Houston's heart turned to stone. With a choking cry, he fell to his knees and put his head on Jackson's skinny chest while his own body shook with grief.

After a few minutes, it came to him that the general would not approve. The thought helped him regain control. He rose to his feet and turned to Margaret and little Sam, who were standing hesitantly in the doorway, not sure whether to go or stay. He reached out one hand and gently motioned his son to his side. The shy boy lurched forward and Houston picked him up.

Eyes filled with tears, Houston looked down at the man he loved and followed for so long.

"My son, always remember this moment," he said. "You have looked upon the face of the greatest man who ever lived."

Houston wordlessly handed the boy back to Margaret and stepped outside to the cool of the spacious verandah. A few rays of the dying sun weakly filtered through the trees. He shut his eyes and leaned his forehead against one of the white columns, trying to accept the impossible.

Andrew Jackson was a sick man. Everyone knew it. But it didn't seem that he could ever die. It had been six years since Houston last saw the general. He'd looked forward to introducing Jackson to his wife and child. The old man always loved children. He would have adored Margaret and little Sam. If only they got here sooner. If only they didn't linger in New Orleans so he could give another damned speech. If only the steamboat didn't run up on a sandbar north of Vicksburg and delay them a full day. If only...

He felt a touch on his shoulder. It was Marian Adams. Time had been kind to her. While never a beauty, now, well into her forties and with hair turned gray, she was more attractive now than when they first met.

"He was ready, Sam." Her quavering voice cut into his heart. "There was no pain at the end. He knew it was time. I can't explain it exactly, but the fire was gone."

She stared off into the trees surrounding the great house in the distance. One large glistening tear coursed slowly down her cheek.

Houston felt as if his chest might burst open from the hurt. He couldn't imagine a world without Andrew Jackson in it.

"At least he'll be with Aunt Rachel now," he said, drawing Marian close as they held each other in grief.

That night, after helping Margaret and their tired son settle in their room, Houston explained that he had one last duty to perform for the man he followed for so long. In Jackson's library, sitting at the old walnut desk, he wrote the most difficult letter of his life to Jimmy Polk - President James Knox Polk now - with the sad news that their friend and mentor was dead:

Mister President,

It is in deep sorrow that I address to you this hasty note. On this day General Jackson departed this life. Like you, I was denied the satisfaction of seeing the general in his last moments by the delays in the long journey from Texas. I will always regret that I was unable to offer some comfort in the closing

*scene of his glorious life. A great man is gone, and a great part
of our lives passes with him.*

*Your servant,
Sam Houston*

He tried going to bed but he couldn't sleep. He could tell
that Margaret was awake beside him but she had the sense not
to say anything. She always felt his moods and knew when he
needed to talk and when he needed silence.

He slid out of bed and threw on his clothes. At first, he
wandered quietly through the house, stopping at the familiar
items and furnishings: the pair of hand-carved chairs given to
Jackson by the Khedive of Egypt; the marble-topped table
Jackson used to write his orders for the Battle of New
Orleans; the comfortable leather chair, a gift from Supreme
Court Chief Justice Roger Taney; Jackson's precious book
collection, neatly organized in cherry wood bookcases. He
tenderly pulled out a book of poems by Robert Burns. He
remembered the day Jackson gave it to his beloved wife,
Rachel, on her birthday.

After a few minutes, he went outside to walk the grounds
just as he did so many times as a young man searching for his
place in the world. Mortality seemed heavy in the air, hanging
like moss from the branches of the big old trees. They were all
dead now. Jackson had finally joined Rachel, his love of so
many years. Jackson's devoted friend John Overton, the
kindest of men who helped young Sam Houston in ways
beyond measure, died more than ten years ago. Drum, Houston's Cherokee father, was gone, too. Poor Tiana, his
Cherokee bride whose love sustained him during the darkest
time of his life, died of the fever seven years ago. Tiana
deserved better from him and he knew it, a hard thing that
never entirely left him.

The old friends and old loves illuminating the long and winding path of his life were dying out. He'd never thought much about growing old. But now, at fifty two, he felt like a relic of another time.

A great man had died. Houston couldn't help feeling that a great age had died, too.

Sweet Jesus, the general was gone.

2

AFTER TEN YEARS OF STRUGGLE, the on-off-and-on effort to shepherd the Republic of Texas into the United States seemed hopelessly stalled. But suddenly events steamed forward with new energy and purpose. Houston knew better, but he couldn't shake the feeling that Jackson's death was behind it.

"It's as if he's still makin' things happen," he explained, grinning at the preposterous thought. "I can just see him at the right hand of God, impatient as ever and sure he could do it faster and better if God would only have the sense to get out of the way."

"Sam Houston! Don't you be blasphemous!" Margaret was genuinely shocked by her husband's offhand way of putting God and Andrew Jackson on equal terms. "I won't have it, not even from you."

Traveling by easy stages on their way back home to Texas from Nashville, they were lazing the heart out of the day on the front porch of a two-story whitewashed house in Marion, Alabama, trying to catch what breeze there was on a sticky summer afternoon. The house, one of several gracious homes on the comfortable tree-lined street, belonged to Margaret's

8

brother, Henry Lea. Lea and his wife had taken little Sam down to Mobile with their own children and wouldn't be back for a few days. Margaret sipped a glass of lemonade on the gently swaying porch swing, her legs curled up beneath her skirts. Houston sat on a stool beside the swing, occasionally giving it a light push with one hand.

He was thirsty, but drank nothing. Margaret not only disapproved of his lifetime habit of hard drinking, she disapproved of alcohol in any form so he rarely drank around her. Despite the heat, he stubbornly decided that if he couldn't have a whiskey or a beer, then he wouldn't have anything at all. Yes, he knew that he was being stubborn, but a man had a right to be stubborn.

Most of the time, Margaret had a playful sense of humor that he loved. But when it came to religion and all its cumbersome rules, she could be downright grim. At those moments, he saw too much of her mother in her and the thought made him wince. A scolding, parsimonious nag, the sound of Nancy Lea's screeching voice could turn honey into vinegar. Five feet tall and round as a ball, she was a whining hypochondriac who claimed to be forever on the verge of death. Good God! The woman even had her coffin ready and waiting. Every so often she laboriously climbed in to make sure it still fit.

Although the widow Lea kept her own home, she lived with them more often than not. Houston was away so much that Margaret needed help to run the household, the small farm, and the other property that always seemed to demand more money than he made from his law practice. His long retreat from Santa Anna's superior numbers before the final decisive battle San Jacinto paled in comparison to his constant withdrawals in the face of his mother-in-law. After three marriages, he'd learned that silent was often the best thing a husband could be. His first marriage, to Eliza Allen, lasted just two months and the scandal drove him out of

Tennessee. His second wife, the Cherokee widow Tiana Rogers, tried her best to soothe his tormented soul, suffering patiently through his drinking and black moods. He left her at the Wigwam, their sad little trading post, with the promise he'd come back or send for her one day. He never did. He heard that Tiana remarried, but it did not go well. Every time he thought about her he felt a thickness in his throat.

Nancy Lea was no doubt terrorizing east Texas this very minute. She'd talked about buying a promising section of land near Austin, but Houston couldn't imagine the penny-pinching crone letting go of the money. In his well-known opinion, Austin wasn't worth it anyway; a no-account shanty-town so far from most of the rest of Texas' population that the Comanches boldly raided up to the town limits. It was a poor place for a capital, but he couldn't convince anyone else to see it.

Who knows? If his mother-in-law did go to Austin maybe the Comanches got her? The thought made him positively cheerful.

"Sam, do you remember the first time I saw you?" Margaret asked, interrupting his meandering, self-absorbed thoughts.

She impishly ruffled his chestnut hair with one small hand, although there wasn't quite as much hair to ruffle these days. Considerable gray in it, too.

Margaret loved these moments when she had him all to herself. They didn't come often. With his law practice, his two terms as President of the Republic, and one crisis after another, it always seemed as if her husband was just back from somewhere, about to leave for somewhere else, or gone altogether. The man just couldn't stay still, at least not for long. It made a hard and lonely life sometimes, although she tried not to let him see it.

"I cut a poor figure that day," he admitted.

"Oh, you were a dreadful sight." Her pert nose twitched at the memory. "I was just a girl then and the great Sam Houston, conqueror of the Mexican horde, wasn't what I expected."

"At that moment, I wasn't what anyone expected, except perhaps the Grim Reaper," he laughed. "Your future husband almost died before you met him."

At San Jacinto, a Mexican musket ball shattered his leg just above the ankle. Once the fight was over and his berserk army amused itself by slaughtering the helpless, Houston was laid under a tree and his bloody boot cut off so the doctor could remove the largest of the bone splinters.

They found Santa Anna the next day, lost and whimpering from fear and hunger. Shocked at the sight of his invincible army being cut to pieces, *El Presidente* ran from the battlefield in a blind panic. Unfortunately for the self-proclaimed "Napoleon of the West," he helplessly floundered in the marsh until two scouts found him and hauled him back to camp, not knowing what they'd found.

Laying in the shade of the big tree, Houston ordered a guard to protect the mud-splattered dictator and make sure that the hotheads still in a rage over the massacres at the Alamo and Goliad didn't lynch the frightened man. If they killed him, Santa Anna would be just another dead Mexican, and they already had plenty of those. Houston needed a live dictator to make this peace stick. He had uses for *El Presidente*.

Three days later, as the army moved up the bayou to get away from the stench of the bloated and rotting corpses, who should show up but David Burnet, President of the Republic of Texas. As usual, Burnet, who resembled a bilious pigeon, was intent on seizing as much credit as possible for something in which he played no part. With Santa Anna beaten, he'd stopped running and suddenly transformed into the greatest military mind in the country, not to mention the bravest. To be fair, before San Jacinto the army did its share of running, too. If they hadn't turned to fight when they did, Houston knew that he might have lost control of his men. Some still claimed that the army led its general to the fight, not the other way around. The lie grated, but there wasn't anything he could do about it

The newly arrived Burnet had the gall to complain that San Jacinto wasn't enough, as if more than a thousand Mexicans killed, wounded, and captured against fewer than forty casualties didn't matter. The army was disorganized, its general crippled, and its officers fighting among themselves. Nevertheless, Burnet demanded that Houston move out, find the armies led by Filosola and Urrea, and beat them, too.

The days passed in a blur. Houston ignored Burnet, worked out terms with Santa Anna, nursed his leg, found a way to feed his starving men, and fended off dozens of outraged citizens demanding the impossible, the ridiculous, and the stupid.

He remembered one in particular. "I believe I told you about her, Margaret," he said. "Her name was Peggy McCormick, the Irish widow who owned the land where we fought."

"I've met the lady." Margaret took a sip of her lemonade and crinkled her nose in disapproval. "She's filthy, chews tobacco, drinks whiskey straight from the bottle, and swears worse than most men."

"That's our girl," smiled Houston. "She marched up bold as you please and demanded that I get 'them stinkin' Mexicans' off her property. Not that I blamed her. There were hundreds of corpses. The little lake - the one they call Peggy's Lake now - was so full of 'em you could walk across on the bodies. I tried to put her off by tellin' her that one day this spot would be celebrated in history, but she wasn't havin' any of that. 'To hell with your damn history,' she said. 'Get rid of them stinkin' Mexicans!' She didn't mind the smell, you understand.

They didn't smell much worse than she did. She was afraid the cadavers might come back and haunt her land. I've heard that she's held a séance or two since then to cut down on the ghostly traffic."

The best of the army's three doctors, a red-haired Scot named Alexander Ewing, warned Houston that if he didn't go to New Orleans for proper treatment he'd likely lose his leg. With Burnet and his cabinet, plus Santa Anna and the dictator's small staff, Houston was carried on board the Yellowstone, a small steamboat on its way to Galveston.

By coincidence, the warship Liberty, which was exactly one-half of the Texas navy, was leaving Galveston for New Orleans when they chugged into port. But Burnet, who'd long resented the sting of Houston's sarcasm, refused to let him board.

"I'm afraid there's no more room." Houston still remembered the pompous blowhard's smirk. "I'll send another boat shortly."

He wanted to break Burnet's fat head open like a melon. But when he tried to rise, he was too light-headed to stand, although it was satisfying to see Burnet jump.

With the faithful Ewing, Houston found passage on the Flora, a tiny coastal schooner that resembled a floating manure pile, but only after he pledged one league of his Texas land as payment to the captain. As usual, the government hadn't paid him in months and he had no money.

With news of the remarkable victory at San Jacinto traveling faster than the Flora, when the schooner sailed into New Orleans eleven days later, the wharf was jammed with hundreds of people eager to get a look at the hero of the hour.

"I was part of that mob, a naïve schoolgirl from Mobile visiting relatives," Margaret recalled, brushing a strand of dark hair out of her face. "You were *quite* the hero. All I wanted was a glimpse of the great man."

Houston bowed to his wife as best he could while sitting on his stool. Talking about the wound made his leg hurt. He'd suffered so many wounds in his life that his big body was a network of scars. Besides the leg shattered at San Jacinto, his right shoulder and upper arm were badly shot up at Horse-shoe Bend. He took a barbed arrow in the thigh at the same battle, where Jackson broke the power of the Creek Indians more than thirty years ago.

With luck, there'd be no more wars to fight, he thought. Good thing, too. He was running out of pieces.

"When the crowd started to cheer and call your name, they propped you up so we could see you," Margaret continued. "You tried to say something but all that came out was a pathetic croak. It was *awful*. You were barefoot, dirty, and so weak you barely kept your head up. You didn't even have a shirt on underneath your coat."

"A hard appearance for a man who appreciates fine cloth-ing," admitted Houston. "They'd used my shirt for bandages and cut my boot off to treat my leg. They cut part of my pants leg off, too. I was barely decent."

"It took three men to hold you up," she said, giving her husband's rough hand a fond squeeze. "You were in such a bad way I wanted to cry. I'll never forget the awful gasp from the crowd. When you fainted they took you away on a stretcher. It was a dramatic entrance, I must say."

"I always try to make a memorable first impression," Houston responded, flashing a smile.

They carried him to the home of Doctor William Christy on Girod Street in the *Vieux Carre*. With both of the major bones in his lower leg shattered, the wound had the faint but unmistakable smell of gangrene. After removing more than twenty splinters of bone, Christy did what he could to repair the shredded muscles. If Houston didn't tell them that he'd rather die than live as a one-legged cripple, they might have cut off his leg.

At Houston's insistence, the physicians placed maggots in the wound, a treatment he learned from the Cherokee when he lived with them as a boy. The maggots ate the rotting flesh and kept the gangrene from spreading. He not only kept his leg, but was back on his feet before anyone thought possible, although he'd always walk with a slight limp. The leg pained him sometimes, too, especially with bad weather on the way.

"My poor husband, so many scars." She ran her hand along his cheek. "You know, you're still the handsomest man I've ever seen, scars and all."

It occurred to Houston that they were alone. Even with their many separations over the years, his desire for Margaret was strong as ever. They met three years after she first saw him on the Flora. Her sister introduced them when he passed through Mobile on a horse-buying trip for the Texas government. He knew that she was special from the moment he saw her. With eyes of such a deep blue they sometimes seemed violet, her hair was light brown with a few streaks of gold around her forehead.

That afternoon, Houston accepted an invitation to attend a strawberry festival with her family. He didn't give a damn about strawberries, but didn't want Margaret out of his sight. At the festival, he found some pink carnations growing in the garden, carefully picked one and presented it to her with a flourish.

"A pink carnation for the sweetest rose of Alabama," he said, hoping that he didn't sound as idiotic as he felt.

Houston knew he said the right thing when she smiled and put the carnation in her hair.

As Houston was introduced around the festival, he was separated from Margaret and quickly grew bored. She caught him pouring a bottle of rum into the punch, led him away by the hand, and scolded him for a good ten minutes. He didn't mind. By then, he'd do anything to keep her near.

They married a year later, much against her mother's wishes, the bitch. He was forty-seven and she was twenty-one. To be fair, everyone he knew thought the marriage was a terrible idea.

"If ever a man was *not* meant to be married it's you," warned his friend Bernard Bee, a rising political star but a poor judge of happiness in marriage. "Look at your history, not to mention your habits! It'll be calamity for both of you."

Bee didn't understand. None of them did. He needed Margaret. Even when they weren't together, he needed to know she was there. In a life that was anything but tranquil, he needed something to hold on to, and that something was her.

And he wanted her now. He rose to his feet and took her small hand in his. He drew her to her feet, held her close so he felt her lush body along the length of his own, and kissed her long and passionately.

Sighing, "Maggie," his pet name for her, he looked down into the dark pools of her eyes and saw eager consent. Holding each other, they moved toward the door leading into the house.

As they stepped through the doorway, Margaret heard a sound and glanced over her shoulder toward the street.

With a gasp, she said, "Oh, my goodness, that's Ash Smith."

3

ASHBEL SMITH WAS a Connecticut Yankee with a Yale medical degree who'd also taken honors in Greek and Latin classics, which made him the most learned man Houston knew. Not the least of Smith's virtues was a trick where he simultaneously wrote Greek with one hand and Latin with the other.

His family was rumored to be wealthy, although, like everyone in Texas, he was cash poor. Everybody made do with whatever they got their hands on. The currency was a hodgepodge of Texas red-backs, American dollars, Mexican pesos, English pounds, German marks, French francs, and barter, mostly involving livestock or land, the most abundant thing in Texas. Land was so plentiful sometimes people didn't attach much value to it. Years back, Houston watched a Kentuckian named Alphonso Steele trade five-hundred acres for a ragged mongrel dog with part of one ear chewed off. If the dog had both ears, it might have cost Steele another five hundred.

But Smith was never so cash poor that he wasn't generous. The two men shared a cabin before Houston married

Margaret, and Smith loaned Houston two hundred and fifty dollars to attend his own wedding in Alabama. Later, when Houston tried to pay him back, Smith refused the money and claimed that it was always intended as a wedding present. They both knew better.

Although they disagreed on everything from politics to women, Houston enjoyed Smith's company and trusted him without question. Ash Smith was his friend, it was that simple. Houston knew himself to be a man with hundreds of acquaintances, but not many friends. He learned a long time ago that a man was lucky if he had three or four close friends over a lifetime.

Smith dismounted and fondly patted his horse's neck. He opened the gate in the picket fence and walked up the flag-stones to the whitewashed porch.

Surprise written all over her face, Margaret offered her hand. Smith, whose hair and carefully trimmed mustache and goatee were prematurely silver, took it, bowed and gently kissed it.

"Margaret, you're more beautiful than ever," he said. "If ever you feel the need to leave your disreputable husband and move up, I'm at your service."

Margaret laughed, her eyes dancing. Only Ash Smith could talk to her that way. She enjoyed the teasing relationship they'd built over the years.

"Ash, you're a fine one to talk about disreputable," she said.

"And Sam," Smith said, reaching out to shake Houston's hand, "you look well."

"As do you, Ash," Houston replied with a grin. "As do you."

It occurred to Margaret that her husband expected Smith. She felt like a dunce for not realizing it when he rode up. How did he know they were here without Sam getting word to him that they would *be* here?

"You knew he was coming, didn't you?"

"Well, maybe not at this *exact* moment," Houston growled, his eyes still hard from wanting her. "My friend the doctor has mighty poor timing."

Margaret felt her face grow warm and knew that she was blushing. Worse, Smith would guess the reason. Under the circumstances, the only thing to do was to retreat with all flags flying.

"Well don't you flatter yourself, *Mister* Houston!" she said. "I wouldn't be *quite* so sure of myself if I were you!"

She hitched up her skirts and sashayed through the door into the house, pleased at her recovery.

With Margaret safely out of earshot, the two old friends laughed at her embarrassment.

"I see marriage still agrees with you," observed Smith.

"Yes, yes, it does, by God."

"Mind walking a bit?" Smith asked. "I've been on the road a while. It'd feel good to work out the knots."

They strolled out through the gate to the hot dusty street, staying in the shade of the oak trees when they could. Smith reached into an inside coat pocket and produced a flask covered with finely worked silver filigree. He offered it to Houston, who accepted gratefully, taking a long swallow of what he discovered to be excellent brandy.

"Thank you, Ash," he said, wiping his mouth with the back of his hand. "I needed that. Margaret wields a heavy hand. I haven't had a drink in weeks. Tell me, how are things back home?"

"Chaos, as usual." Smith said cheerfully. "Getting worse, too."

"You know, I suppose any new territory is bound to be invaded by a class of noisy, second-rate blowhards clamoring for some damned foolishness or another," mused Houston.

"But I swear there are times when Texas seems absolutely overrun by that sort. I'll never understand..."

"We need you back," Smith interrupted. "Odds are that annexation will go through. There's even a referendum set to ratify a state constitution. But the French and British will do anything to keep us out of the Union and they're applyin' some heavy pressure. Even Mexico's makin' pleasant noises. It's terrified at the notion of havin' the United States on its border. After all these years, it finally offered to officially recognize Texas as a free and independent country. The concessions we'd get from France, the British, and Mexico for stayin' independent are so temptin' that some of the leadership is startin' to wonder if annexation might be the wrong way to go, after all. They figure we've come this far, maybe we should continue to stand on our own? It's a small group, but it's noisy and needs to be squelched."

They walked awhile. Houston accepted another drink, and Smith took one of his own.

"And how's Anson, *President* Jones, holdin' up durin' all this?" Houston asked.

Smith replied with an impatient snort. "He's like a spinster with three or four suitors who doesn't know what to do with any of them. I just hope that when his head stops turnin' his face is to the front again."

Amused by the description, Houston confessed, "I never imagined that Anson was such a leaky vessel. Give him an order and he'll see it through right enough. He just never should have been President. He's not a bad man; he's just not good enough."

Houston pulverized a hard clod of Alabama dirt with an impatient kick from his boot.

"I thought Burnet was bad. Hell, I *know* Burnet was bad. My successor, the dashing Maribeau Buonaparte Lamar, spendthrift and bad poet, was no bargain either. He left us so badly in debt I thought we'd drown in it. But in his way Jones might be worse. At a time when we need leadership, the man misplaced his spine."

"Sam, you're makin' my argument for me," Smith said. "It's time to come back. Not everybody likes you, but no one back home else carries the weight you do."

Margaret would not be pleased. Houston knew that much. She'd enjoyed their travels, the most time they'd spent together since they were married. Jumping back into the maelstrom would be hard on her, but there wasn't any other choice. He had to do it.

He caught himself, amused at his duplicity. At least be honest with yourself, he thought. Even if there was another choice, he wouldn't take it. He simply *must* see Texas into the Union. It was his dream, and Jackson's dream, too. Then there was his considerable vanity. He just couldn't stay away from the center of things for long. There was no sense pretending different.

"Who for our first governor, do you think?" Houston asked. "And don't say me. We need a man who satisfies everybody, or close to it."

Smith thought for a moment. "Ed Burleson?"

"Good God, no!" exploded Houston. "I'd rather have Jones."

"Burnet?"

"Now I *know* you're joking. Did you know he challenged me to a duel once?"

Smith chuckled to show that he wasn't serious. He enjoyed teasing his large friend. It was so easy to get him riled up.

"That doesn't exactly put him in an exclusive crowd," he said. "I'm one of the few who haven't challenged you. I'm startin' to feel left out."

It happened during Houston's campaign for a second term as President. He ran against Burnet, who wanted another term of his own. As usual, the invective was ugly. When Burnet, always self-conscious about his short stature, issued the challenge, Houston archly replied that he did not fight downhill. It humiliated Burnet more than if he'd fought and lost.

"It was damn peculiar," Houston recalled. "I called that man a fraud, a coward, a drunk, and a hypocrite. I said he was a moral leper and a scoundrel. But he didn't challenge me until I called him a hog thief, which might have been insultin' to hog thieves. I'm surprised one of *them* didn't challenge me."

Without speaking, they turned around and headed back to the white-washed house.

"I'm thinkin' of Pinckney Henderson," Houston said. "Pink's not brilliant, but he's steady."

"Did you know Pink was the one talked me into comin' to Texas back in '37?" Smith asked.

"Is that so?" Houston joked. "I won't hold it against him."

"And our senators?" Smith asked. "The legislature'll pick 'em, of course."

"What about you?" Houston asked. "How does Senator Smith sound?"

A scowl crossed Smith's tanned face. "Terrible, is how it sounds. I'm a doctor, not a politician, or a damn fool."

"Tom Rusk?"

"A little high strung, but he'd likely grow into the office and do no harm while he's at it."

"What about the other one?" asked Houston.

"You?" asked Smith.

"Yes," Houston said. "Me."

"I thought so." Smith nodded.

They walked a little further.

"Does Margaret suspect any of this?" Smith asked, nodding toward the house. "I can tell it's been on your mind for a while."

22

"Good God, no," Houston said. "She won't like it at all, not one bit."

"When are you goin' to tell her?" Smith asked.

"Not for a while," Houston said. "A man's got to build up to these things."

4

L<small>IEUTENANT</small> P<small>ERCIVAL</small> M<small>OUND</small> was not a happy man.

Most of the time, his duties as President Polk's secretary were congenial enough. It gave the ambitious young officer every opportunity to meet the celebrated and powerful, exactly what he intended when his influential family pulled the strings that got him the assignment. But he didn't count on Polk's non-stop work habits. Not only did it wear Mound out, it cut deeply into his social life. Why be at the center of power if he couldn't flaunt it in public and use it to his advantage?

Feeling under-appreciated, overworked, and irritable from lack of sleep, Mound looked into the small mirror hanging on the wall in his tiny room and sourly reflected that at least the bags under his eyes added character. Only twenty-four, like most young men he took himself too seriously. His wheat-colored hair, blue eyes, and sharp handsome features combined with bustling self-importance to give him the appearance of a dashing young officer on his way up, which was exactly how he saw himself.

What he was on the way up *to* he did not yet know, but he

was sure that he would discover it in time. As he liked to say, anything is possible in a world where carpenters are resurrected and a plodder like Polk becomes President.

For now, Mound's eyes felt gritty, his head throbbed, and all he wanted was sleep. As usual, he began work at six a.m. only to find the President already hard at it. Sixteen hours later Mound decided that he'd had enough. Leaving the indefatigable Polk at his desk, the weary lieutenant retired to his room off the main hall of the President's House.

As Mound sat on his bed and tugged off his boots, he heard a timid knock at the door.

"Damn you!" he shouted, knowing it was one of the servants. "Can't a man have some peace?"

"Sir, I'm sorry to bother you, but the President has a visitor."

Mound recognized the voice, but couldn't remember the name. It was impossible to keep all their names straight.

"At *this* hour? Tell the madman to go away and come back tomorrow."

Remembering Polk's insane work ethic, he caught himself. It might be someone important.

"Wait! Do you know who it is?"

"No, sir. Perhaps you should see for yourself."

In his stocking feet, Mound shuffled to the door. He opened it just enough to peek down the hallway to the entrance off the north portico. He saw a big, rugged-looking man dressed in a rich black velvet suit with a cape of the same material lined with white satin. He wore a crimson sash around his waist, a ruffled white shirt, and black boots with silver spurs. The broad-brimmed hat in his hand was topped with what appeared to be a white egret feather.

"Who is this peacock?" Mound muttered, reluctantly tugging on his boots.

In a few moments, crackling with an air of disdainful effi-
ciency, Mound confronted the colorfully dressed visitor.

"Well, what do you want?" he asked impatiently, taking a
closer look at the colorful apparition.

Whoever he was, the man radiated power, not so much
physical strength as force of personality. The face was broad
and weathered, with a network of wrinkles around the crisp
gray eyes. The graying chestnut hair was thinning, but still
thick and curling around his ears. Under his arm, he carried a
slim walking stick with a gold head in the shape of an eagle.

"I have an appointment with the President," he said.

"I'm sorry, but he's retired for the night," Mound
announced, assuming that would end the conversation.

Incredibly, it didn't.

"Son, I've known Jimmy Polk for longer than you've been
alive and I doubt that very much," the man said. "He's
expectin' me, so why don't you just run along and tell him I'm
here?"

Mound bristled at being told to "run along." He didn't like
being called "son" either. But something about the man made
him hesitate. Instead of losing his temper, he decided sarcasm
was safer.

"And *who* should I saw is calling, *if* I may be so bold?"

Instead taking offense or snapping in return, the big man
seemed amused.

"Tell Jimmy that Sam Houston is calling, or trying to."

Mound gaped. Mound knew that Houston was in Washington to take his place in the Senate, but he didn't know
about any meeting with the President. His ignorance was
nettlesome. It was his job to be aware of what the President
did every minute of the day, which was easy enough considering that Mound made most of the appointments. Because he
controlled access to the President, indirectly, at least, it made

him one of the most powerful men in Washington, not that it did him much good. Power unused is no power at all.

Being from Tennessee, Mound was raised on stories of Sam Houston: war hero, congressman, governor, and protégé of Andrew Jackson, the state's patron saint. Adopted by the Cherokee as a boy and a hero of the Creek Indian War, Houston was run out of the state after a scandalous marriage and went west to live with the Cherokee again, where it was rumored that he took another wife and fell into the bottle. Three years later, he dramatically returned to Washington and practically beat to death a congressman named Stanbery for insults spoken on the House floor. After a trial that captivated the country, he escaped with a mild reprove, really more of a triumph than a penalty. Houston went to Texas, almost certainly as Jackson's unofficial agent, defeated the Mexicans, was twice elected President of that rowdy republic, and now represented the nation's newest state in the United States Senate. Controversial, larger than life, and improbably resilient, he seemed capable of anything.

And now the legend stood before him in the flesh.

Mound realized that he was staring.

"I'm sorry, Senator," he stammered. "I didn't know. I'm..."

"Of course you didn't know, son," Houston said, soothing the rattled young man. "That's the point. No one is supposed to know. Jimmy and I would appreciate it if you didn't babble it about."

Houston waited, but Mound didn't move. He looked as if he was dazed by a blow on the head.

"Why don't you tell him I've arrived," urged Houston, holding back a smile.

"Yes, sir, I mean Senator. I'll take care of it myself."

Backing down the long hallway to the staircase leading to Polk's private office on the second floor was awkward, but

ROBERT WISEHART

Mound thought that he pulled it off with as much dignity as possible.

5

JAMES KNOX POLK hadn't changed. He looked older, of course, but still the same man Houston had known for more than twenty five years.

While he always respected Polk, and they often worked together in the old days, he never succeeded in liking him more than he had to. For one thing, Polk was the most utterly serious man Houston had ever known; the hardest working, too. Politics was his religion, his liquor, and his love. A year or two younger than Houston, Polk more or less followed his tracks. When Houston was elected governor, Polk won Houston's old spot in Congress. A few years after Houston left Tennessee, Polk was elected Governor.

He married well, to the vivacious, dark-haired Sarah Childress. Houston never understood what she saw in Polk, but there was no accounting for what some women saw in some men, or what some men saw in some women.

The President briskly stepped out from behind his desk to shake his visitor's hand. Polk's most prominent feature was the dark recessed eyes in a nearly square head. His light brown hair was swept back and fell over his collar

Polk looked Houston up and down. "Senator, I see that you're underdressed, as usual. It's been a long time."

"More years than I care to count, Jimmy...excuse me, Mr. President."

The slip was intended. Houston wanted to remind Polk of their history. Until he left Tennessee, crushed by scandal, it was Houston's star that shined brightest. Despite the popular nonsense about Polk being called "Little Hickory" after Jackson's "Old Hickory," Houston was closer to the general and they both knew it.

"When did you arrive in Washington?" Polk asked.

"This mornin'. I checked into Brown's Hotel, found your message waitin', and here I am. I take my place in the Senate tomorrow."

"I know," Polk said. "I thought it best that we talk as soon as possible."

The President returned to his big leather chair and waved Houston to a much less comfortable chair on the other side of a messy desk piled high with papers and documents. An awkward silence filled the room as they settled in. Polk was never comfortable with small talk and Houston didn't intend to help him. He had no idea why the President called him here. Although they were old friends, and Polk helped defend him with energy and ability during Houston's trial for beating Stanbery, they were never particularly close. He wanted the other man to make the first move.

"I hear you're to be a father again," Polk said, finally discovering something to talk about as he labored like a man crossing a muddy, plowed field. "Your second, I believe."

Houston nodded. How did Polk know already? Margaret told him just two week's before he left for Washington. She'd planned to come with him, but, with a baby on the way, the long trip to Galveston, across the Gulf to New Orleans, up the Mississippi to the Ohio, east to Pittsburgh, followed by coach to Washington might be too much for a woman in her condition. He missed her already.

"Senator...Sam, have you ever thought about how things might have been different? It could easily be you in my place."

Yes, he *had* thought about it. Houston couldn't help but compare this massive house to the shabby two-room cabin with the hard-packed dirt floor that served as his residence during his first term as President of the Republic. Washington still wasn't much of a city, surrounded by swamp and overrun by bad weather, mosquitoes, and wandering livestock. But it was much bigger than he remembered and growing fast, certainly more of a city than anything Texas had to offer.

"I *have* thought about it and I won't deny it," Houston replied, breaking another uncomfortable silence. "But it doesn't matter now, does it? You're the President and I'm not and that's the simple truth."

Polk visibly relaxed. He leaned back in his chair, seeming to be satisfied by the answer.

They talked about how pleasing it was that so many of Jackson's men were doing so well. One, James Buchanan, was Polk's Secretary of State, although Houston thought it a poor choice. When it came time to make hard decisions, he doubted that Buchanan could make them. The Senate was full of old friends. Old foes, too. The power in Washington hadn't changed much over the years. Henry Clay, the unpredictable Kentuckian who ran against Jackson back in '24, and then ran against Polk twenty years later, remained one of the most powerful men in Congress. The same for that old wine sack Daniel Webster, still a glorious orator on those occasions when he was sober. John Calhoun, the hatchet-faced South Carolinian who once threatened to court-martial young Lieutenant Houston, still blew that tired old trumpet of state's rights in the Senate. Missouri Senator Thomas Hart Benton, an old friend and ally, was the most powerful politician in the West.

And there was plenty of time left in his own political life, Houston reflected. Polk might not be here long. During the campaign against Clay, he made the astonishing promise to serve only one term, although Houston didn't believe it. It was too hard to give up power once a man held it in his hands.

"Jefferson Davis is in the Senate now, too," Polk said. "I believe you know him."

With a dismissive wave of his hand, Houston replied, "I know Davis, but we're hardly friends. He's as cold as a lizard and as ambitious as Lucifer. To be fair, he thinks even less of me than I do of him. Did you ever hear how we met?"

Polk shook his head, obviously relieved to have Houston carry the conversation.

"It was out at Fort Gibson, in those days the most godfor-saken outpost in the country," Houston recalled. "Davis was on temporary assignment. My little tradin' post wasn't far away and I sometimes stayed at the fort for a day or two. I was in my cups one evenin', woke up in the middle of the night, and wandered outside buck naked to take a piss."

Polk winced at Houston's earthy expression, which was the reason Houston used it. For no particular reason, he wanted to keep Polk off balance, a test of strength between two sometime friends and sometime rivals who hadn't seen each other in years.

"In my, ah, *confused* state I lost my sense of direction, wandered into Davis' tent, and crawled in with him," Houston continued. "He squealed like a stuck pig. One way or another, he's been squealin' about me ever since."

Polk laughed mirthlessly, not because he thought it was funny, but because he knew that he was supposed to find it amusing.

"You'll be happy to know that my drinkin' to excess is a

thing of the past," Houston said. "My wife, Margaret, taught me the virtue of moderation."

"That reminds me, may I offer you a libation?" Polk asked. "I don't indulge myself, as you know, but Sarah convinced me it's hospitable to keep something on hand."

If by "libation" Polk meant a whiskey, brandy, rum, wine, or a beer, even a small beer, Houston desperately wanted one. Making small talk with Polk was like rolling a boulder up hill. It didn't used to be that hard, but whatever sense of ease Polk once had was long gone.

The President rang a silver bell on his desk. A servant entered the room before the sound died in the air.

"A glass of wine for the Senator," Polk ordered. "I'll have tea."

Offering his visitor a glass of wine seemed to relax Polk in some mysterious way.

"Have you met Senator Benton's delightful daughter, Jessie?" he asked.

Houston replied that he hadn't.

"She's a very attractive and, dare I say, brilliant young woman," Polk said. "She's married to John Fremont, who's been so much success with his explorations of the West."

Houston *did* know Fremont. In his opinion, a greater combination of self-promoting blowhard and fatuous blockhead never lived. Based on everything he heard about Fremont's explorations, the so-called "Pathfinder" was more lucky than good. Without an experienced hand like Kit Carson to guide him, Fremont probably couldn't find his ass with both hands and a lantern. Houston tried reading Fremont's monumentally self-serving chronicle. But "A Report of an Exploration of the Country Laying Between the Missouri River and the Rocky Mountains on the Line of the Kansas and Great Platte Rivers" was such hard going that he quickly lost interest. The words were so dead they didn't even stink anymore.

"I'm happy to hear that you've cut back on your consumption," Polk said. "I remember how much the general worried about you, and I've heard some, ah, unfortunate stories since then."

"Which stories might those be?" Houston asked, feeling his innards clench. "There are so many."

"One, in particular, had to do with the Alamo," the President explained. "If I may be candid, supposedly the reason you didn't lead your army to its relief is that you were dead drunk most of the time."

There it was again. Houston knew that he'd never live it down. Over the years, he'd offered different defenses and justifications at different times, although none of them seemed completely satisfactory, not even to himself.

"Mister President, I tell you candidly that it isn't true, or at least it's not the whole truth," he said. "Yes, my condition was not always the best, but we were engaged in formin' a government and I was certainly sober enough to participate in that, as even my enemies will agree. The Alamo was under siege for several days before we knew it. Was I to lead a ragged army of a few hundred men against Santa Anna's thousands? We had no choice but to wait and grow our army. You know better than anyone life is full of hard choices."

Nodding in agreement, Polk abruptly changed the subject.

"Have you heard the latest from Mexico? We received official word this morning, although we've known unofficially for some time."

Houston shook his head and accepted a glass of wine from the servant. He took a sip and nearly gagged. If this was Polk's idea of drinking then no wonder he didn't indulge. He didn't know where Polk found this swill, but he wouldn't varnish a floor with it.

"Mexico's broken off diplomatic relations as s a result of our annexation of Texas." Polk steepled his hands in front of his chin. "Of course, you realize this will almost certainly mean war."

That *was* alarming news. It wasn't so much that Mexico broke off relations. Houston expected that. Despite the informal offer to recognize Texas as an independent country if it remained apart from the United States, officially Mexico still refused to recognize that it even lost Texas. What made Houston nervous was Polk's bristling militancy. This wasn't like the cautious man he remembered.

"Why does it have to mean war?" he asked, taking another tentative sip of Polk's ghastly wine. "Mexico will come 'round eventually. What choice does it have? Mexico's temporary pique isn't worth fightin' over."

"True, but the territories of California and New Mexico *are* worth fighting over," Polk replied. "Oregon territory, too, although that's another situation. It is our destiny to extend all the way to the Pacific and this administration will be the one that accomplishes it."

Houston's eyebrows shot up. What Polk described would happen eventually. It was inevitable. Desirable, too. Houston could even see a time when Mexico itself might be part of the United States. If ever a country deserved better government, that country was Mexico. But why push it so hard? He'd heard the war talk, of course, even down in Texas. Polk was elected on just that platform. But he dismissed most of it as the usual campaign rhetoric.

"Although it was coined to apply to the Oregon situation, there's a phrase I've grown fond of," Polk said. "It came from one of our gentlemen of the press."

He reached into a pile of papers on the desk, pulled out a newspaper and pushed it across the desk.

"Here, Senator," he said, "please read it."

Ever since John Quincy Adams negotiated a treaty between the two countries back when Adams was Secretary of State under Monroe, the disputed territory in the Pacific Northwest had been under joint occupation by the United States and Great Britain. Under the stipulations, with a year's notice, either country could break the treaty. In the meantime, citizens of both countries were free to occupy land there. But when the British moved their Hudson Bay Company headquarters north to Vancouver Island, they all but conceded control of the disputed area from Puget Sound south to Mexican California.

Even so, Great Britain still hovered over the territory like a thundercloud. British warships paid frequent visits to the west coast as far south as Acapulco. Did the British covet California? Would they try to buy it from Mexico? Or would they seize it outright? Did the British have designs on Mexico itself?

In a message to Congress after his election, Polk proposed to give Great Britain notice regarding the United States' claim to Oregon. The move surprised no one, least of all Great Britain. Expansion into Oregon territory and the annexation of Texas were key issues in Polk's campaign. The Texas issue was more or less settled, although the boundary was in dispute with sporadic fighting along the border. Mexico maintained that the Nueces River was the traditional boundary, while the United States claimed the territory south to the Rio Grande, and the area between became a deadly no man's land. At the same time, nobody knew for sure exactly where Texas' western boundary was, although everyone had an opinion. Some claimed that it stretched all the way to California.

As this hodgepodge of politics and national ambition swirled around in his thoughts, Houston scanned the newspaper until a phrase jumped out at him: "It is our manifest destiny to overspread the continent allotted by Providence."

Apparently John L. O'Sullivan, writing in the United States Democratic Review, saw it as a God-ordained right that the United States should extend to the Pacific Ocean. If it meant war, O'Sullivan declared, "Then so be it. Mexico can never exert any real authority. The Anglo-Saxon foot is already on its borders. Already the advance guard of the irresistible army of the Anglo-Saxon emigration has begun to pour down upon it, armed with the plow and the rifle."

Houston doubted that O'Sullivan had much acquaintance with either a plow or a rifle. As usual, the newspapers stood ready to fight to the last drop of someone else's blood. War with Great Britain wasn't likely. As Houston understood it, negotiations were going well. But if this kind of thinking became popular - and Polk wasn't likely to endorse it other-wise - then war with Mexico was inevitable. Polk wasn't satis-fied with Texas and Oregon. He wanted California and New Mexico, too. But Mexico had already lost an enormous portion of its country. It would not sit idly by and lose more.

Houston tossed the newspaper on Polk's desk.

"I had no idea the Almighty spoke so clearly to newspaper editors," he said. "In that case, there's hope for us all."

Polk's responded with another one of his mirthless smiles.

"Even they can be right sometimes. I've come to like the phrase 'Manifest Destiny.' It has the ring of history."

"It sounds dangerous."

"I'm surprised Sam Houston fears danger."

"All wise men do. I've seen too many wars. Did you exhaust all attempts at negotiation? Remember, I've been travelin' for almost a month. I don't know the latest."

"It's difficult to negotiate when Mexico will not even receive our ambassador, John Slidell," Polk said dryly.

"What about buyin' what we want?" Houston asked. "That

was always the general's preference. He preferred spendin' money to losin' men."

"I am prepared to offer as much as five million dollars for New Mexico territory and twenty four million dollars for California," Polk explained. "But, as I said, Mexico won't even receive Slidell. Informal communication failed, too."

Houston got the impression that Polk wasn't disappointed. A man eager to use war to get what he wants isn't interested in negotiation, unless it's to show a public face of good intentions.

"There is one other possibility," Polk said mysteriously.

"What is that?"

"Santa Anna," the President replied, eager to see the effect of his surprise on Houston.

"Santa Anna! Has the Mexican Lazarus risen again? What's he up to now?"

"As you know, Santa Anna is in exile in Havana," Polk explained. "Through Slidell, he assures us that if we can get him into Mexico, with the greatest of secrecy, of course, he can regain control of the government, although it will require a considerable amount of money on our part for bribes and other expenses. In exchange, he will arrange for a peaceful sale of territory to the United States. It promises to be very neatly done."

Houston couldn't believe it. If Polk put his trust in Santa Anna, then war was inevitable. For all of his intelligence and charm, the Mexican was the most amoral human being Houston had ever met. The only thing Santa Anna ever regretted was failure. Once in power, he would no more go along with Polk's scheme than he would join the priesthood.

Houston fought down the urge to stand up and pace the room to work off his growing agitation.

"Mister President, I know this man. If you put him back in power he'll turn against us and use our own money in the process. He cannot be controlled or trusted, not now and not ever. Anyone who thinks otherwise is a fool."

Polk's dark eyes flashed as his compact body jerked upright in his chair.

"Are you calling me a fool? You may be...well, you may be who you are, but remember that I am the President of the United States. You will respect this office even if you don't respect me!"

Houston was disappointed with himself. He said the wrong thing at the wrong time. People who assumed moral superiority were inevitably blinded by self-righteous pride. It would do no good to argue.

"No, you're certainly not a fool, Mister President," he said. "We go back too far and I know better. But I sincerely believe that you are wrong. Santa Anna is not to be trusted. I know the man. He can charm the dead back to life, but he'll turn on you like a viper."

"It doesn't matter." Polk's anger disappeared as quickly as it came. "I'm convinced that it's a gamble worth taking. If it fails, we can always defeat the Mexicans in the field. Pardon me if I say that if your Texans did it, the army of the United States can certainly do it."

Polk rose from his chair and briskly walked to a cabinet on the other side of the room. He opened the door, pulled out a big rolled-up map, spread it out on a table, and gestured for Houston to join him.

"I'm sure you know that Zachary Taylor's at Corpus Christi with a substantial force." He bent over the map and moved his finger to show Taylor's position. "What you may not know is that General Taylor soon will be heavily reinforced. At that point, he will move south to the border, a position the Mexicans will find provocative."

"I know the general he'll probably face; Mariano Arista," Houston said. "Arista won't be hard to provoke."

Polk looked pleased, even a little smug.

"If, as you suggest, Santa Anna lets us down then the war will begin there, where Taylor and this Arista meet. When it does - I'm sorry, *if* it does - Taylor will brush Arista aside and move into Mexico."

Houston leaned over the table and concentrated on the map. He weighed his options and took his time before speaking.

"That won't be enough." He rose to his full height, almost a head taller than Polk. "Mister President, that won't be enough at all."

Polk scowled. "What do you mean?"

"To liberate Texas is one thing. We were fortunate to capture the dictator himself. But to defeat Mexico, to truly defeat Mexico, is another matter. To do that you'll have to cut out Mexico's heart, and Mexico's heart is here," he said, placing his finger on Mexico City.

Polk studied the map. After a moment, he said, "That's too far for Taylor, although we do plan another invasion further west, in conjunction with his move south."

"It's even worse than it looks, hundreds of miles of brutal country that burns a man in the summer and freezes him in winter," Houston said. "The Mexican cavalry is as good as ours. Maybe better. They'll be fightin' in their own country, too. They'd hound Taylor all the way, killin' ten men here and twenty men there. He'd be lucky to arrive with half his force. They will oppose Taylor in the north. That much is certain. Maybe Taylor should stay in the north while we strike at Mexico's heart?"

Polk thought it over. Reluctantly, he asked, "What do you suggest?"

"Start here." Houston put a finger on Vera Cruz, on Mexico's Gulf Coast. "Do what Cortes did. Invade from the coast and move on Mexico City while Taylor threatens the Mexicans from the north. Think of it as a vice."

"That command should go to Winfield Scott, unless he refuses just for spite," Polk said. "General Scott is *not* a congenial man."

Houston saw that Polk was thinking about politics when he should think about war.

"I've heard Scott's not easy to get along with, but he's the best we have," Houston said. "Anyone who thinks Mexicans can't fight hasn't seen them in action. They may be badly led at times, but there's not a thing wrong with their fightin' men. I agree with you. I believe we'll win. But it will be a damned bloody war. If anyone tells you different, they're only sayin' what they think you want to hear."

"Senator, General Scott is *very* hard to get along with," Polk said glumly. "The man's impossible, hard headed, vain and stubborn. He not only ignores civilian authority, he seems to go out of his way to provoke it."

In short, thought Houston, Scott was just the man for the job.

"Scott has the Presidential bug, too," Polk added. "And if he's successful, I'm sure Taylor will get the itch. The acclaim is too much to resist. Washington and Jackson were generals. Harrison, too, though at least that simpleton had the decency to die a month after taking office. Win a battle or two and high office is assured."

Polk straightened up from the table. He placed the palms of his hands in the small of his back, stretched backward, and stopped in mid-stretch, as if a thought occurred to him.

"You certainly did well enough against the pride of Mexico," he said.

Swallowing the last of Polk's gruesome wine, Houston said, "Luck was on our side. Santa Anna made a mistake and broke his army into pieces. We beat the biggest piece and grabbed him at the same time."

"Nevertheless, you did defeat him," Polk said. "And you didn't just defeat him, you annihilated him."

The President returned to his desk with his head down and his hands clasped behind his back, as if thinking something over. To Houston's eye, there was something a little too practiced about it. Polk was just now getting to his real point.

"I would like to offer you a commission," Polk said. "You'd outrank everyone but Scott. You'd report only to Scott...and to me. After all, who else has your experience and knowledge of the enemy?"

Houston had to admire the President's skill. In just a few minutes, Houston went from more or less opposing the war, or at least feeling reluctant about it, to being offered a position as second in command. If it had truly worked, Houston wouldn't be aware of Polk's attempt to maneuver him. Even so, it was well done.

"Mister President, I hope you don't think me presumptuous when I say that you're very good," Houston said. "The general would be proud."

"Thank you...Sam." Polk didn't bother to hide his pleasure. "Our conversation is stimulating. It reminds me of the old days. You're right about too many men saying what they think I want to hear. It's the curse of this office."

Polk escorted Houston to the door, one hand on the bigger man's shoulder.

"Over the next few years, the future of the country will be in the hands of a few men. This is a critical time. Will you accept my offer?"

"I'd like to think on it."

"Of course, but don't take too long. Events will move swiftly once they're in motion."

Houston turned down the offer of a carriage to take him

back to the hotel. It was a pleasant evening. He wanted to walk and think.

As he watched Houston step into the night, Polk thought that it was good to see him again. Perhaps he should have told him that, but this was no time for personal considerations. Great men make few friends, a price he was willing to pay.

As he walked back to the hotel on the deserted Washington streets, Houston searched his pockets for a match to light his cheroot. He got it drawing as he marched through the darkness and considered the pros and cons.

He was tempted by the President's offer, of course, but there was much to consider. Margaret would hate it. The thought of her husband going off to fight a war a thousand miles away would crush her, although she'd never admit it. Physically, he was more than up to it, as strong and vital as ever. He was younger than Scott and Taylor, too. He didn't like the idea of reporting to anyone, and he especially didn't like the implication that he'd be Polk's spy in Scott's army, but there'd be no ignoring Polk the way he ignored Burnet.

It was an odd way to come to the conclusion he supported the war after all. He hoped for another way, but never really thought it likely. Mexico swore to fight if Texas was annexed. The fact that Polk was doing everything possible to provoke a war didn't change the fact that there'd certainly be one no matter what Polk did. The United States wanted what Mexico had.

Houston tossed the stub of his cheroot into the gutter and walked up the steps into the old hotel. A saying popular in Mexico came to mind: "Poor Mexico, so far from God, so near the United States." True enough, he thought.

As he undressed, Houston remembered that he would be sworn into the Senate in a few hours. He'd forgotten all about it. He carefully laid out a new black suit for the occasion. With the exception of a new and glorious addition to his wardrobe, there would be none of his usual flamboyance. The moment called for dignity.

Of course, that exception was magnificent, a vest made from the spotted fur of a Mexican jaguar, a going-away gift from a group of San Jacinto veterans that touched him deeply. He held the vest in one hand and caressed the fur with the other.

"My God, you are a beauty," he said.

He remembered Margaret's reaction when she saw it.

"My goodness!" she cried. "Do you actually mean to wear that thing?"

She held the vest up to his shoulders and tilted her head back, trying for a sense of how it might look.

"There's no doubt of one thing," she said.

"And what is that, my dear?"

"It takes a man to wear this vest."

6

As THE SWELTERING months dragged on, Sam Houston cut a swath through Washington. As a freshman senator he had no seniority, but, after reluctantly turning down Polk's offer of command because he refused to be the President's spy in the army, Houston was named chairman of the powerful Military Affairs Committee, which helped oversee war preparations. Polk relied on him so much there were rumors Houston had designs on the Presidency in 1848, when one Jackson Democrat would succeed another.

The truth was nothing of the sort, but he didn't bother to deny it. He *was* thinking about the Presidency, but the next election was too soon, although he kept the thought to himself. One of the first lessons of politics is that what people think to be true can be more useful than the truth itself. All of his life, he rarely denied the wild tales that sprang up around him like dandelions. And when he didn't deny them, they became the truth. He also possessed a politician's skill of seeming to listen carefully to what everyone had to say, which gave the impression that he agreed, even when he did not. As a result, he was often accused of duplicity. He didn't bother to deny that either. There were times when it came in handy.

He agreed to work with an eager young scribbler named Charles Edward Lester to write a book, "Sam Houston and His Republic." If nothing else, he welcomed the potential income. His Washington expenses ran higher than anticipated. Expenses had a way of doing that all his life.

They labored for three months, usually in Houston's room in the National Hotel on Pennsylvania Avenue, six blocks from the White House. He'd moved out of Brown's, his longtime favorite. The old place was practically falling down around his ears. He especially enjoyed the comfort and convenience of a private bathtub. The National was one of the first hotels in the country to offer such a luxury. He liked to dictate to young Lester at the end of the day while soaking in the tub with a cigar in one hand and a glass of whiskey in the other. Margaret would have been appalled.

Although the title was Lester's idea, Houston liked it. For one thing, it was sure to infuriate the opposition back home. Unfortunately, the sales were disappointing. The book was too hurriedly written to be of any real value. While there was no money in it, he was pleased to hear from Ash Smith that the title did what he thought it would:

My Controversial Friend,

You would take pleasure in hearing Burnet and Lamar rant about your literary effort. When anyone mentions the book Burnet's face turns purple and he begins raving, 'Houston and his republic! His republic!' I don't think he's read a word of it, you understand. He can't get past the title.

Before Lamar joined Taylor as a colonel of cavalry (God help the cavalry!), there was a going-away fandango in Austin, mostly to celebrate the fact that Lamar was going away. When

Sam Maverick asked Lamar if he'd read your book, his nibs
sneered, 'It's just like that drunk old Cherokee to try to turn
Texas into his own private ranch!'

Lamar and Burnet aren't the only ones piqued. Once again,
you have made yourself controversial. Or is it that you continue
to be controversial? The name Sam Houston is either revered or
loathed. Sometimes even your friends aren't sure what to make
of you.

The latest charge is so magnificent in its stupidity that I
must share it with you. In your exalted state of vanity, suppos-
edly you have taken to signing your name 'I Am Houston' rather
than plain old 'Sam Houston.' Personally, I like the idea and
believe you should adopt it immediately. Not many have the
flair for it, much less the name. For example, 'I Am Smith'
wouldn't do. It lacks the proper grandeur.

Your servant and friend,
Ashbel (I Am) Smith

Houston was used to exaggerations and rumors, but
anything this bizarre demanded an immediate investigation.
Alone in his hotel room, he found a sheet of paper, dipped his
pen in his battered old ink pot, and signed his name. Unfortunately, he felt so self conscious that instead of the usual bold
signature with the elaborate rubric beneath, he produced a
cramped scrawl that resembled a timid schoolgirl's "thank
you" note for attending her tea party.

Amused by his self-consciousness, he opened a drawer and
searched through some recent correspondence. Triumphantly
withdrawing a sample, he tried to pretend that was seeing it
for the first time.

Damned if he didn't see what they meant. Thanks to his
odd shaping of the capital "S", and a slight space between that
letter and the following "a", he saw where some brainless dolt

might interpret his signature as "I am Houston." As he knew from experience, there were a good many brainless dolts out there.

Houston smiled and returned the correspondence to the drawer. Ash was right about one thing. "I am Smith" didn't pack the same majesty.

The only blemish in his Washington life was that he missed Margaret terribly. Although they wrote to each other constantly, sometimes more than once a day, there were times when he didn't hear from her for a week or more. Just as he'd begin to fret, he'd get several letters at once, and read them over and over until they were tatters.

He liked to write at his desk in the Senate while one of his peers gassed along about a subject neither he nor anyone else cared about, which was most of the time. He enjoyed whittling there, too, with his long legs crossed at the ankles on top of the desk while he accumulated a satisfying pile of shavings at his feet. He usually gave away what he whittled as a gift. It might be anything from a miniature gavel to a tiny replica of the clasp knife he used to do the whittling. Occasionally, he'd whittle a miniature heart and include it in a letter to Margaret.

Fortunately, the session ended in time for Houston to hurry home for the birth of their second child, Nancy Elizabeth. Margaret insisted the baby be named for her mother, although Elizabeth was his mother's name.

When their first child, little Sam, was born, he made the astonishing discovery that he enjoyed being a father. He watched Nannie - he couldn't bring himself to call her Nancy - for hours at a time, whether she waved her little red fists and gurgled, or slept peacefully. Little Sam was jealous of the attention given the tiny newcomer and turned stubborn and willful, driving Margaret's mother to distraction. She waddled around the little house muttering, "Well I wonder where the boy gets *that? Certainly* not from his *mother!*"

The more she fumed, the more Houston spoiled his son. He especially enjoyed racing around the house with the shrieking boy riding on his shoulders. When he took little Sam down to the creek to fish, they usually wound up splashing and laughing in the water. Soaking wet, they'd try to sneak back into the house to avoid being scolded by Margaret and always got caught. The scene was repeated many times during those golden months: Father and son pretending to be contrite while wife and mother pretended to be angry.

With himself, Margaret, two children, Nancy Lea's long visits, and their frequent visitors, the little house near Huntsville they called Raven Hill seemed ready to explode. Two rooms split by the dogtrot on the first floor and one large room above wasn't enough for a growing family. Someday he'd do something about it, but just now there were too many demands on his limited resources.

Between his speeches and the politicking that comes from holding high public office, he found a little time to practice law, too, which required frequent trips to Nacogdoches. They needed the money from his law practice. The farm was barely self-sustaining. The little house at Cedar Point above Galveston, where they'd often go to escape the hot and sticky summer weather was a drain, too. After paying his Washington expenses there wasn't much left of his Senate salary. He'd never been any good at making money and it looked like he wasn't getting any better with age.

After four months, Margaret had recovered from giving birth and Houston was eager to get back to Washington. She could run the place without him now, especially with her mother's help.

His dual nature made life difficult. That he was aware of it only made it worse. He longed to be at the center of things, but at the same time hated to leave home. As a result, he felt vaguely guilty no matter what he did, although he suspected leaving home didn't bother him as much as it should, which made him feel guiltier still. He decided that he must be a monstrous hypocrite.

One evening a few days before he was to leave for Washington, Houston watched Margaret practice her guitar in the parlor. She was already an accomplished pianist, although the piano she bought in Mobile and transported to Raven Hill at great expense was too big for the room, another reason to find a bigger place. Now she was determined to learn the guitar and practiced every day. That was the image he'd carry with him to Washington: His beautiful brown-haired Maggie with the guitar in her lap, shoulders hunched over the instrument as she gently chewed her lower lip in concentration. She wore her tiny gold spectacles when she practiced, although she refused to wear them in public.

When he teased her about it, she blushed like a schoolgirl.

"I'll be a little old lady soon enough. I don't want to look like one until I *am* one."

To him, she looked adorable. The thought of leaving her all but broke his heart.

Margaret practiced so long her hands began to cramp and she stopped. The children were asleep and Nancy Lea was at her own home for a change. This might be their last chance to talk privately before Sam left.

Nothing had been said, but Nancy Lea was getting on in years and they both knew that she'd be spending more and more time with them. Not, Houston thought, a happy prospect.

Trying to head off trouble before it started, Margaret abruptly asked, "Sam, why can't you use some of your famous charm on my mother? I know she's difficult sometimes, but you never give her a chance. Your hackles rise the minute she walks in the room. You're like a big dog looking for a fight."

Houston put down his book, "The Iliad," a lifelong favorite, and crossed the room. He sat down, lifted the guitar from her lap, set it on the floor, and took her in his arms.

"All right, Maggie, just for you." A wisp of her gardenia-scented hair tickled his nose as he nuzzled her ear. "From now on I'll love the old lady like my own mother."

In mock anger, she punched him in the chest with her small fist.

"Don't you try that on me! I know very well you didn't get along with your mother. You know exactly what I mean."

He promised to do better. He'd never get along with Nancy Lea, much less like her, but he hated to disappoint Margaret. He told her what she wanted to hear and left it at that.

He meant it, too, as much as he was able.

7

POLK COULDN'T HAVE FOUND A BETTER man than Zachary Taylor to pick a fight.

The man was as subtle as a sledgehammer. In the field, Taylor wore a linen duster and an old straw hat pulled down to his ears. Mounted on his horse, Old Whitey, he looked like a hardscrabble farmer riding into town to check crop prices.

The general marched his three thousand men south to a position on the Rio Grande across from Matamoras, where they started work on a fort where the elevation would allow Taylor's gunners to fire across the river and rake the Mexican town. The fort was nearly finished by the time the Mexicans marched into Matamoras with five thousand men. While the two armies glared at each other, an American patrol discovered an abandoned rancho twenty-five miles up river. Intending to spend the night behind the crumbling adobe walls, the patrol was surprised by a detachment of lancers. With sixteen Americans killed in the sharp little action, the Mexicans had the clear advantage.

But Taylor had what he wanted - an excuse to make war -

and sent a courier galloping to Washington with the rousing message: "American blood has been spilled."

Two weeks later, Taylor met Mexican army in the first battle of the war, with both sides spread out in the saw grass on a treeless prairie at Palo Alto. The Mexican cannon opened fire, but the range was too great, the gunners too inexperienced, and the quality of powder too poor. By the time the round shot reached the American lines it bounced harmlessly along the ground like a child's ball and the ranks simply stepped aside to let it pass.

Returning fire, Taylor hit the enemy with his more accurate eighteen-pounders and used flying batteries of small six-pounders to break up the dangerous Mexican lancers. By the time the skirmish ended, fifty Americans were killed or wounded, with Mexican casualties twice that number.

The next day, the Mexicans made a stand in a long shallow ravine that formed an arc facing a called *Resaca de la Palma*, the main road to Matamoras. Under heavy fire, the American infantry surged forward through thick underbrush. At the same time, raked by grape and canister, Taylor's dragoons charged the enemy cannon. The charges routed the inexperienced army and the Mexicans retreated south, leaving behind more than four hundred wounded. With fewer than one hundred and eighty casualties, Zachary Taylor had won the first battle of the war.

In Washington, when Polk received Taylor's message he sent a message of his own to Congress claiming that Mexico had invaded American territory. Since war was already underway, the President wanted the means to wage it. A bill to raise fifty thousand troops passed by a vote of forty two to two in the Senate and one hundred seventy four to fourteen in the House.

There was more opposition to the war than the votes indicated, but it was thin, badly organized, and unpopular. One of the leaders was an Illinois Congressman named Abraham Lincoln. Houston didn't think much of him, a gawky lawyer who needed seasoning.

As Houston warned Polk, Santa Anna turned on the Americans as soon as the crafty Mexican was smuggled into Mexico. Using American money for strategically placed bribes, he ousted the ineffectual government of Jose Joaquin de Herrera and the newly reinstalled *El Presidente* vowed to push the invaders back across the Nueces.

Despite Santa Anna's bluster, when Houston left Washington Taylor looked like a winner. By the time he returned, the outlook was dim and opposition to the war was growing.

"I told Polk! Hellfire and damnation! I told him that very thing!"

Houston's fist came down on General Winfield Scott's desk with a crash that startled a big gray cat out of its nap in a corner chair. The cat languidly stretched, slithered off the chair, sauntered over to Scott, and softly hopped up on the general's spacious lap.

A big man in more ways than one, Winfield Scott stood six feet, four inches tall and weighed two hundred seventy pounds, much of it around his bulging belt line. With his hawk nose and grim slash of a mouth, the irascible Scott was known as "Old Fuss and Feathers." A hero of the war of 1812with almost forty years in the army he was a brilliant professional who scorned amateurs, especially politicians. His men adored him, politicians were wary of him, and most of his generals were afraid of him.

Sensing a kindred spirit, Scott didn't mind when Houston vented his spleen. God knows he'd vented his own enough lately to recognize the need for it.

"It's even worse than you think." Scott's rumbling voice sounded like distant thunder. "In forlorn effort to find a general with the correct politics, while you were away Polk offered command to practically every Democrat in town. He seems to think that the Mexicans will be beaten by paper thunderbolts hurled from Washington. He also mistakenly assumes that I have designs on the Presidency when it's Taylor who wants the job."

Houston said nothing in reply. He did not for a second believe Scott's claim he wasn't interested in the Presidency.

"And the fact that you turned down his offer of a high position only reinforces you reputation as an independent man," the general continued.

Houston shrugged. Scott's sources were excellent. It was time to test him a little.

"This is a different kind of war, or will be once we get movin' again," Houston said. "There's no question you're the best choice. And the last thing we need is another self-important general breathin' all the air. Two of us would be one too many."

Scott's astonished look was priceless. No one had dared speak to him like that in years. Then his great slab of a face turned red and he began to laugh. His big belly jiggling under his blue coat startled the cat again. Houston feared the coat's brass buttons might fly off like dangerous projectiles.

"By God, you, sir, are a truthful man!" The general wiped the tears of laughter from his eyes. "You see? I may be vain, but at least I admit it. You and I are a great deal alike."

As he gently stroked the cat, Scott responded to Houston's smile with the satisfied smirk of a man who sees things turning his way.

"However, I do believe the last straw is upon us," Scott said. "I assume you know about Benton?"

All of Washington knew. How could Tom Benton be such a fool? The Missouri Senator, whose military experience consisted of a few months as an officer in the Creek War a generation ago, marched into Polk's office and offered to "accept" command of the American forces in Mexico, but only if he was appointed lieutenant general, the highest rank in the army, one currently held by only Winfield Scott.

Although he was too polished to let it show, Benton's arrogance had Polk seething and he quietly let it be known the assignment would go to Scott.

"It would serve that pusillanimous pip squeak right if I refused," Scott grumbled. "Why should I place myself in the most perilous of all positions, with fire upon my rear from Washington and fire in front from the Mexicans?"

"Because there'll never be another campaign like this one," Houston replied bluntly. "You couldn't pass it up even if you wanted to."

Despite his confident words, Houston wasn't so sure. Several Senators were worried that Scott might reject Polk's long-delayed offer of command. They'd asked Houston to make a pilgrimage go to the great man and convince him to take it.

"Promise the blustering old bugger anything he wants," advised Webster, who, despite his frequent alcoholic daze, was still as canny as they came. "All he has to do is say the word. We're fighting a war without a competent general to command it. Taylor won't do. Everybody knows that. Scott detests most of us, with good reason. But he's too ambitious *not* to take this command. He just needs to be wooed."

As Houston began to make his argument, Scott raised his hand.

"You needn't bother, although I'm sure it would be a pleasure to hear it all. I know why you've come and I know what the concerns are in that den of thieves known as the United States Congress." Scott tilted his head toward Houston. "Present company excepted, of course. Despite what people think, I'm too old a soldier to refuse an order, although winning this war will be a devil of a lot harder than people think, which means neither the army nor I will get the credit we deserve."

Scott dumped the cat on the floor, ponderously rose to his feet, and walked back and forth across his office in great stomps. It felt like an earthquake. If Scott gained any more weight, Houston wasn't sure that he could mount a horse.

"Your plan to invade Mexico from the Gulf is sound," Scott said. "I thought the same thing myself. What people like Polk and Benton don't understand is that artillery, training, supplies, guts, and strategy win wars, not babbling politicians. War is always the same; old men talking and young men dying."

"What will you do about Taylor?" asked Houston. "He's bogged down, just as I feared."

"Yes, you were right there, too," replied Scott, who stopped his pacing. "Are you sure you wouldn't like some high command in this little *soiree,* say second only to me? Unlike Polk's offer, you wouldn't be a spy for the administration. With Taylor out of the way, I think Mexico's big enough for two bombastic generals."

Houston hoped that Scott might ask. Now that he'd met the man, he knew they'd get along. The opportunity was too glorious to ignore.

"General," he said, "I'd be honored."

"Excellent!" Scott cried, pumping Houston's hand. "Give me a few days to clear the paperwork and then I'll get you caught up."

With that, the general went back to his thunderous pacing. Houston pitied whoever had the office below.

"To answer your question, what I propose to do with Taylor is leave him where he is. I will pull the best units from his army, add them to the men I'll ready for the invasion, and we'll take Vera Cruz."

After a promising start, Taylor's position had fallen apart.

After his army's initial success, he rashly moved south to Monterrey, where he barely defeated the overmatched Mexicans in the bloodiest battle of the war. In three days of house-to-house fighting that saw blood run like water down Monterrey's cobblestone streets, Taylor lost more than twelve hundred men, a fifth of his army. Worse, the badly shaken general then settled for an eight-week armistice that made the sacrifices of his men count for nothing. The Mexicans were allowed to withdraw while Taylor camped outside the city.

To the public, it looked like a victory. But every experienced hand knew better.

Stung by the mounting criticism, Taylor marched to the mountains south of Saltillo and blundered right into Santa Anna's hands. In a remarkable burst of energy, *El Presidente* threw together an army of fifteen thousand men and moved north in a man-killing march across hundreds of miles of desert. He took Taylor by surprise and hit the Americans with everything he had, an all-or-nothing gamble.

Scrambling for a defensive position to gain time to reform his shattered troops, Taylor fell back to a gully-seamed plateau with steep mountains on one side and impassable ravines on the other, just south of a walled rancho named Buena Vista. Mistaking the withdrawal for retreat, Santa Anna momentarily stopped his advance and offered Taylor a chance to surrender. "You are surrounded by twenty thousand men and cannot avoid a rout where you will be cut to pieces," read the dispatch, exaggerating the Mexican numbers.

The pause gave the Americans time to organize a defensive position before Santa Anna drove his exhausted and starving men into the enemy one more time. It almost worked. The Mexicans found an opening between the mountains and the American flank and came within a few minutes of a shattering victory. Taylor's army was saved by the bravado of his flying batteries and hard fighting by the Texas

Rangers and Mississippi volunteers under Jefferson Davis who filled the breech until reinforcements arrived.

Houston was pleased to see the Rangers distinguish themselves. One Ranger captain, young Jack Hays, adapted Sam Colt's new repeating handgun as a cavalry weapon. When the other Rangers saw the new weapon at work, especially after modifications by another Ranger named Sam Walker made the weapon more durable, they all wanted the new repeaters. With one "Walker Colt" on a Ranger's hip and another holstered on his saddle, one company now possessed the firepower of a regiment.

But despite their stout service as scouts and irregular cavalry, the Rangers' record was marred by atrocities that shocked the country. Feared even by their own army, *Los Tejanos Diablos* refused to obey any authority but their own. Rangers collected Mexican scalps and hung them from their bridles, while making disgusting necklaces of Mexican fingers, teeth, and ears.

As a result, Houston found himself in the uncomfortable position of defending the Rangers in Washington while deploring their behavior back home. Although he denounced the reports of atrocities as lies and exaggerations, they were all too true and he knew it. He saw the same thing during the Creek War and again at San Jacinto. The only noble thing about war was the end of it.

Taylor was lucky. Santa Anna had gambled and lost. With his troops exhausted from the forced march and terrible fighting, *El Presidente* quietly left the field, leaving Taylor to claim another victory.

"And there he sits," concluded Scott. "What *is* the good general to do? He can't move forward and he won't move back. But, Houston, believe me when I say this: If Taylor is not killed or court-martialed then that man *will* be President. The voters will find him irresistible, damn them."

An aide entered the room and reminded Scott of his next appointment. As the aide bustled around the office gathering Scott's papers, the big-bellied general made arrangements for Houston to meet with his staff the next day.

Feeling light-headed at the momentous decision and wondering how he'd break the news to Margaret, Houston walked back to his hotel. Checking at the desk, he was delighted to find a letter from Ash Smith and eagerly broke the seal. Smith's letters were always entertaining and informative.

Hearing an anguished cry, the hotel clerk looked up from his work. His illustrious guest seemed stricken and suddenly pale.

"Senator? Are you all right?"

"It's my wife..." The letter was three weeks old. Margaret might be dying. She might even be dead already.

8

THE SKY WAS the color of mud and the rain fell in warm sheets that turned the world to ooze.

Smith had turned his collar up so that his slicker covered him from his ears to his boots. A blue kerchief tied around his neck kept the rain from trickling down inside his shirt, and a broad-brimmed hat kept his head more or less dry. His tired horse stopped in front of the house, its head hanging between its legs as if to hide from the pounding rain, and Smith slowly dismounted, his boots squishing into the soft ground.

Joshua, a handsome slave who'd been with Margaret since she was a little girl, came out of the house holding an umbrella. He took the reins of the horse with one hand, held the umbrella over Smith's head with the other, and nodded toward the house, ignoring the rain that drenched him in seconds.

"We're awful glad to see you." Joshua's voice was so soft Smith could barely hear it. "The Misses is in the bedroom. There's a pitcher of water and a wash bowl inside the door to the parlor so you can clean yourself. The Misses said she'd 'preciate it if you'd take your boots off. I set a pair of the Mister's boots out for you."

Smith smiled at the thought of his small feet rattling around in Sam Houston's big boots. It was just like Margaret to demand that he take off his muddy boots before entering her house, as if she didn't have other things to worry about.

"How is she, Joshua?"

"Don't know." Lines of worry etched his usually expressionless face. "She won't tell us a thing, not a thing."

With a nod, the slave handed Smith the umbrella. He led the weary horse to the barn, man and beast holding their heads down against the terrible unending downpour.

Smith never knew what to make of Joshua. His soft-spoken reserve made some people uncomfortable. An expert blacksmith and a fine hand with horses, somewhere along the way he acquired an education or sorts, probably from Margaret, who loved to teach. Joshua spoke as well or better than most whites Smith knew. He could read, write, and do sums, too. His position in the household was more overseer than slave. Smith did not doubt that Sam and Margaret would give Joshua his freedom if he asked for it, but where would he go? A free nigger didn't have much future in Texas, and it was a long way to anywhere else.

Some thought Houston soft on slavery, both as slave owner and politician. They hadn't talked about it for years, not since they shared a cabin back in Houston's rough and tumble bachelor days, but Smith suspected that Houston was one of those slave owners who are uncomfortable with the notion of men owning other men. Like others in a similar position, he preferred not to talk about it, as if he could make the contradiction go away by ignoring it.

And that, Smith told himself, was peculiar thing to be thinking just now.

After cleaning himself as best he could, Smith combed his

hair with his fingers and slid his feet into Houston's massive boots before knocking on the bedroom door. Hearing Margaret say, "Come in, Ash," he entered the room and put the black leather case with his instruments on the table by the bed.

He gently sat on the edge of the bed and looked down at his patient, with her masses of brown hair splayed out around her head on the pillow like a nimbus around the sun. To his practiced eye, the rigidity of her body revealed the turmoil inside. Smith knew the look. He'd seen it often enough. Frightened and fighting to control her fear, the horror of what might be happening inside her body was a hot light that flickered deep in her eyes like the blazing fire of an open furnace.

This part was the worst. The first few moments were too soon for either patient or physician to know anything for sure, but the cold hand of the unknown always made the possibilities seem worse than they were, and they were bad enough. There wasn't anything he could do except assume an air of casual professionalism so that she might take comfort in his competency.

"I appreciate your comin', Ash." Only a barely noticeable throaty quality in her voice gave away her fear. "You made good time in this weather."

He forced a smile that he hoped looked breezy and confident.

"I came soon as I got your note. Forget about me, Margaret. Tell me about yourself. Tell me everything, no matter how insignificant you think it is."

Not long after her husband left for Washington, she noticed tenderness in her right breast. At first she thought it was from nursing Nannie, but it was more painful than anything she experienced when she nursed little Sam. When she stopped nursing, it got worse instead of better. Then she felt the lump. Although it hurt to do it, she examined herself everyday. After a few weeks the lump grew smaller until it disappeared, although the pain never went away. Sometimes it hurt worse than at other times, but it was always there.

"Women get these things, Ash, you know that," she said. "It never happened to me before, but I'd heard about it. When the lump disappeared I figured it was over with. I didn't see a reason to say anything, even with the hurt."

Smith nodded and gently patted her hand. Covered to her shoulders with blankets, her left arm was outside the blankets, bent and lying over her hip. Her right arm was beneath the blankets, across her body beneath her breasts. As awkward as it looked, Smith suspected any movement of the right arm must be painful and this was the most comfortable position she'd found.

After several weeks, the lump reappeared. Small at first, it grew larger and more painful than before, seeming to get worse every day. The pain was agonizing. Her breast was sensitive to the lightest touch and even a simple movement of her arm made her cry out from the pain.

Finally she couldn't bear it any more. Although there was a perfectly competent doctor in Huntsville, she sent a slave to Austin with a note asking Smith to come as quickly as possible.

Knowing Margaret's habit of not admitting problems existed until after they were solved, asking for help was the most alarming thing she could have done. Smith canceled his appointments, referred his patients to another doctor, and rode out of Austin on his powerful mare only two hours after receiving her message, leaving the slave to get back in his own time.

"Margaret," Smith asked, "why isn't Sam here? What's he doin' still in Washington? Come to think of it, where are your mother and the children?"

She smiled one of her quiet smiles that made her look so much wiser than her years. It was easy to forget Margaret was not thirty. Sometimes Smith thought he might be half in love with her. Practically everyone who knew her knew felt the same way.

"Mother doesn't know," she explained. "You know how she gets. She's in Grand Cane with my sister and her husband. The children went with her."

Margaret hesitated, knowing that she'd be scolded.

"Sam doesn't know either. If he knew he'd be here, or on his way. You know that. You know him as well as anyone."

Ashbel Smith lost his temper. It never happened to him before, at least not with a patient. It wasn't a professional thing to do - it was a damned stupid thing to do - but the words came out before he knew it.

"Margaret, for Christ's sake, why haven't you..."

She reached up and gently touched him on the lips to stop his outburst.

"No need to get worked up." She used her quiet voice to soothe him, as if she was the physician and he was the patient. "If I wrote and told him about it, he'd come right away. You know that. But what good would it do? He'd just fret himself to death. With this awful war, he needs to be where he is, doing what he can do."

He took her small hand in both of his and looked into her violet eyes.

"Margaret, I'll only say this once: If I had you at home, I swear I'd never leave. The world could go right to hell."

In the silence, they knew they would never again speak of what had just passed between them.

"All right, it's time for me to take a look," he declared, breaking the intimate mood. "The sooner we get started, the sooner you'll be well."

Smith gently lifted the blankets and folded them down the

bed. He loosened her bed clothes and began his examination. He remembered what a professor told him many years ago: "To have a sensitive touch it should be as if you have eyes at your finger's ends." Keep it clinical, he told himself. This isn't Margaret. This is just another patient.

The lump was obvious, a large, angry swelling above the nipple of her right breast. The skin wasn't broken and there was no discharge of watery blood. He took it as a good sign, though he didn't know why. Some instinct told him it was good. He was constantly amazed by how much modern medicine didn't know. He didn't want to think about that either. The lump was hard and close to the surface. It must seem huge to Margaret. Nursing the baby must have been incredibly painful. How did she ever stand it?

As gently as possible, he felt the lump with his forefinger and thumb as she squirmed under his touch. He hated to hurt her, but there was no choice. He'd seen tumors drawn out by an arsenic plaster, but that was after they'd burst open. He didn't think it would work this time, and he didn't want to wait until the tumor burst to treat her. Still, the right poultice might help. It was something to consider.

He examined the rest of her body to see if the cancer - *if* it was cancer, he reminded himself - spread in any of the usual ways. The glands under her arm looked fine. There was no problem anywhere else that he saw, although it was painful for Margaret to move her arm. He was relieved to see that there was no white coating on her tongue, sometimes a sign of advanced cancer. She was weak and feverish, probably worn out from worry and lack of sleep. No one should carry a burden like this alone.

Examining her body, gently rolling her to one side, then the other, he felt her tension. As much as she trusted him, Margaret was a modest woman. The examination must be humiliating. She'd given birth to two children, but this was different, a violation in a way no man could understand.

He finished, tenderly readjusted her clothes, and carefully placed the blankets back in their original position.

"I'll have to operate," he said. "I 'spect you knew that already, or thought it likely."

She nodded. Her hair made a faint rustling sound on the pillow.

"I'd hoped it wouldn't come to that, but I'm not surprised," she said. "Now, tell me what you think, Ashbel. And don't try to fool me. I'll know if you're lyin'. You're not very good at it."

"Oh, you'd be surprised what I'm good at," he joked, taking a moment to gather his thoughts. How he said what he was about to say was important. A patient's attitude had as much to do with healing as anything else. Despair was the worst disease of all.

"I can remove the lump," he said. "There's no question of that. It doesn't look like it's spread. None of the obvious signs are there. There's no sign of cancer anywhere else I can see. You won't lose your breast, at least I don't think so. Just because there's a tumor doesn't mean it's cancer. That's a thought I want you to hang on to. I'll learn more when I operate. Beyond that I'd only be guessin'. I wish you'd got hold of me right away, but I'm glad you didn't wait any longer than you did. Right now, that's all I know."

"Ash, I'll need a day or two to take care of things...you know."

He nodded and squeezed her hand. "I'll give you a day, but no more." He hesitated, but decided to say it. "Margaret, write to Sam. I'll do it for you, if you'd like. He deserves to know and you need him here. It's terrible that you've gone through this by yourself. "

"I will do no such thing." Margaret pushed herself upright

in the bed with one arm, winching at the pain it caused her. "By the time he got my letter it'll be over...either way. It wouldn't make me any better and it'd only cause him pain. Whatever happens to me is God's will. Not even Sam can change that."

Seeing Smith's dubious expression, in a pleading voice he never heard before, she begged, "Promise me you won't tell him. If you're my friend, if you truly are, you'll make that promise."

He looked down at her, tenderness in his eyes. With a resigned smile, he bowed his head.

"Margaret Lea Houston, you are a stubborn woman," he said. "And yes, I promise."

He gave her something to make her sleep. Rest would do her more good than anything. She must be strong for what had to happen.

As soon as she was asleep, Smith sat down in the parlor and scratched out a short letter to Houston. One of the slaves could get it to the post in Huntsville. He'd broken his promise and it troubled him not at all.

She was right, though. By the time Houston got the message, much less got back to Texas, it'd be over, no matter which way it went. If a cancer was spreading somewhere inside where he couldn't see it, then Margaret Houston was already dead. He'd seen women die during the operation, too, although he'd do everything in his power to make sure that didn't happen.

He felt desperately tired. It came over him like a curtain falling. He leaned back in the chair and rubbed his eyes with his thumb and forefinger. He heard the pounding on the roof. God, how he hated this damned rain!

9

HE STOOD at the ship's rail and looked out over water as flat as a table top. The only sounds were the creak of the rigging and a soft hiss as the ship knifed through the strait between Florida and Cuba. Hovering just above the horizon, the moon was huge and perfectly round as moonlight glistened off the dark gulf.

Within an hour after reading Smith's letter, Houston hired a coach to take him from to Baltimore, where he boarded the Hope, a schooner bound for New Orleans. When the Hope's captain, Thomas Lyte, discovered the identity of his passenger, every day for the first three days of the voyage the gray-whiskered captain invited Houston to dine with him in his cabin, which was considered an honor aboard ship. Houston rebuffed the invitations, along with all of Lyte's attempts to strike up conversation. The captain finally gave up and left his moody passenger to himself.

Houston didn't speak to the other passengers either. He didn't care about them, the ship, the cargo, or the crew. Tormented by what might be happening - or already happened - back home, he could barely control himself when the Hope took in all sail and anchored off Cape Hatteras, where it rode out a storm that rolled the little ship like a cork for twenty-four hours.

Usually a poor sailor who became seasick with embarrassing ease, except for the storm Houston barely noticed the weather. He didn't drink and rarely ate or slept. All he wanted was to get to New Orleans. From there, he'd book passage on a ship to Galveston, if one was immediately available, then overland to Huntsville. If he couldn't find a ship, he'd find a horse and kill the beast getting home.

He knew that Lyte was pushing as hard as he dare. The captain owned a third share in the cargo of wine, spices, and fine linen. But if the Hope sprouted wings and flew it wouldn't be fast enough for Houston. Margaret might be dead. He couldn't force the thought out of his mind, like a scream welling up inside until he choked from the horror of it.

When he could walk without reeling around the deck, he spent the days pacing. Head down and hands clasped behind his back, he walked for hours at a time. Seventeen strides in one direction, turn, and seventeen strides the other. On Lyte's orders, the crew did not disturb him. The hard-bitten seamen were almost comic as they gingerly avoided him while carrying out their duties.

Such was his reputation that the ship's officers, crew and passengers wondered what new devilment Sam Houston was planning. Judging by his dark look, it was bad news for someone.

Whatever it was, they agreed that someone was in for it. The passengers found the prospect thrilling. It helped enliven a dull voyage.

10

ASHBEL SMITH WAS READY.

Assisted by Doctor Josef Bauers of Huntsville, a round Dutchman whose soft pink appearance helped put most patients at ease, Smith decided to operate at Raven Hill, where Margaret was most comfortable. His instruments were neatly laid out on the table beside the bed.

The only problem was his patient.

"No, Ashbel, I will not drink it, no matter what you say!"

The agitated doctor ran his fingers through his silver hair. Wonderful, he thought. This is what every doctor wants, an argument with the patient before an operation. He had nothing to dull the pain except a bottle of brandy and the teetotaling Margaret wanted none of it.

"Margaret, I know how you feel about alcohol, but this isn't drinkin'."

He tried to sound reasonable when what he really wanted to do was shake some sense into the stubborn woman.

"I'm not askin' you to get drunk. I'm askin' you to take this for the pain. It's all we have. I use it for most of my patients. So does Doctor Bauers here."

71

Smith looked at Bauers for support. The Dutchman energetically nodded his head, his multiple chins waggling.

"Yah, Schmidt is right," he said. "We have not'ing else. You must trink little lady."

"I will *not* drink alcohol and that's the end of it!"

"Margaret, I..."

"Ashbel!"

"Dammit, Margaret..."

"Ashbel!"

He felt Bauers' hand on his arm. "Schmidt, we cannot force her. This is no goot."

Bauers was right, of course. But of all the damn silly...he caught himself and set his mind to the task at hand. All right, he thought, but it sure won't make the operation any easier.

Smith walked across the bedroom to the gray coat he'd slipped over a chair. He reached into a pocket and pulled out a silver dollar. Returning to Margaret's bedside, he balanced the dollar on the back of his fingers just above his knuckles, adroitly flipping it from one finger to the next, a trick he learned back when he played entirely too much poker as a young man. Back and forth went the coin, from one side to the other and back again. He found that it had a calming effect. He didn't like tricks, but sometimes tricks worked.

"All right, Margaret, you win," he said softly. "I give up."

He kept the dollar moving while her eyes followed it back and forth across his fingers.

"I want you to take this dollar and put it between your teeth. It'll be quite a souvenir when this is over. You can tell your grandchildren how stubborn you were."

She was calm now that she'd won the argument.

"I'll be fine, Ash. I trust you as much as any man I know."

With a tight little smile, Smith handed her the dollar. He walked over to a basin on the other side of the room and scrubbed his hands and forearms. His hands always felt more sensitive when they were freshly washed.

Scalpel in hand, he bent over his patient. He wasn't a religious man, but this might be a good time for prayer. Fortunately, Margaret was religious enough for both of them. At least he hoped so.

11

HOUSTON SWUNG his leg over the saddle to dismount, joints creaking in protest. After riding all night, it was a little after dawn on a beautiful morning. The quiet was eerie. Even the birds seemed asleep.

As Houston dismounted, Ash Smith stepped out of the parlor. The doctor put his finger to his lips and motioned Houston away from the house with his other hand.

Consumed by anxiety, but feeling better thanks to Smith's reassuring presence, Houston practically hopped up and down with impatience as they walked. Smith waited until they were in the trees to break the silence.

"She'll be fine, Sam," he said. "I just wanted a word before you see her. Margaret's asleep. She's recoverin' nicely. The ligatures are still in but I'll take 'em out in a week or so. I've been sleepin' in the parlor since the operation. The children are with Margaret's sister."

Houston bowed his head, overwhelmed by the rush of emotions.

"Ash, I..."

"Not a word, Sam." Smith grasped Houston's forearm.

"There's plenty of time for that. Anyhow, there's somethin' I need to explain."

Smith wore dark trousers tucked into knee-high black boots, dark suspenders, and a white shirt with the sleeves rolled up to his elbows. He looked tired, but more than that, he looked worn out. There was no sign of his usual sardonic vitality.

"This is a little awkward, and might be more personal than you'd like, but it needs to be said," Smith explained. "We saved Margaret's breast, but there's some scarrin' that couldn't be helped. It's not much compared to what might have been, but to Margaret it's a whole lot. To keep up her strength, I give her five grams of quinine three times a day before meals. Before I leave I'll give you instructions for a poultice that you'll have to change every day. But more than that, there's somethin' she'll have to overcome in her own mind, somethin' no man can really understand, I think. She'll feel disfigured. Maybe she already does, now that the relief has passed. She won't feel like the same woman. She won't feel desirable, if that's the right word. It's up to you to show her she's wrong. I wanted you to know it before you saw her. What happens now on depends on you, on *both* of you, especially you sayin' and doin' the right thing. I thought you should know in advance."

Smith grinned. "And thus ends Doctor Smith's lecture. Now go see your wife."

As Houston eagerly turned toward the house, Smith called out a last warning.

"Take it easy. She's been through a hard time."

Houston slipped through the door of their bedroom. Margaret was asleep, propped up in a sitting position. His heart was so full he couldn't say anything.

She either sensed his presence or heard his breathing. She

75

jerked awake and gave a little cry. Suddenly she was in his arms. He wasn't even aware he'd crossed the room.

Without thinking, he pulled back, fearful of the contact. He didn't want to hurt her. Margaret took it for something else and began to cry, soft at first, then with deep sobs.

He was afraid to hold her close because he didn't want to hurt her. But with Smith's words fresh in his mind he knew that he'd made a terrible mistake. He awkwardly sat on the edge of the bed with his hands on her arms. So far, he'd done everything wrong. Worse, he didn't know how to make it right.

He tenderly touched her wet cheek with the back of his fingers. "Maggie, what is it?" he asked. "Tell me. I didn't mean..."

Margaret violently shook her head. She stopped crying and pushed herself up straight. She looked like a soldier working up his courage before charging a well-defended position.

"I've got somethin' to say, Sam, and I don't want you to interrupt me."

He saw Margaret fighting herself, misery etched on her face.

"Sam, the operation..."

She took a deep breath and the words came in a clumsy rush, as if she'd practiced what she wanted to say, but never found the right way to say it.

"I'm not the woman I was. I mean, I'm not the woman you married. I'm scarred and ugly. You can't love me, not the way I am. Look at me!"

She angrily yanked at her nightgown with her left hand. The cloth tore with a gentle ripping sound and exposed her breast. A series of frightening red scars puckered across her breast at the deep depression where Smith removed the tumor. The ligatures in the incisions bristled like dark hairs.

"If you leave me, I'll understand," she said, her voice catching. "I wish I'd died when Ashbel cut me!"

Margaret lowered her head as the tears rolled down her face and fell lightly on her exposed breast.

Houston stepped back to the white-washed bedroom wall. He tugged off one boot, then the other. The boots made a thumping sound as they hit the floor. The sound made Margaret look up. He tossed his coat to the floor, shrugged his suspenders from his shoulders, pulled his shirt over his head, unbuttoned his pants and let them drop to the ground.

Stark naked, he stepped out of the pile of clothes at his feet.

"Look at me, Maggie," he said.

With tears rolling down her red cheeks, she tugged the nightgown over her breast and looked down, refusing to meet his eyes.

"Look at me!"

He'd never used that voice with her, the booming voice he used to command men or to reach the distant recesses of the Senate. Unconsciously, Margaret obeyed, her senses struck numb.

He watched her eyes rove the scarred body she knew so well: the terrible wound where a Creek musket ball left a colorful web of red and purple scars where his shoulder met his collarbone; more scars etched in the big muscle at the top of his arm where another Creek musket ball put him down; the discolored skin hardened like pine in the fist-size hollow where a barbed arrow caught him in the thigh; his San Jacinto leg, a pale depression above his ankle where hair wouldn't grow on the scar tissue thanks to a close-range blast from a Mexican musket that almost cost him his leg.

"Look at me, Maggie," he said. "I'm scarred and nicked and battered. I was this way when you found me and changed my life. I believed you when you said you loved me. Why do you think I can't love you? Why is it you can love me the way I am, but I can't love you? What are a few scars between us? They're nothin' at all, just a sign we're alive."

Margaret saw something else, too. Houston had been away for months, which meant he was without a woman for months. Even so, after an all-night ride it was the last thing he expected, to be standing naked in his own bedroom with a massive hard on while his wife wept in despair.

He didn't know what to do about it so he did nothing while his pecker pointed at her like a post.

Margaret started to laugh. At first she laughed and cried at the same time. Then the crying stopped and it was all laughter.

He started laughing, too. His pecker didn't seem to mind. You could hang a hat on that thing.

"It looks like you *are* glad to see me," gasped Margaret, laughing so hard new tears rolled from her eyes.

She reached out and drew him into bed. After a few minutes she gently put him on his back and mounted him with her knees outside his hips. When he protested that he didn't want to hurt her, she only laughed.

"Hurtin' is not what I have in mind."

––––––––––

THEY SAT in twin rockers on the porch of the little house. It was near dusk, with the smell of a good spring in the air, fresh and humid and raw like the earth itself. They heard the cicadas in the woods, a comforting sound Houston associated with the end of the day ever since he was a boy. They kept their voices low so not to disturb the sleeping Margaret. Holding a bottle in one hand, Smith balanced two glasses in the other as he poured drinks. He handed one to Houston and reached out and clinked Houston's glass.

"This is the brandy Margaret wouldn't drink," Smith explained. "I figured I'd save it for just this occasion, the best and highest use I can think of."

Houston took a deep swallow and felt the satisfying burn. Now that he wasn't drinking much, when he did drink it made the occasion seem special.

Holding the glass in his lap with both hands, he said, "Ash, there's no way I can explain how grateful I am. I can't..."

"Oh, shut up," growled Smith.

After a few minutes while they listened to the sounds of dusk, Smith broke the silence.

"I don't mean to pry, Sam, but is *that* what you call takin' it easy? Judgin' by the sounds I heard until I decided it was time to take a walk over to the creek, my advice must have been just this side of brilliant. I just didn't think you'd turn it into action so soon."

"It surprised me, too," Houston admitted. "I don't know. It just...came up."

"I suppose it did." Smith kept his face expressionless.

He reached into his shirt pocket.

"Thought you might want this as a keepsake," he said.

He flipped it toward Houston, who caught it in mid-air; a silver dollar marred by teeth marks on both sides.

12

MARGARET'S ILLNESS convinced Houston that the house at Raven Hill was too remote, especially with a growing family that was about to grow by one more. Margaret was pregnant again.

After some considerable searching, he found a beautiful piece of land, almost two hundred acres on the edge of Huntsville with a pretty little year-round spring and an abundance of trees for shade from the summer heat. The ground was so fertile they could grow almost everything they needed for food.

It was good land for cotton, too. Houston was determined to give cotton a try. Some of the fields along the Texas river bottoms yielded as much as two thousand pounds an acre. Flatboats and steamboats traveled up and down the east Texas rivers collecting the harvest in five hundred-pound bales and carrying them to Galveston. From there the bales were transferred to ships bound for the mills in the northeast or across the Atlantic to England and France.

Cotton was hard work and they'd need more slaves. God

knows how they'd find the money. But with cotton selling for fifteen cents a pound a good crop on fifty acres would go a long way toward solving their money problems.

The possibilities seemed endless. Walking the property with Margaret to show her everything it offered, near the spring Houston got down on one knee, dug his fingers into the soft dark earth, and held it up for his wife to see.

"I swear, Margaret, this soil is so rich if we put ten-penny nails in the ground it wouldn't be long before we'd have a crop of iron bolts."

Margaret giggled. "Sam, if I didn't know you better I'd think you were the biggest liar in Texas."

He tossed the dirt aside and brushed his hand on his trousers. Caught up in the happiness of the moment, he swept Margaret up in his arms and whirled her around.

"I may be just that," he laughed. "There's some who say so."

Their hopes and dreams aside, the property cost more than they could afford. Selling Raven Hill wouldn't nearly cover it all. It was a stretch, that's for sure. Maybe too much of a stretch, he wondered?

What convinced Margaret and nudged Houston into making an offer was Huntsville itself. A few years ago, it was just another east Texas village no one would have missed if it disappeared overnight. Now it was the proper town where Margaret always wanted to live. She never got used to the isolation of Raven Hill.

With Huntsville booming, progress flowered everywhere. Working with an ambitious young Virginian named Henderson Yoakum, Houston used his influence to have Huntsville named the county seat, which allowed him to do more of his legal work at home. Yoakum, who had nine children, started an academy for the Huntsville youngsters. The nine Yoakums were the first to enroll. Little Sam was tenth.

There was a Baptist church for Margaret, too. Houston was skeptical about organized religion, but made it a point to attend from time to time, bellowing out hymns with the best of them. If nothing else, it was good politics. Margaret was dying to convert him. He felt her waiting to pounce. But she was canny enough to wait. She knew that pushing only increased his resistance.

Once they decided to buy the property, the sale was quickly consummated. A house was only part of the complex Houston had in mind, one that he already called Woodland. His eagerness to see it become a reality ran roughshod over his common sense. Too impatient to build in stages, he borrowed the money and did it all at once. To their considerable irritation, he supervised the laborers, carpenters, and masons detail by detail. Seeing Woodland rise from nothing was one of the most satisfying events of his life.

His eagerness put them in serious debt, their creditors barely held in check by the modest income from his law practice, which he neglected more than he should to get Woodland up and running.

But no matter how much he worried about money, as their new home took shape Houston knew that it was worth it. Until he married Margaret he never really had a home. He lived wherever he happened to be, each place as temporary as the last. Even Raven Hill never felt like home because he was so rarely there. Woodland was different. He felt it in his bones. Even before they cut the first log, he knew that he belonged here.

The complex included the main house, his office, and a detached kitchen to keep the cooking fires away from the main house. There were quarters for their dozen slaves, a cotton barn, a privy, a smoke house, the stables, a chicken coop, a carriage house, a corn crib, and a spring house. He changed his mind so often about what he wanted and how he wanted it that by the time the place was close to finished it looked like some giant hand haphazardly had thrown it down like dice.

The house was larger than Raven Hill, but by no means grand. He laughed at his old dream of one day having a home to rival the Hermitage, where the slave quarters alone were bigger than everything they had at Woodland. To make it seem like more than it was, the squared logs were covered by hand-hewn, white-washed boards. The boards not only gave the impression of gentility, they offered extra insulation in the winter. The house was built around a dog run, a wide-open hallway from front to back to let the cooling breeze pass, not to mention dogs, poultry, and the occasional varmint. Their bedroom was on the ground floor on one side of the run, with the parlor on the other side. Unlike the small house at Raven Hill, the parlor comfortably held all of their furniture, including Margaret's rosewood piano. There were two more bedrooms upstairs. If the family kept growing, and he saw no reason why it shouldn't, there'd be one bedroom for the boys and another for the girls.

There was a small pantry behind their ground-floor bedroom and an even smaller bedroom behind the parlor, which is where he'd put visitors, including Nancy Lea. The little room was barely big enough for a single bed, a chest, and a wash stand. Margaret's only objection was that it had no direct access to the parlor. To get from the bedroom to the parlor, her aging mother had to walk out to the back porch, turn into the dog run, and then into the parlor.

"She'll have to go outside just to get to the parlor with the rest of us," Margaret objected.

"Yes, I'm afraid she will, my dear," Houston agreed, the house plans clutched in his hand as they walked through the empty skeleton of their new home, the air alive with the pounding of hammers and the grind of saws. "There are times when suitable architecture demands sacrifice."

She was skeptical. He saw that clear enough.

He walked around the unfinished parlor and waved his arms to show he knew what he was talking about. He remembered Jackson doing the same thing when the general led a tour of the yet-to-be-built Hermitage, the grand version that was still years in the future.

"To put a door to her bedroom along the back wall of the parlor would cost us the use of that wall and there's no other place for your piano, not with windows on the opposite wall and the fireplace over here. I'm afraid that practicalities overrode my consideration for your mother."

Margaret gave him a level look and walked away. He secret hoped if his mother-in-law was sufficiently inconvenienced she wouldn't visit so often. He suspected that Margaret knew it, too.

The house was almost finished before Houston realized that he'd built a smaller version of his old family home in Virginia, before they pulled up and moved to Tennessee after his father died. Wasn't that the damnedest thing? The idea must have been in the back of his mind all these years.

The feature that gave him the most pleasure was his office, the first proper office he ever had. It was nothing fancy, just a small cabin of unfinished logs away from the main house, with his battered desk, an oak chair with a rawhide bottom, an old buffalo rug to help keep the chill out in the winter, a stone fireplace, and a raised wood-plank floor. The walls were covered with shelves for his law books, his volumes of Shakespeare, and several translations of The Iliad, his lifelong favorite.

The office was his private sanctum. No one but Joshua could enter. Fortunately, Margaret understood the need. He could think and write and receive clients and friends. He felt free to smoke, too. He was fond of cigars and enjoyed the occasional pipe. His wife disapproved of smoking almost as much as she disapproved of drinking, cursing, and most of his clients.

"These people need a lawyer precisely *because* they're in trouble," he explained. "Everyone, no matter how low, is entitled to legal representation. In a perfect world there would be no need for lawyers. Or politicians either."

He tried to look downcast and put upon, a look that he'd pretty much perfected over the years.

"And for myself, it's well known even the most virtuous man needs *one* vice."

Eyes sparkling, Margaret stood on her tiptoes and gave him a kiss on the cheek.

"Sam Houston, I love you dearly," she said, eyeing him in her shrewd and knowing way. "But you could do away quite a few vices and still have a sufficient number left over."

He supervised all the building until he couldn't contain himself and jumped in to lend a hand. They felled the timber on another section of the property, cut the logs to length and hauled them by oxen to the site. With the logs properly notched, they raised the walls by rolling the logs one on top of the others by means of skids. Two men hauled the logs from above with ropes while two other men pushed the logs up the skids from below. Three men rived shingles and shaved them down with draw knives. From dawn to dusk the warm days were full of the sharp pounding of big axes, the thumping of mallets, and the shouts and cries of men at work.

The happy days turned into weeks and then into months. With the Senate back in session, he knew that he should be in Washington. But there were too many reasons not to go. Margaret's health, for one. Although she'd recovered from her ordeal, she still wasn't her old self. She'd lost weight, although she was gaining it back with the pregnancy. She'd changed in other ways, too. Her face seemed longer, her cheekbones more pronounced, and her body harder than before. Some of it was maturity; the Alabama girl that he married was replaced by a strong woman who'd borne children and suffered illness, loneliness, and hardship, someone who coped with life in a way she never thought possible.

Yes, his Maggie had changed. But by God she was still a beauty and he loved her all the more for it.

Even as grim and bloody a job as hog butchering held new attraction for him. The work began early in the morning when a slave threw slops in the trough and the pigs waddled up to feed. Joshua quickly stepped up behind each one and struck it between the eyes with the flat of an ax, an expert blow that killed with one swing. Another slave moved in to slash the dead pigs' throats to bleed them. The blood gushed out of the jagged wounds and made a stinking red mud of the ground. One by one the animals were dragged to great tubs of water boiling over fires set in deep holes so the rims of the tubs were even with the ground. The pigs were dumped into the tubs and scalded. With the hides scraped free of gristle, the carcasses were hung from a tree by the heels and gutted. They were washed out, scraped of fat and butchered. The hams and middlings were hung in the smoke house. Most of the fat was fried into cracklins, and some of that mixed with cornpone. What wasn't fried was turned into lard or soap.

He hadn't done any hog butchering since he was a boy. But that didn't stop him from pitching in. His clumsy efforts boundlessly entertained Margaret, little Sam, the slaves, and even the hired help.

Backing up in the soft bloody mud as he hauled one carcass to the fire, Houston's feet slipped and he fell flat on his back with the foul gory thing on top of him like a lover. A stricken silence fell over the yard. Everyone in sight waited until he began to laugh at his predicament, and only then did they join in.

At the end of the long day, with their clothes stiff and stinking with blood and the air foul with the scent of killing, the men stripped naked and washed themselves in the beautiful little spring out of sight of the house, laughing and shouting with the pleasure of it. The fastidious Houston knew that he couldn't bring himself to ever again wear the old shirt, trousers, and threadbare moccasins he wore for the butchering, so he gave the clothes to one of the hired hands. He was sore and aching in a way he hadn't felt in years, but it was satisfying, too. Despite the filthy work, the feeling of well-earned righteousness was cleansing.

"What's happened to me, Henderson?" he asked Yoakum a few days later as they left a meeting of the Huntsville school association, where Houston donated his legal services for free. "As a youngster I hated farming with every thought and muscle. Now I can't get enough of it."

Yoakum fiddled with his briar pipe to get it going in the darkness as they walked across the town square to their horses.

"I suspect it's the difference between *havin'* to do it and *wantin'* to do it," he replied. "You can walk away whenever you want. Most people don't have that selection in life. Even with your new-found zeal for the task I doubt you'd want to butcher hogs for the rest of your days."

Riding home through the dark, letting the horse find the way, Houston considered Yoakum's point. It was true that he could pick and choose in many things. Yes, there were worries, but he could take pleasure in what to others was grinding labor that rarely allowed them look up and see life, much less enjoy it.

Sam Houston was a lucky man and he knew it. For that reason, and others too many to count, he didn't leave for

Washington simply because he didn't want to. For once in his life, the pleasures of home were stronger than the great events of the day. He knew there would come a time when the call would be too strong to resist. But for now it felt good to be home.

13

HE WAS NOT a patient man by nature. But by now anyone would be fed up with the rascals who were holding up his re-election out of sheer spite.

When Houston and Tom Rusk were named Texas' first Senators, they drew straws to see who got the full term and who drew a partial term so that both seats wouldn't be up for election at the same time. Houston got the short term and now it was past time for the legislature to re-elect him, but instead it dawdled and fiddled.

Some even had the *cojones* to question Houston's Washington expenses. He replied with detailed records justifying his accounts to the penny, even if he improvised most of it in his office. The investigation concluded that Sam Houston might be the only politician in history to *lose* money on expenses. His friends had a good laugh at that one.

Although he groused about the investigation, he didn't really mind. Yes, it was aggravating, but it was politics. What rankled was that Texas still owed him a considerable sum for his two terms as president of the Republic. In those days, he rarely got expenses, much less his salary. No one ever mentioned payment for *that* little service, and he was too proud to bring it up.

It was time to go to Austin and put an end to this nonsense. The world was calling again.

———

HIS BELLY full from a spectacular meal of consume, capons with truffles, chestnut puree, pears, vanilla pudding, and chicory coffee fresh from New Orleans, Houston pushed his chair back from the table. He crossed his long legs at the ankles, lit a match with his thumbnail, and applied the flame to his cigar until he got it drawing properly.

Two or three of his dinner companions were out at the privy in back of Columbine's, a new restaurant, tavern, and sporting room on Congress Avenue near the capital. Although he still didn't like Austin, he had to admit that Columbine's was impressive. The fringed wine-red velvet curtains were as thick as rugs, with the subdued music from a string trio playing at the far end of the room. Not even the smallest detail was neglected. The oil in the lamps was so expensive that it burned virtually smokeless

As far as Houston knew, Ash Smith was the only one who didn't like it. The widely-traveled doctor wrinkled his nose, sniffed, and declared that it "looks like a high-priced Paris whorehouse."

Smith was entitled to his opinion, but until something better came along Columbine's suited Houston just fine. At one time, he might have enjoyed a high-priced Paris whorehouse, too.

It had been a fine evening, with a break after dinner while the old friends, sometime rivals, and acquaintances there to celebrate Houston's re-election went out back to relieve themselves, out front to get some air, or just relax around the table.

Houston didn't drink as much as he once did. These days he hardly drank at all. His dinner companions marveled at the abstemious gentleman who'd replaced their old friend. But he hadn't entirely stopped either. Right now a glass of port was just the thing to aid his digestion. A glass after dinner wasn't really drinking, especially measured against his past standard of consumption.

"You know," he said to James Taylor White, who was seated to Houston's right, "there was a time when I regarded Austin as the most miserable place on the face of the earth."

White, whose attention was distracted by a series of small belches, was an illiterate Louisiana farmer who'd come to Texas twenty years ago and settled near Anahuac with three cows and two ponies. Now he was one of the richest men in the state. Houston was working up to asking White for a loan until he collected some long-owed debts for legal services. After a few minutes alone with the man he wondered if the loan was worth the work. White didn't seem interested in anything except the price of beef and the price of land. Considering how much of both he owned - forty thousand acres and thirty thousand head of cattle, they said - maybe there wasn't room for anything else in his square head?

"But even my enemies will tell you that I admit when I'm wrong," continued Houston, whose enemies said no such thing. "Bein' fair-minded, I concede that Austin may only be the second or third most miserable place on earth."

Instead of the expected laugh, White responded with a low growl.

"Land around here's too expensive." The cattleman's belching grumble added peculiar emphasis to his words. "They want ten dollars an acre for it. Wasn't long ago they'd take half that and been happy in the bargain."

"...and it wasn't long ago nobody wanted it, most of all Senator Houston here," interrupted Governor Pinckney Henderson, back from his turn at the outhouse.

A gangly man with a long head and weak chin, Henderson was recently returned from the war, where he commanded a regiment under Taylor. The experience convinced Henderson that Taylor would be the next President, assuming that Polk kept his word and didn't run for a second term.

"He's got the disease, make no mistake," explained Henderson. "He'll invade Washington just like he invaded Mexico. Say what you want about him, but once he puts his head down Taylor's a hard man to stop."

In ones and twos, Houston's dinner companions filed back into the luxurious dining room. First through the door was Sam Maverick, who owned even more land than White, although he wasn't nearly as wealthy. As usual, the gray-bearded Maverick appeared to be looking for someone to disagree with. A former San Antonio mayor and occasional legislator, he was renowned for his unpredictability. He could be a good friend one day and unforgiving opposition the next. Houston found that short men like Maverick were often cantankerous.

The prematurely balding Frank Lubbock was right behind Maverick. A rising star in state politics, Lubbock jabbered away like a terrier yapping at the older man's heels.

Ash Smith chatted amiably with Gail Borden, the former newspaper editor who made a fortune thanks to some new way of producing milk. Unless Borden bred a new kind of cow, Houston couldn't imagine what the secret might be.

Memucan Hunt, who represented Texas to Washington in the early days of the republic, was deep in one-sided conversation with Ben McCulloch, a San Jacinto veteran turned Ranger. Hunt was peddling shares in a proposed railroad from Galveston to the Red River. As he took his chair,

McCulloch glanced at Houston and rolled his eyes to indicate that Memucan was as boring as ever.

Another Ranger, Big Foot Wallace, was so drunk that all he could do was mumble threats about the "goddamn Meshkins." Everyone at the table wished that he'd pass out and be done with it. It didn't look like there was long to wait.

Seated on the other side of Wallace and keeping to himself, as usual was John Meusebach, who ran a syndicate that brought German immigrants to Texas. Taking over the operation from Prince Carl of Solms-Braunfels, who escaped just ahead of a lynch mob when he was caught pocketing the money that was supposed to support the Germans their first year, Meusebach had already settled more than ten thousand Germans in and around New Braunfels and Fredericksburg, mostly hard-working farmers and artisans. Although Meusebach claimed he had difficulty with English, Houston suspected that he understood more than he let on.

Lighting his cigar, Henderson grinned at Houston over the flaming match.

"Sam, remember when you tried to steal the capital out from under Austin's nose?"

As it always did, mention of the failed coup drew a laugh. Houston enjoyed telling the story, even if it was at his own expense, and motioned to the waiter for another glass of port.

"Nearly pulled it off, too," he said. "If it wasn't for that boardin' house woman the capital would be in my namesake city."

Founded as a tiny settlement named Waterloo on a bend of the Colorado River, Austin was too isolated from most of the rest of the population for Houston's liking. The fact that Austin was Lamar's idea had something to do with it, too. When Lamar succeeded Houston as President, he appointed a committee to find a permanent capital. Lamar pushed for

Waterloo over Houston City, in part to spite Houston, and in part because he genuinely thought it a superior location.

Even Houston had to admit that Houston City wasn't much in those days. Two brothers, John and Augustus Allen, bought twenty two hundred acres of swamp and marsh fifty miles above Galveston. Reasoning the seat of government would attract business and high real estate prices, the brothers spread the word about their "million dollars of capital" to transform the swamp into "the great interior commercial emporium of Texas." They even offered to erect a proper capital building at their own expense. Columbia was the capital that year, but the capital moved so often most folks couldn't say for sure where it was anymore. With republic so badly in debt, the offer of a free capital building got Congress' attention. In return for his support, the Allens offered to name the new city after Houston. His readily accepted the offer.

Lured by dreams of fat government contracts, merchants and craftsmen poured into the city. The Allens hawked lots at prices as high as three thousand dollars. But most newcomers preferred to wait until they got a feel for how things might take shape. Instead of buying lots at inflated prices, they threw up a clutter of shacks, *jacales*, cabins, and tents in areas outside of what the brothers staked out to sell.

The promise of easy money drew another kind of newcomer, too. Houston City quickly became home to every drifter, whore, cardsharp, thimblerig artist, lawbreaker, reprobate, drunk, deserter, and lunatic who passed that way. With so many murders there and in nearby Richmond, an enterprising tavern owner rigged up a tote board allowing customers to bet on which town had the most killings every month. Gangs of youngsters, most of them little more than children, ran wild in the streets, swearing, fighting, thieving, and tormenting the innocent. The town never shut down, but nothing ever got done. There were more than twenty taverns and bars, but not one church. The bayou's water was foul, but the residents drank it anyway. They paid the price for it, too. In one year, more than two hundred residents died from the yellow disease. The stricken included John Allen, whose death took the starch out of his brother, Augustus.

The extent of the brothers' gamble didn't become public until their creditors discovered that the vaunted "million dollars of capital" didn't exist. The Allen brothers were broke, and intended to finance their wild promises from the sale of the town lots, except they were lucky to get a tenth of the asking price for the few that did sell. Augustus Allen narrowly avoided tar and feathers by blaming everything on his dead brother.

"I won my lot in a poker game," Lubbock said. "I paid two hundred and fifty dollars to have a cabin built, but the damn fool carpenter didn't put in any windows. Anytime I needed more air I just kicked a board out of the wall."

That got everyone laughing again. The merriment penetrated Big Foot Wallace's stupor. He jerked upright and looked around in alarm.

"Boys, I tol' you 'bout them damn Meshkins," he shouted.

Warning delivered, Wallace's head fell to the table with a crash. McCulloch seized Wallace's mass of tangled hair, lifted his head, assessed the Ranger's condition, and released his hold so that Wallace's head hit the table with another crash.

"Gentlemen, Big Foot is out for the duration," McCulloch announced. "That's all right. He's heard this story before. So have I, but I don't mind hearin' it again."

With a dramatic wave of his arm, he cried, "Carry on, Senator Houston, carry on!"

With Houston City such a mess, the orderly and well planned Waterloo had the votes to become the next capital. The town was divided by Congress Avenue, a broad central

ROBERT WISEHART

boulevard, and a public auction sold three hundred and six building lots. The new capital was named for Stephen Austin, the *empresario* who died not long after Houston crushed him in the first presidential election. Austin was more popular in death than he ever was in life. The way it was going, Houston figured he'd make sainthood in another ten years.

Construction began with riflemen standing guard on a stockade that was built to protect workers against Comanches. Five months later, the capital officially moved to Austin. Even then anyone who ventured out of town after sundown risked their scalp.

Three years later, a thousand Mexicans under Adrian Woll, a French soldier of fortune turned Mexican general, crossed the Rio Grande and moved on the capital, forcing the government to get out of town in an undignified hurry. Woll held Austin for more than a week before a force of Rangers and militia led by Jack Hays decoyed him out and drove him back to Mexico.

During his second term as president, Houston tried to convince congress to move the capital to Houston City.

"For all the good it did I might as well have been talkin' to Big Foot there," he explained. "So I decided that what I could not do legal and honest I would do illegal and dishonest." He held out his arms as if to embrace them all. "In short, I decided to steal the damn thing. The archives were the key. Congress might meet anywhere, but wherever the archives rested was the capital."

A militia captain named William Pettus was sent to collect them. Unfortunately, word of his mission moved faster than he did. When Pettus rode into Austin he was instantly surrounded by a mob and pulled from the saddle. They cut off his horse's mane and tail as a warning, put the humiliated captain back on his horse, and sent him galloping out of town.

"A setback, yes, but I was undeterred," Houston continued. "I decided on other means and another man."

Another captain, Tom Smith, was sent to steal the records. At midnight on December 30th, Angelina Eberly - whose popular boardinghouse would go bust if the capital left Austin - heard a noise on the street. She peered out her window and saw Smith loading the archives into a wagon.

"In her, ah, sleepin' attire, by which I mean the woman was practically naked, she ran to a cannon on the square that was loaded with grapeshot in case of a Comanche attack," Houston said. "She let loose with a blast that aroused the town and spooked the hell out of Smith's horses. The wagon with the archives clattered off on its own, with Smith gallopin' hell for leather behind. And behind *that* parade thundered an angry group of Austin's finest. They caught up with Smith at the same time he caught up with the wagon. But Smith was no Pettus. Both sides drew their weapons and there was a testy little stand off until cooler heads agreed this was not the time for Texans to be shooting each other. The whole opera decided to hell with it and marched back to town. My coup had failed again."

Despite its dubious start, Houston City went on to flourish almost in spite of itself. The incredible tonnage of cotton shipped downriver increased legitimate business many times. To bring order to the river traffic, the Port of Houston was created by town ordinance and it wasn't long before the city boasted a thriving shipyard. With legitimate money came legitimate enterprise. Today it had more schools than any other city in Texas. There was a new college, too. It looked like civilization was winning, for a change.

With a flourish, Houston rose to his feet and raised his glass.

"So ended the Great Archives War. Austin, that miserable

little fart of a town, remains the capital and I remain damned unhappy about it."

14

Houston and Governor Henderson watched with amusement as Maverick and McCulloch staggered out the door and down the street, one carrying the unconscious Wallace's arms and the other his long legs.

"Old Big Foot's in for a hell of a hangover," Houston said, wincing as he remembered a few hangovers of his own.

"I can't think of a man who deserves it more," Henderson said. "Sam, I'd like a word with you. It'll only take a moment. Can I interest you in a cup of coffee?"

They returned to the restaurant, settling at a small corner table, and ordered their coffee. Houston added milk and stirred it while he waited for Henderson to say his piece.

"Now that your re-election's out of the way I imagine you'll be headed to Washington," Henderson said.

"Once I get back to Huntsville I'll leave within a week or so," replied Houston. "What's on your mind, Pink?"

"Sam, why do you think they held up your election so long?" the Governor asked.

"It was the work of a few scoundrels who care even less for me than I do for them."

"I'm afraid there's more to it than that." Knowing how touchy Houston could be, Henderson chose his words carefully. "I hate to say it, but a risin' number of men don't trust you anymore, including some you regard as friends. They don't know what you're up to, but they fear the worst."

"Pink, I'm not up to anything," Houston protested. "And what's this about 'fear the worst'? What does Texas have to fear from me? I was re-elected with only one less vote than I had the first time, more than two-to-one in favor. They tried to beat me and they lost. To hell with 'em."

Henderson's thin cheeks puffed as he blew air out between his lips. He clasped his hands on top of his head, leaned back and gazed toward the ceiling, carefully measuring his words.

"You just laid out the problem for me," he said. "You're the most sure-footed man I know. If anything you're *too* sure of yourself. More to the point, you act like it. Those who like you call it confidence and those who don't call it arrogance. You keep your own counsel, rarely reveal anything to anybody, smile pleasantly to one and all, and then do as you damn well please."

Seeing Houston's skeptical look, Henderson warned, "Don't be so quick to dismiss what I'm sayin'. Look at your past. A lot of folks think if you'd hanged Santa Anna at San Jacinto like he deserved we wouldn't have this war with Mexico. But you had to go your own way. And what about the archives? How'd you put it? You couldn't do it legal and honest so you tried it illegal and dishonest."

"That was a joke and you know it."

"I *know* it was a joke," the Governor responded. "But you *did* do it. People aren't sure they can count on you like they used to. Some think you've got your eye on the presidency and to get national support you've gone soft on what matters here. I even heard you intend to vote for Oregon as a free territory."

Henderson waited for Houston to deny it. When he didn't, the Governor pushed a little harder.

"Well?"

Houston drained the last of his coffee.

"Here's how I see it: The Missouri Compromise kept this country together for almost thirty years. Under the compromise, everything north of the line is free soil. I don't see sufficient reason to change that."

Henderson threw up his hands.

"In other words, you *will* vote for a free Oregon. You'll be the only southern Senator who'll do it. You know that, don't you?"

"I've been alone before. Tell me, who's given more to Texas than I have? Or doesn't that matter anymore?"

"There's nobody and you know it," Henderson said. "But Texas is changing. All these new people care about is today and tomorrow, not what happened ten or fifteen years ago. Look at your own party, Sam. It's falling apart. Everything Jackson built is in ruins. "

It hurt to admit it, but Houston knew that Henderson was right. The old alliance of Jackson Democrats was dead. When Polk refused to break his promise and run for a second term, the Democrats turned to Michigan senator Lewis Cass. The problem was old Matty Van Buren, vice president back during Jackson's second term who followed Jackson as president. Led by Van Buren, a noisy mix of antislavery Democrats, Whigs, and independents put together something called the Free Soil Party. They weren't strong enough to win a national election, but intended to give their abolitionist views a good airing. The South already felt skittish. The Free Soilers' rise made it worse. Even southerners who didn't own slaves felt the pressure.

Van Buren even found an Adams - Charles Francis Adams, John Quincy's son – for a running mate. The two of them gave the Free Soilers a legitimacy they hadn't earned. With most of the Free Soil votes coming from Democrats, the new party just might be enough to cost Cass the election and put Taylor in the White House, assuming Taylor ran like everyone expected him to.

"There comes a time when a man has to choose," Henderson warned. "Maybe it's not here yet, but it's coming. Count on it. At such times, it's best to choose your own people."

Impatient to be finished with this nonsense, Houston rose from the table.

"Look, Pink. I can't control what other people say. If some folks don't like what I stand for, or if they have some mistaken notion of who or what I am thanks to this reputation of mine, then my reputation be damned."

"Sam, I'm afraid that one of these days your reputation is going to damn you," Henderson said.

15

"FOR THE LIFE of me I don't see how any civilized person could live in Texas, not with the ticks, that horrible black mud, the sand flies, and those gigantic mosquitoes. I spent a week in a pest hole called Nacogdoches and the miserable place almost did me in. I was bedridden for a month. You may be a man of national reputation, but you represent the most perfect purgatory on the face of the earth. Do you know the *real* reason why I oppose our war with Mexico? I oppose it because a victory will only gain us more territory that resembles Texas and I never want to encounter that again this side of hell."

Houston didn't know who this fool was, but he had enough of being poked in the chest by his pudgy finger.

He'd looked forward to this reception after so long away from Washington. The Polks didn't give many and that made each one an event. He took special care with his appearance, wearing his jaguar-skin vest, a broad-brimmed, smoke-colored hat with a half-inch fur nap, and a white silk shirt with ruffles at the neck and wrists. His buff-colored coat came to his knees, with black trousers worn over black leather boots polished until he saw his image.

He thought about wearing his sword with the curved Damascus blade and elaborate engraving in a gold floral pattern, with the hilt of pearl and brass tapered to a lion's head. His military rank entitled him to it. But he decided that it might be too much of a martial statement. Instead he carried a gleaming walnut cane topped with a gold knob inscribed with his name.

He wore three rings, too. There was his wedding ring, plus a thin gold band on the small finger of his right hand with the word "honor" inscribed on the inside, a gift from his mother when he left home to join the army. The third ring was a topaz stone in a gold setting on the index finger of his right hand.

Flamboyant dress was a habit he picked up from the Cherokee, who believed it was a man's duty to be noticed. Houston couldn't agree more, although some men were more worthy of notice than others. Several turns before the mirror in his hotel room confirmed that he still possessed the broad shoulders and narrow waist of a younger man.

Unfortunately, Houston had barely passed through the double doors of the East Room when he found himself cornered by this fool who was nearly done in by the bite of a Texas mosquito. He was polite at first. Pretending to pay attention to some bore was the hazard of a political career, but a few minutes exposure to this windbag would test Jehovah.

Stepping closer, he towered over the balding man with the soft pink hands and double chin.

"I'll strike a bargain with you, sir," Houston said, hardening his eyes. "Either you go away and bother someone else or I will give your fat head a dunking in that punch bowl yonder."

The man's small piggy mouth fell open, his eyes bulged in

surprise, and he took an abrupt step back as if he expected Houston to strike him. He looked so comical Houston fought the urge to laugh.

Safely out of range, the man found his voice.

"Senator Houston, you are a barbarian not fit to consort with decent people!" he blustered. "I've never been so insulted."

"That *was* my purpose," drawled Houston.

The man drew himself up.

"I don't waste my time talking to scoundrels."

"I'm afraid that I do," Houston replied mildly.

With that final insult, the man flushed, turned on his heel and waddled away.

"Congratulations, Sam. Unless I'm mistaken, and I make it a point never to misidentify the rich, you've just offended Charles Ramsbottom, reputed to be the wealthiest man in New England."

Houston knew that voice. A smile was on his face even before he turned to confirm that it was Stephen Douglas.

Although they often disagreed, he enjoyed Illinois Senator's company. You could argue with Douglas all day and have a convivial dinner with him that night. He did have a tendency toward pomposity, but most politicians did, including, Houston admitted, himself from time to time.

"Senator Douglas," he said, shaking Douglas' hand. "Delighted to see you in good health."

"Never better, Sam. Never better. Apparently eating and drinking too much agrees with me. I am a medical phenomenon."

Douglas was an odd-looking man. He resembled a stuffed pigeon, with a thick chest and torso on tiny legs. His outsized head was striking, with abundant dark hair, heavy brows, piercing eyes, and big jaw. The overall effect was grotesque, as if he was assembled from leftover parts.

With his short legs, the Illinois Senator was more impressive sitting down than standing up. He knew it, too. It wouldn't be long before he'd be sitting in a corner surrounded by admirers, like a potentate holding court.

"Tell me, how does a fool like that become so wealthy?" Houston asked.

"Mills, factories, a remarkable skill for keeping his heel on the necks of the poor and downtrodden," replied Douglas. "They say no virtuous man can ever be rich."

"In that case, I must be the most virtuous man in the country," Houston said.

"You've been missed, Sam," Douglas said. "I trust I'll see you tomorrow?"

"You will indeed," replied Houston. "We can resume all of our old arguments and start new ones."

"I look forward to it," Douglas said with warm smile. "And now I believe I'll find a glass of the Polks' deplorable champagne. If their taste runs true to form, it won't drown my sorrows as much as poison them."

In his eagerness, Houston arrived as the reception was scheduled to begin, which meant he was early and the crowd still thin. He strolled the room, nodding to people he knew. The walls were covered with elegant lemon-yellow wallpaper and the high windows hung with yellow-and-blue curtains. Overhead, suspended from the twenty-two-foot ceiling, were three monumental crystal chandeliers, each one lit by eighteen oil lamps with glass shades. Although it was the dead of winter and pitch black outside, the room was as bright as a summer day.

It was Jackson who had the chandeliers installed and they reminded Houston of one of the more peculiar events of the Jackson administration. Someone made the President a present of a fourteen-hundred-pound cheddar cheese. It arrived in a fancy cart drawn by twenty-four magnificent gray horses. No one knew what to do with the absurd gift. The cheese sat in the entrance hall until Jackson finally declared that the people should eat it. It took all day for the mob to devour the thing. The faded stain could still be seen on the floor.

He still missed Jackson. They didn't see each other often in the last years, but he longed for the comforting presence of the man who took him under his wing when he was still a raw-boned boy with more brawn than brains.

Tom Rusk entered the room, limping as a result of a recent carriage accident.

"How do, Sam," he said. "I was lookin' for you. There's news about Seguin."

"Good news, I hope."

"Looks like he's comin' home," Rusk said. "Keep it to yourself. It won't be official for a while. He'll file a petition admitting to everything he did and some he didn't, but it's done."

"That's a fine piece of work, Tom," Houston said. "It's a sad thing to know that in a fair world Texas should apologize to Juan, not the other way 'round."

"Who is this Juan fellow and why is he so much trouble?" interrupted James Buchanan, who'd quietly slipped up without their knowing it.

Shaking hands with the Texans, Buchanan added, "When I saw you two talking so eagerly I knew something was going on. Is this Juan fellow someone I need to worry about? I hope not. I have enough on my plate."

It was typical of Buchanan, thought Houston, nettled by the reference to "this Juan fellow." The Secretary of State's only interest was self interest.

Buchanan was one of the young men who orbited around Jackson in the old days, although he eventually fell out of favor. The general sent him into exile by naming him ambassador to Russia. He eventually recovered to win election to the Senate representing Pennsylvania during the Van Buren administration. Buchanan was one of several who made a bid for the presidency in '44, but lost the nomination to Polk. One of the new President's first acts was to name his old friend Secretary of State, the worst decision Polk ever made, in Houston's view.

Buchanan was tall but soft, with graying blonde hair. A meticulous, though somber, dresser, he was nearsighted in one eye and had a habit of tilting his head as if his neck hurt. Some thought it a charming gesture. Others were distracted by it.

Houston regarded Buchanan as a weakling who shifted his beliefs, assuming he had any, according to which side would likely win. He was so consumed by ambition that it made him fearful, as if his advancement was a delicate thing that might shatter any moment. He'd never married and there were scandalous rumors that he preferred boys, but Houston didn't think there was room in Buchanan's heart for anyone except Buchanan.

"So tell me about this Juan of yours," Buchanan said.

The story of Juan Seguin made Houston angry every time he thought about it. Unfortunately, by the time he knew his old friend was in trouble it was too late. Buchanan wasn't really interested and Houston knew it, but he decided to tell the story. Buchanan asked, so let him listen.

The Seguins were an old and respected *Tejano* family. Juan's father, Don Erasmo, was *alcade* of San Antonio and a member of the Mexican congress. They owned one of the largest ranchos in Texas and were among the first *Tejanos* to cooperate with Moses Austin and his son Stephen to bring *norte americano* settlers into the colony. Juan followed his father to become *alcade* of San Antonio before he was thirty.

Seguin's liberal politics made him a natural opponent of Santa Anna. As the dictator's iron hand closed on Mexico,

Seguin joined the Texas independence movement and helped take San Antonio from Santa Anna's brother in law, General Martin Cos. The humiliating defeat spurred Santa Anna's drive north to Texas.

Seguin joined Houston's ragtag army as a captain of cavalry and shortly found himself back in San Antonio, riding into the Alamo with Buck Travis, where Travis and Jim Bowie agreed to fight instead of follow Houston's order to blow up the place and get out. A few days into the siege, Travis sent Seguin galloping out of the crumbling mission with a message for help. He took Jim Bowie's horse, the fastest mount in the compound, and outran the Mexican patrols. He was headed back to San Antonio with the few men he'd managed to scrape together when he got word the Alamo had fallen. Seguin commanded Houston's rear guard during the desperate retreat after the disasters at the Alamo and Goliad, beating off the Mexican cavalry. After San Jacinto, Houston promoted him to colonel.

The flood of settlers in the next few years brought a new kind of people to Texas, people who treated the *Tejanos* worse than they treated niggers. As military commander, senator, and then mayor of San Antonio, more than once Seguin had to use force to defend his fellow *Tejanos*. The spirited defense of his people led to the ridiculous charge that he was in treasonous correspondence with the Mexican army during Mexico's brief invasion in '42.

"We didn't know it was as bad as it was until Juan took off for Mexico with his family, barely ahead of a mob," explained Houston. "The Mexicans grabbed him as soon as he crossed the border."

Seguin was given a choice - join the Mexican army or rot in jail. Fearing for his family if he went to prison, he joined the army, protecting against Rio Grande crossings by the Anglos and turning back Comanche raids.

"He probably saw action against Taylor, too," Houston said. "That's only a rumor, but any sensible man would want Juan Seguin on his side in a fight."

The resourceful Seguin escaped and went into hiding in northern Mexico. He sent out feelers about returning to Texas, but wasn't sure how he'd be received. Houston asked Rusk to take charge of the issue. If word got out that Houston had taken up Seguin's cause, some would oppose it just because Houston was for it.

"We'd appreciate it if you wouldn't say anything until Juan gets home," Houston concluded.

"Not a word," Buchanan said, utterly devoid of sympathy. "Well, we all have our burdens. I'm sure it'll work out. Good to see you, gentlemen."

With that, he strolled away to find a less depressing conversation.

"Helpful, wasn't he?" Houston said.

"At least he's consistent," Rusk said. "You know that you can *never* count on Jim Buchanan."

For the next hour, Houston enjoyed the reception. The President and First Lady appeared, but Polk stayed only a few minutes, leaving Sarah to shoulder the social burden. During their time in the White House, Polk had the odd habit of barely attending his own infrequent parties.

Houston felt someone squeeze his elbow, an army captain with an empty sleeve.

"Senator, the President would like a word alone with you," the captain said quietly. "Later, you will be joined by others. He apologizes for the interruption, but promises that it will be worth your time. To avoid drawing attention, why don't you wait a few minutes after I leave and meet me down the hall?"

Houston waited ten minutes before following the one-armed captain up the curving stairway and down the wide hall to a conference room with a large table and a dozen chairs. Polk sat at the head of the table, reading what looked like a military dispatch.

"Senator, it's a pleasure to see you again," he said, rising to shake Houston's hand.

Polk seemed to have aged twenty years since they last saw each other. His deep-set eyes were bloodshot and rheumy and his complexion was sallow. He unconsciously rubbed his chest as if soothing some deep ache. His breathing was labored, too, like he couldn't get enough air in his lungs.

"Please, sit down," Polk said. "I wanted some time with you before the others came in."

To hide his shock at the President's appearance, Houston blurted out the first thing that came to his mind.

"Mister President, whatever happened to that lieutenant on duty the first time I visited you here," he asked, "the one who seemed so infernally pleased with himself?"

"You mean Mound, a handsome and somewhat self-important young man?" asked Polk.

"That's him."

"He joined General Scott in Mexico," Polk explained. "He believed that serving in the war was a necessary addition to his record. For one so young, Percival was very ambitious."

"Sounds like us at that age," Houston said. "Is he still with Scott?"

"I'm afraid not," Polk said. "A Mexican cannonball took his head off at some meaningless skirmish deep in the interior. The only way they recognized his body was by one of my letters in his pocket."

Polk looked stricken. Houston had rarely seen him so emotional.

"For all his airs, Percival was a promising young man," Polk placed a hand over his eyes. "I've known his parents most of my life. It was a hard thing to tell them of their son's death. Part of my interest is selfish, I suppose. He was the closest I'll come to a protégé. I would have enjoyed watching a young man grow."

The silence was almost unendurable. The Polk Houston knew was usually so detached and cool. Something was wrong. Was it illness? The strain of the Presidency? Polk never gave up the habit of doing everything himself; holding together a squabbling coalition that almost certainly would fall apart the minute he left office while at the same time leading the country in an increasingly unpopular war.

"Don't misunderstand me, Rogers out there is a good man," Polk said. "He lost his arm in a munitions explosion. There isn't much future for a one-armed captain. I had him assigned here until his retirement. It seemed the least I could do."

Drawing on some inner reserve, Polk reverted to his old crisp business-like self.

"I didn't ask you here to watch me wallow in self pity," he explained. "I have news. The dispatches arrived within the hour."

Holding up a sheaf of papers, the President announced, "The war is over. Scott's taken Mexico City. Santa Anna's probably out of the country by now."

Polk placed the papers on the table.

"I'll leave you alone to take a look at this before the others arrive," he said. "I'll be back in a half hour."

16

HOUSTON SHUFFLED THROUGH THE MATERIAL; dispatches from Scott, reports from the President's men with Scott's army, and private letters from Scott's staff and other officers.

Obviously the letters were sidetracked to Polk before going on to their intended recipients, a violation of law that did not trouble Houston in the least. Jackson did the same thing. A candid private letter could be more informative than any dispatch.

The more he read, the more he appreciated Winfield Scott's extraordinary feat of arms. He felt a pang of regret he wasn't able to accept Scott's offer to join him. It would have been glorious.

The general assembled his army at Tampico and sailed south, where he engineered a faultless landing near Vera Cruz. The city was captured two days later. From there, Scott led his army of fourteen thousand men inland. Facing hostile territory and superior numbers every step of the way, he defeated the Mexicans at Cerro Gordo, Puebla, Contreras, Churubusco, and Molina del Rey.

Between the heavy casualties and garrisons left behind as

they moved inland, by the time the Americans shouldered their way through the pass that flanked the great smoking volcano the Mexicans called Popocatepetl, they were down to nine thousand men. The army came up over a high ridge and suddenly the great Valley of Mexico spread out three thousand feet below.

"It was like looking at a fairyland," a young officer named Sam Grant wrote to his wife Julia. "Hard to believe there was so much danger waiting for us."

Three large lakes ringed the fabled city of the Aztecs like gigantic mirrors. Although Mexico City was more than twenty miles away, in the crisp air the city's towers seemed close enough to touch.

"A panorama to dazzle the gods, perhaps not much different than what Cortez saw more than three hundred years ago," Scott wrote. "I was nearly overcome by the weight of history."

But Mexico City was not Scott's immediate target. In the hills above the city loomed Chapultepec Castle, Mexico's proud military academy. A forbidding stone fortress that seemed to belong to some long-lost age, Chapultepec was said to be impregnable. Scott's scouts and engineers agreed it had to be taken before the army could safely turn on Mexico City. It had to be soon, too, the army was growing weaker every day.

The next morning Scott opened an artillery bombardment that lasted until it was too dark to see. At dawn the next day, the artillery resumed its destruction, with showers of stone chips flying from the old walls.

At mid-morning, the general gave the order to attack. Under heavy fire from the determined defenders, many of whom were students at the academy, the Americans charged the great walls, breached and crumbling in a half-dozen places. Huge clouds of dust rose from where the fighting was hand-to-hand so that when Scott peered anxiously through his telescope, it was impossible to see. For all he knew, his men were being slaughtered. It required all of the general's self control to remain calm and give the impression that he had no doubt about the outcome.

The invincible Chapultepec Castle fell after only an hour. The first Scott knew of it was when he saw the American flag above the walls.

Now Santa Anna and ten thousand troops waited in Mexico City. Some of the troops were the best in Mexico, but others didn't even know how to aim and fire their weapons. Anticipating it might come to this, but never quite believing it would, *El Presidente* had put the city under martial law weeks earlier, emptying the prisons and forcing prisoners into military camps. If they weren't proper soldiers, at least they could haul water, ammunition, and supplies. He ordered every able-bodied Mexican between fifteen and sixty into the army. Press gangs roamed the streets, battering the "recruits" into unconsciousness before dragging them away. Construction crews built new defenses and reinforced existing ones. The marshes surrounding the city were flooded to confine Scott's men to the causeways as they approached.

Certain that Scott would have to rest his tired men, Santa Anna assumed that he still had time to firm up his defenses. Retreat was impossible. There was no where to go. The war would be won or lost here and both sides knew it.

But with the prize so close, Scott did not rest. Only minutes after the American flag was raised above Chapultepec Castle, he demanded one last effort of his men. The army bound its wounds, gathered itself, and stormed down the hillside toward the gates of Mexico City, an irresistible force that took the defenders by surprise and swept everything before it.

When he saw the *norte americanos* burst into the heart of

Mexico, Santa Anna lost his nerve and ran, just as he did at San Jacinto. The Mexicans were brave and many of them fought well, but, abandoned by the charismatic leader who promised so much, one-by-one or in small groups they threw down their arms.

A report from one of Polk's officers described the scene: "There was still fighting in the city and the flag was not even raised over the National Palace when General Scott, dressed in full uniform and mounted on a heavy bay charger, dashed into the grand plaza with his staff and a squadron of dragoons. His gold epaulets and showy plumes were resplendent under the brilliant sun, typifying the glory of his unkempt and limping army."

Although Scott suffered more than eight hundred casualties against two thousand Mexicans killed and wounded, the war was over.

Houston looked up from his reading when Polk returned to the room.

"This is extraordinary," he said.

"I quite agree," Polk said, absentmindedly rubbing his chest. "Unfortunately I doubt that General Scott will get the credit he deserves. Perhaps history will be kind, but for now the war is too unpopular and victory too far away. The masses expected us to win. It never crossed their minds that we wouldn't."

"And Taylor will try to suck up all the credit like a drunk with a keg of rum," Houston said. "Ever since Scott skimmed off the best of his army for the invasion, Taylor's done everything he could to undermine him. He claims that he could have won the war in half the time with half the casualties."

Polk reacted to the mention of Taylor as if he'd smelled a foul odor.

"Twice the time and twice the casualties is more like it. Even so, there isn't much doubt that man will ride all the way to this office. I'm told that he's positively giddy with the idea of the Presidency."

It seemed inevitable. With Polk leaving the White House, no one else had the political clout and public popularity to stop Taylor.

"Mister President, this is fascinatin', and I appreciate your confidence, but what do you want of me?" Houston asked.

"Don't you know?" Polk replied. "I haven't relied on you as much as I have only to ignore you now. In a few minutes, several members of my cabinet and key members of Congress will meet in this room. I'll announce that the war is over and we must decide about the peace. I need you here for that meeting. But before it begins, I want your thoughts about what we can get out of the Mexicans, especially considering our success in California, too."

Houston combed his fingers through his hair. He felt the old urge to pace the room. Movement always freed his mind. Of course, he'd thought about it. Like everyone else, he assumed the war would be won, no matter how difficult. The alternative was unthinkable.

Compared to Scott's accomplishments, despite the best efforts of John Fremont, Commodore Robert Stockton, and General Stephen Kearny to inflate their deeds, the "conquest" of California was like plucking ripe fruit from a tree. The dons there had no great love for Santa Anna. Ignored by their country's government for decades, many of them supported the Americans. Based on what Houston heard, Margaret and Little Sam could have taken Sonoma. The northern California capital was little more than a pathetic soldierless village. Down in Southern California, the most vicious fighting took place among the three American leaders who were frantic that there wouldn't be enough credit to go around.

There probably wasn't, reflected Houston, considering each man wanted *all* the credit. Fremont was in Washington now, facing Kearny's charges of insubordination, charges that would likely lead to a court-martial.

It was ironic that Fremont's reputation just might be the greatest casualty of the campaign. It would serve the bumbling amateur right, Houston thought, although Tom Benton probably wouldn't let his son in law suffer too much damage.

"Mister President, we can get anything we want out of the Mexicans," Houston said. "Their country is in our hands. It's a question of agreein' among ourselves as to what we want. At the very least, I'd expect to get every mile of Mexican territory west to the Pacific. To ease their loss, it might be wise to offer the Mexicans financial considerations. That might blunt the criticism about the war being a glorified land grab, too."

"Do you realize that this doubles the size of our country?" Polk asked, pride strong in his voice. "With the Oregon agreement, this administration will have added more than one million, two hundred thousand square miles of territory to the United States. We'll stretch from sea to sea. No small achievement in only four years."

Houston hated to interrupt Polk's pleasure, but something needed saying.

"Why stop there?"

"What do you mean?"

"Why not seize all of northern Mexico, down to Tampico at least?"

Houston quickly made his case. There wasn't much time.

"A few months back, a faction opposed to Santa Anna requested that we occupy the Yucatan. Maybe the offer's still open? The Mexicans fear the same thing we do. From their possessions in the Caribbean and off South America, it'd be easy for the British to move on a weakened Mexico. The country's been in chaos for fifty years. There's no reason to believe that'll change with another government. Our army's already in place. We can justify our occupation on humanitarian grounds; savin' Mexico from the chaos that engulfs it, somethin' like that."

Polk went to a sideboard. He poured a glass of water from a pitcher and raised his glass, as if offering a toast.

"You never deal in half measures, do you?" he said. "You have an unexpected ally, by the way. Jefferson Davis came to the same conclusion, only he wants the whole country. It will be interesting to watch the two of you try to get along. Keep in mind that Davis was Taylor's son in law until his wife died. They're still close. He'll never make a good friend, not to any man, but there's no doubt he'd make a bad enemy."

Polk returned to the table, thoughtfully rolling the glass between his palms.

"I don't know. Moving south of the Rio Grande may be biting off too much. The abolitionists would howl about the new slave territories. They're already screaming about what's to become of California and New Mexico territory. Nevertheless, I agree with most of what you suggest. As to the rest, we'll see."

Polk pulled a watch from his vest pocket and checked the time.

Nodding toward the door, he said, "And now it's time. Let the peace begin."

17

HOUSTON WAS curious to see and assess Polk's choices. At the same time, he knew that finding Houston in the room with the President before they arrived would disturb a few. Time alone with Polk was the most valuable commodity in Washington.

Postmaster General Cave Johnson entered the room first. Polk's closest advisor and an old friend of Houston's, the long-faced Tennessean's influence far exceeded his position. He wouldn't say much, but his opinion carried weight.

Attorney General John Mason followed Johnson, his deceptively youthful face framed by masses of curly brown hair. Mason was brilliant, but cautious. Houston marked him down as probable opposition to his Mexico scheme.

George Bancroft was the Massachusetts historian Polk inexplicably named Secretary of the Navy. He sidled into the room as if he'd rather not be noticed. Usually content to observe rather than participate, Bancroft was easy to underestimate and used it to his advantage.

William Mary, the pugnacious Secretary of War, glared at

Houston with a dislike he didn't bother to hide. He'd be trouble.

The balding Treasury Secretary, Robert Walker, spent the last eighteen months scrambling to pay for the war, an incredible one hundred million dollars, the most expensive undertaking in the nation's history. If Walker felt the strain he didn't show it. Seeing Houston, he nodded congenially, his thumbs hooked into his waistcoat and fingers splayed across his soft belly.

Seeing Houston, Buchanan's eyes widened in surprise before the usual bland mask closed over his face. He would add nothing to the discussion until late, when he joined the winning side.

South Carolina's John Calhoun marched into the room as if he owned it. Constantly on guard for plots against his state and the south, Calhoun assumed there was much to guard against. It was hard to say where he might come down. The potential slave territory might be too much to resist.

Douglas raised his eyebrows when he saw Houston. On his way to take a seat, Douglas bent over and whispered, "Our next meeting came sooner than I expected."

Tom Benton looked weary and older than his years. Houston laughed to himself that saving his son-in-law's skin must be hard work. Benton wasn't the man he used to be, but the dedicated expansionist was still a powerful ally.

Next came Dan Webster. With his towering reputation, he'd be invaluable when it came time to sell the treaty to Congress and country, whatever it might say.

The temperature in the room seemed to fall when Jefferson Davis took his place at the table. Dressed in gray, with a wide forehead and narrow chin, the Mississippi Senator's Achilles heel was pride, a man who confused compromise with weakness.

For all the foils, idiosyncrasies, and vanity on display, it was an impressive group, and Houston was proud to be part of it.

———

OVER THE NEXT THREE HOURS, pride took a beating.

The stink of anger and frustration was thick in the room. Tempers flared and patience wore thin. The more they argued, the more their differences became clear. It wasn't only North against South, slave states against free, and how more than a million square miles of new territory might tip the balance of power. There were factions within factions and personalities clashed like thunder. It was hard to believe that with so much at stake they could be divided in so many ways. Polk looked like he might collapse from the strain of keeping the meeting under control.

Thanks to Calhoun, Houston was struggling with his own temper. Over the years, while they'd sometimes been on the same side, they never liked each other. Calhoun was the long-time champion of nullification, the idea a state can nullify federal laws if it disagreed with those laws, which came out his passion for state's rights, the position that every state was sovereign and independent of the union.

To Houston's surprise, Calhoun rejected any long-term occupation of Mexico and refused to entertain the thought it might someday join the United States, even as a protectorate, and warned Polk that he'd do everything in his power to block it.

Houston was prepared to let it pass for now and fight another day, but Calhoun wouldn't let go.

"Annexing Mexico or any part of that country would degrade American whites and destroy our own institutions," Calhoun said, his voice harsh and his manner insulting. "In my opinion, we would be better off today if we'd sent the

Mexicans in Texas back to Mexico before we annexed it. As a people they're no better than niggers. The women are slatternly and the men lazy, probably from an excess of nigger blood."

Houston might have ignored someone else, but Calhoun always got under his skin like a field tick. Glaring at the old buzzard, he sneered, "Senator, at least you're consistent. You were a fool when we met more than thirty years ago and you're a fool today. The degradation belongs to South Carolina for putting you in the Senate and keeping you there."

Calhoun rose to his feet, a vein throbbing on his forehead. "By God, sir, I demand satisfaction!"

"Gentlemen! Control yourselves! If we can't disagree without threatening each other then we're no better than barroom brawlers. The country expects more from us. It *deserves* more from us."

Polk realized that he made a mistake by bringing all these men into the room at the same time. It would have been better to approach them one by one. He must be in worse shape than he thought. It was the kind of blunder he never would have made if he'd been himself.

After a pleading look from the President, Houston curtly apologized. This isn't working, he thought. If these men represent the country, the country is in trouble. There must be another way. There always was. All it took was the brains to find it and the skill to make it work.

When the failed meeting ended, Houston interpreted a glance from Polk as an invitation to linger. Once the others filed out of the room, the President slumped in his chair.

"This will not go down as a great moment in the annals of statesmanship," he said. "What a shameful display!"

"Are you all right?" Houston asked, alarmed by Polk's frailty. "Can I get you somethin'?"

"Please, don't trouble yourself," Polk rubbed his bloodshot

eyes. "I'll be fine as soon as I get out of this hellish place. You have no idea what it's like here. The burden is unbearable. If you have any thoughts about this place for yourself, I urge you to resist them. I don't see how General Jackson stood it for eight years. I can barely manage four."

Drawing once more from some inner reserve, Polk rose from his chair and escorted Houston to the door.

"I'm sorry," he said, placing one hand on Houston's shoulder. "I didn't mean to burden you with my self pity. My complaints are unworthy of this office. We have an enormous task ahead and the country needs better service than we gave it today."

As Houston left, Polk wanted to cry out. He wanted to shout, "No! I'm not all right. Can't you see? Please stay a while." He wanted a warm and genuine talk between old friends. He wanted to open up and say how much he regretted the invisible wall around him. He wanted a friend.

But he could not do it. The hard habits of a lifetime were too strong. He watched Houston walk down the long hallway. Once he was out of sight, Polk returned to his chair, where he shut his eyes and lowered his head to rest against his arms on the table. But he couldn't sleep. There was too much to do.

18

THE TREATY of Guadalupe Hidalgo was signed on February 2, 1848. In return for fifteen million dollars, the disputed boundary between Texas and Mexico was set at the Rio Grande. Further, Mexico officially recognized Texas as belonging to the United States.

Mexico also ceded all of New Mexico territory stretching from Texas to California, and California itself north to Oregon territory. The definition of "New Mexico territory" had a wide reach, including virtually all the Rocky Mountains, great sections of the southern plains, and most of the land between the Rockies and the Sierra Nevada. All told, the territory gained exceeded even the Louisiana Purchase.

In return, the United States assumed responsibility for its citizen's claims against Mexico, some of them going back twenty years. Houston doubted the claimants would ever see a dollar. Getting money out of the government was never easy. The legal work could take years. He might even take some of the cases himself.

During the senate debate over the treaty, Houston introduced a resolution calling for the absorption of northern Mexico into the United States. Jefferson Davis rose to second, but the resolution failed to gain even minimal support.

Houston was terribly disappointed. The moment might never come again. Why didn't anyone but Davis see it?

He vented his frustration in a letter to Ash Smith:

My good friend,

The timing of our debate couldn't have been worse. A few days before the vote, word came from California about a gold strike in the foothills east of Sacramento. The whole country is buzzing about it. I'm afraid the Senate had California gold, not Mexico, on its mind.

I fear this treaty will ultimately satisfy no one and we'll have the devil to pay or it. The abolitionists are horrified by the possibilities for new slave territories. Many southerners, coveting the fertile lands of California, argue that the line drawn by the Missouri Compromise should be erased as if it never existed. Only a few of us feel that more of Mexico should be taken for the good of both nations. A more compact Mexico has a better chance at internal stability. At the same time, bringing so much territory into the United States from the south might ease the South's fears of being surrounded and threatened by the North.

Time will prove me right, but that doesn't give me pleasure today.

Your obedient servant,
I am (Sam) Houston

The Senate ratified the treaty by a vote of thirty eight to fourteen. Most of those who voted against it were opponents of the war. Four Senators abstained, Houston and three anti-

slavery Whigs from the north. He didn't want to vote against
the treaty ending the war, but couldn't bring himself to vote
for it either.

19

THE SHIPMENT FINALLY ARRIVED. Margaret was pleased and happy and that was all he needed.

Instead of overloading himself with baggage when he left Washington, Houston had it shipped. It was only now, weeks later, that the boxes and packages arrived - small mountains of toys for the children and dresses, bonnets and parasols for Margaret.

Although her pleasure was obvious, she pretended to be shocked at the extravagance.

"Sam Houston, what on earth *ever* possessed you to buy all this?"

He grinned and kissed her on the cheek.

"My darling Maggie, it's simple. I not only love to see you smile, but I want to keep you smilin'."

"But how will we pay for it all?" she asked, introducing a discordant note of practicality into the happy occasion.

"Don't worry, my love," he said. "I took care of it."

Despite his breezy assurance, he knew that the bills waited in Washington, along with others from the hotel, his tailor, and his tobacconist. There was time for all that later.

With Margaret in the middle of the parlor floor, skirts spread around her, little Sam climbed all over the boxes and packages, searching for the next surprise with all the exuberance a boy can muster. He'd find something with his name on it, tear it apart, shriek with delight, then dig for something else while Houston roared with laughter.

The boy was especially captivated by a large wooden box of colorfully painted lead soldiers.

"He shows martial inclinations, just like his father," Margaret said, reaching out to remove one of the soldiers, a general, by the look of him, from the youngster's mouth.

Nannie, not yet three, sat in her mother's lap, her thumb planted firmly in her mouth while she pensively looked out at the noisy world. Occasionally she'd reach out to touch her new music box, then jerk her hand back as if she'd touched a hot stove.

Their third child, Margaret Lea, or Maggie, as they called her, slept peacefully in her crib, oblivious to the world.

After Margaret's terrible experience with the tumor they worried about having another child. But the birth went smoothly. They already had hopes that another child was on the way. Margaret said that she'd know better in a week or two.

"Mother," Margaret called out, "come and help me try on these lovely new things."

As if poised outside and waiting for her daughter to call, Nancy Lea waddled into the parlor almost before the invitation echoed off the walls. The old dragon glared around the room with a disapproving eye.

"Did you manage to buy anything practical?" Her voice sounded like rancid lard. "Or is it all fripperies?"

Rather engage in another skirmish with his mother in law, Houston decided to retreat. As he left the room, he blew his wife a kiss and got a beaming smile in return.

Stepping out on the verandah, the love he felt for their home swept over him like a cool breeze. The strong feelings the place evoked always surprised him. Margaret did a magnificent job in his absence. The parlor floor was covered with an elegant hand-woven rug of rose and gold, with her beloved piano against one wall, facing a serpentine sofa of carved rosewood. On the wall above the sofa was a Seth Thomas clock, one of the first in Texas, side by side with Margaret's small collection of Wedgwood China.

Houston didn't much care about such things, but Margaret cared and that was enough for him as long as she let him keep Santa Anna's silver chamber pot. Except for his bad leg, it was his only memento from San Jacinto.

Across the breezeway from the parlor, their bedroom was modestly furnished; a four-poster bed, a trunk at the foot of the bed, an armoire, a standing mirror, a smaller mirror and dressing table with Margaret's female unguents, Maggie's cradle, and the ornate chamber pot.

From the verandah, he looked out at the front yard bordered with carnations and chrysanthemums. A colorful explosion of lilacs, narcissus, jonquils, and Easter lilies decorated either side of the walk. Along the fence, Margaret planted bed after bed of lilacs, roses, and irises. At the corner of each flower bed was a Crepe Myrtle tree, sixteen in all. In back of the kitchen were more than a dozen fruit trees - apple, quince, fig and peach. A bit further out, the large vegetable gardens helped feed the family and the slaves. They sold what they didn't eat.

Houston walked to the pantry at the rear of the house, pulled off his boots and replaced them with an old pair of moccasins. The beadwork was gone and the leather discolored and worn. He picked up the one remaining package. This one was for Joshua and his family, who had their own cabin.

They probably weren't there now, but a walk would be pleasant.

Five months since Zachary Taylor was sworn in as President, it felt good to be free from the worries of Washington.

Although Louis Cass never had a chance, Houston worked hard on his behalf. At one point, he made speeches in nine cities in thirteen days, traveling by carriage, steamboat, horseback, and railroad. Toward the end of the campaign, William Ricky, an old friend from the Creek War, invited him to speak in Zanesville, Ohio. In a personal letter accompanying the invitation, Ricky wrote,

> *If you are not familiar with this district, be assured that this district is familiar with you. We are still plagued by an evil influence you put down in your unique way many years ago. I saw the gentleman a few days past. He is still bitter in his feelings toward you. He is a Taylor man and brags that you don't have the nerve to show your face in 'his' town. His name is William Stanbery.*

Houston was tired and his voice hoarse from too many speeches, but he couldn't refuse. Years ago Congressman William Stanbery stood on the floor of the House and accused Houston of any number of crimes. It was a difficult time in Houston's life and he was in no mood to accept insults. After running from Tennessee with his tail between his legs, he spent most of three years wallowing in drink and self pity. In a last chance to save himself, he headed for Washington, desperate for some way to make his life right again, the way a man drowning in a river claws for a tree branch.

Houston challenged the Congressman to a duel. Stanbery refused, but let it be known than he'd armed himself. A few days later they accidentally met on the street. Stanbery's pistol misfired and Houston beat him half to death. The trial in the House of Representatives was a national sensation that helped raise Houston to prominence again. The opportunity to tweak Stanbery one last time was too good to ignore.

Riding a cramped and uncomfortable coach to Zanesville, Houston gave a strong speech in support of Louis Cass. As far as anyone knew, Stanbery did not leave his impressive two-story home in the center of town for the entire three days of Houston's visit, which surprised Houston not at all. Stanbery was a coward then, a coward today, and he would be a coward on the day he died.

To Houston's surprise, the election was fairly close. As the Democrats feared, the difference was Martin Van Buren and his Free Soil Party, a collection of antislavery Democrats, Whigs, and independents. The New Yorker took away enough votes from Cass to give the election to Taylor, with one hundred sixty three electoral votes to Cass's one hundred twenty seven.

The rising talk about Houston running for President in four years appalled Margaret, although she never said a word. He didn't know what she feared most, the campaign itself, or the prospect of living in Washington. He wasn't sure how he felt about it either. He'd see how things developed. Four years was a long time.

As expected, Joshua's cabin was empty. Houston left the package beside the door. He was pleased to hear from Margaret that Joshua had taught his wife to read and started lessons for their child, too, a strapping boy. Houston made a mental note to ask Joshua if he'd like to borrow any of their books. Margaret probably already made the offer, but it wouldn't hurt to repeat it.

He strolled back to the house, taking his time and meandering along. He enjoyed feeling the hard earth beneath the moccasins, a feeling that no boot or shoe could ever duplicate. It was rare that he felt so carefree. The feeling of luxury was indescribable. He felt positively decadent, and laughed to himself that he knew more about decadence than most men.

As the house came in sight through the trees, he saw the post rider out in front, his big government-issue mail bag hanging over the saddle. The rider handed several letters to Margaret and slowly wheeled the lumbering mare around, tipping his hat to Houston as he plodded past, heading out the circular drive and down to the road to the Marylbone place.

Margaret separated two letters, probably from her sisters, and handed the rest to Houston as he walked up. He glanced over the batch. One was from Sarah Polk in Nashville. It was odd to get a letter from her instead of from her husband, he thought. Curious, he set the other letters on the step and broke the seal.

Engrossed in her own reading, Margaret heard her husband gasp. She looked up to see him sag to the verandah and sit down on the edge.

"Sam, what is it?"

He couldn't speak and sat quietly with elbows on his knees and head bowed, the letter in his hand, as Margaret moved to his side and put a gentle hand on his shoulder.

"Sam, please. What's wrong?"

Houston's broad face was so sad that Margaret felt it touch her heart.

"Polk is dead."

He remembered the last time he saw Polk, two days before Taylor's inauguration. He'd accepted the President's invitation to the White House, a chance to say goodbye. The President seemed positively lighthearted. He looked healthier than he had in months, with new color in his face and a trace of his old brisk energy.

"By God, I'll be a happier man in retirement than I ever was in this place," he said. "The thought of freedom is like a tonic. I can honestly claim that I accomplished everything I set out to do. Now it's time to go home. Why don't you and your family come visit us in Nashville? You haven't been back since the General's death, have you?"

Surprised as always that Polk knew so much about him, Houston replied that he just might take the President up on the invitation. The prospect of an extended period of time in the Polk household was not thrilling, but it would be good to see Nashville again.

Their parting was predictably awkward. Neither man knew what to say and didn't want to embarrass the other by trying to say it. They silently shook hands and Houston walked away. Their goodbye was incomplete and they both knew it.

Now there was nothing more to be said.

"What happened?" Margaret asked.

She gathered her skirts to sit beside him, her feet dangling over the edge without touching the ground.

Houston realized he hadn't finished the letter and quickly read over the remaining pages. After the Polks left Washington, they took a month-long tour along the Atlantic seaboard. They enjoyed it so much that they extended the tour and traveled south to the Gulf States, where Polk became ill, probably from the remnants of a cholera outbreak in New Orleans. He broke off the tour and went home, hoping to recover. Characteristically, he spent his last days working on his papers. He died in bed with his family and a few friends gathered around him. He was only fifty-three years old.

Maybe it *was* cholera that killed him, but Houston couldn't rid himself of the feeling he worked himself to death.

"That poor man," said Margaret, who knew Polk only through Houston's description. "That poor lonely man."

Feeling her arm across on his shoulder, Houston reached across his chest and squeezed her hand.

"It *is* sad," he said. "Not many men did so much, but Polk wasn't the sort who'll be fondly remembered, or even remembered much at all. Somehow I think he understood that."

20

20

Too restless even to pretend to sleep, Houston got out of bed, dressed, and walked into the darkness. He needed to be alone with his thoughts and memories.

It was a cool night, the moon a thin crescent, and the only sound was his soft footsteps as he moved deeper into the trees.

He and Polk were never close. There were times when they didn't even like each other, but they were side by side during some of the most important moments of their lives, bound together in a way neither man fully understood or appreciated. He felt connected and yet disconnected from Polk, as if their friendship was incomplete beyond their ability to make it whole.

Despite all that, he was filled with a sense of unbearable loss. The people of his past, of his youth, really, of the fire that forged the man he was today, were all dead now. His only connection was in his memories. They walked beside him only as ghosts walk beside the living.

It wasn't long ago that the world was bright and full of promise. Now the bright future was a past that could never change. With Polk's death, he felt it in a way he never had, not even when the general died. He was not an old man. With luck, he had many good years left. But the feeling of loss beyond one man's death was powerful in the night. He wasn't afraid of death, but he hated the thought of dying, of non-existence. Death would take him away from Margaret. With death there would be no more laughter and no more friends. There would be no more air to breathe and no more great things to do. The world would move on without him and he hated that most of all. He could not fathom the inevitability of it. He did not understand how it could be even as he knew it would come for him as it came for all the others.

And there was nothing he could do about it but mourn.

21

STANDING SIDE BY SIDE, little Sam and Nanny solemnly handed Houston a bouquet of chrysanthemums they'd picked that morning. Nanny was still too young to understand that her father would be gone for a long time, but his son knew it all too well. In the few years of his short life, his father was absent more than he was at home. It tore at Houston's heart to see the boy trying to be brave.

After he kissed the two children - the baby was asleep in the house - Margaret walked with him to the big yellow coach that was waiting to take him to Galveston. Eager to get started, the four horses snorted, stamped, and tossed their heads while the driver strapped Houston's bags in the boot.

Margaret's eyes shined with tears. She was four months pregnant and it was just now showing. Neither one of them said so, but they knew it was unlikely that he would be home for the birth of their fourth child.

They stood beside the coach with their arms around each other, her head buried in his chest so he saw only see the top of her head and the part down the middle of her hair.

He kissed her head, nuzzling his face into her hair.

"Oh, Maggie, I hate to leave," he said softly. "I must be the biggest fool on earth."

She tilted her head back and looked up at him.

"You have to go, but I won't pretend it's easy."

Houston climbed into the coach shut the door. Reaching through the window, he grabbed her hand, kissed it, and held it against his cheek.

"I love you, Maggie. I love you every minute of every day."

She stepped away from the coach and blew him a kiss.

He hit the roof with his hand to signal the driver and the coach lurched forward.

FROM GALVESTON, Houston took a schooner to New Orleans. After the long dust-choked drive in a coach crowded with passengers who smelled too ripe, it felt good to be at sea. Usually a poor sailor, the weather was so pleasant and the sea so calm that for once the passage was a pleasure. He even slept in a hammock slung on deck, where the sounds of the sea lulled him to sleep.

In New Orleans, he arranged for his usual room at the Quintero boarding house on Canal Street, two blocks from the river. By day he prowled the city, buying a small mountain of supplies and arranging to have it shipped to Huntsville. As always, he delighted in New Orleans' exotic sounds and scents. He enjoyed strolling through the bustling wharf and the surrounding markets of the *Vieux Carre*, comparing prices, being careful in his choices, and bargaining hard. He bought bags of magnolia, locust, bois d'arc, crepe myrtle and tobacco seed, plus clover and grass seed for around the house. There were barrels of sugar and rich New Orleans coffee, too.

He couldn't resist buying presents, too, including several books and a new cloak for Margaret, and a small cameo for Nancy Lea. Margaret would be pleased that he thought of her mother. That it gave Margaret pleasure was the only reason he thought of her at all.

The shipping costs were almost as much as the items themselves. Fortunately, Houston had been swamped with legal work. As Texas' population grew so did its need for lawyers. From time to time he patted his waistcoat pocket, comforted by the thick wad of notes. Assuming that most of the clients who owed him money eventually paid him - it was unrealistic to think they all would - he had enough set aside to take care of his Washington debts and still free Margaret from worries about money while he was gone.

By the time he returned to Texas he'd be seriously in debt again, but he'd make that up with more lawyering. He never got ahead enough to stop worrying about money, but there was no way around it. Some men had a natural talent for wealth. He always envied his old friend Bowie for the way money always seemed to roll down hill in his direction. He never saw a man who made and spent fortunes so easily. But Houston knew that he had no talent at all in that area. Of course, all Bowie's money didn't keep him from being hacked to pieces by Mexican bayonets either.

After three busy days in New Orleans, Houston took passage on a sloop bound for Charleston and then on to Baltimore. From Baltimore, he'd travel by coach to Washington, unless the long-delayed Baltimore-to-Washington railroad was finally finished. In that case, it was the railroad for him. He enjoyed traveling by rail. Someday railroads would link every part of the country. It might even happen in his lifetime. He'd already seen so many changes that anything seemed possible.

It was about time Texas moved into the new age of transportation. There already were a few halting steps in that direction, but maybe he could find a way to move things along?

22

"ISN'T THAT A BIT GREEDY, SAM"? Stephen Douglas' orator's voice rumbled. "I mean, introducing bills for both a national road *and* a transcontinental railroad to pass through Texas. Good Lord! How much transportation does one thinly populated state need? Leave something for the rest of us."

One of the most skillful politicians in the country, the Illinois Senator pretended to be the most put upon man in Congress, an act that never failed to amuse his friends.

Houston, Douglas, Cave Johnson, and Ash Smith were strolling down Eighth Street, stretching their legs after a performance by Jenny Lind, the world-famous soprano, at the brand new Capital Opera House. Lind's four encores were almost more than Houston could stand. He was glad to finally be up and moving.

"Texas needs everything it can get," he replied. "We're not like Illinois. We have vast distances to cover. Land's cheaper, too. Right of way is less than half than it is up your way. It's a good arrangement for both sides."

"Don't worry, Stephen," Johnson said. "He knows he won't get both. He'll settle for one or the other. Am I right, Sam?"

Of course, Johnson was right. Johnson knew it, Houston knew Johnson knew it, and Johnson knew Houston knew it. The rest of them knew it, too. If they were any more knowledgeable they might explode right here on the street.

"Seems like everybody wants a railroad, even if it's for nobody's good but their own," Smith said. "There's serious money to be made, especially if you get in ahead of everybody else on the land rights."

Smith had traveled north to visit his family in Connecticut. After several days in New York City on some mysterious business he refused to divulge, he stopped in Washington before heading back to Texas.

"I'm shocked that you could possibly believe that we dedicated public servants are interested in money," Houston said with a wide grin.

Smith replied with an ironic half bow.

"We live in cynical times, Senator, cynical times indeed."

It was too early to turn in and they'd eaten before the concert. The night was pleasant, an enjoyable time to stroll the bustling Washington streets. After a while, they might turn into one of the taverns that seemed to populate every block of the rapidly growing city. A billiard parlor was a possibility, too.

These days, Houston's favorite drink was a glass of bitters with a slice of orange peel. Technically, it broke his promise to Margaret to avoid alcohol, but he told himself that it didn't violate the spirit of the promise, or something like that.

Smith, Johnson, and Douglas accepted his offer of cigars. He'd bought a dozen boxes in New Orleans, imported fresh from Cuba. Everyone said that Cubans possessed the knack of cigar making, though Houston couldn't tell the difference.

"What did you think of the great Jenny Lind?" asked Johnson, stopping for a moment to take a light from Douglas. They made a ridiculous picture. Johnson tall and skinny;

Douglas short and tending toward fat. Johnson had to bend over like a question mark to take the light from Douglas' match.

The most famous singer in the world, "The Swedish Nightingale" was out to add the United States to her long list of national conquests with an eighteen-month tour. Judging by tonight's thunderous ovation, she was well on her way.

"Oh, I don't know." Houston blew a cloud of smoke into the night sky. "Call me a Philistine, but I like something I can tap my feet to."

"Philistine!" cried the other men in chorus.

Houston laughed along with the rest.

"One thing I will agree to, she's a beauty. Her husband is a lucky man, whoever he is."

Smith cleared his throat self-consciously.

"As it happens, the lady is unattached, so to speak" he said. "In fact, I am to meet her this evening for a late supper and a bottle of champagne, an expensive bottle, no doubt. Miss Lind has extravagant tastes."

Douglas and Johnson howled like randy boys while Houston poked Smith in the ribs with his gold-headed cane.

"How in creation did you arrange that?" Houston asked. "You haven't been in town twenty-four hours."

"I met the lady last year in Paris, where we became, ah, friendly." Smith was torn between his natural gallantry and pride that he'd conquered one of the most desirable women in the world. "We renewed our acquaintance in New York and agreed to meet again when her tour came here."

"So *that* was your mysterious business," teased Houston. "And here I thought you'd come see an old friend."

"Put yourself in my place," Smith said. "On one hand there's Jenny Lind, with a voice like a goddess and a body like mortal sin. On the other, there's ugly Sam Houston, with a voice like a croaking frog and a body...well, never mind."

Douglas dropped off when they came to his boarding-house.

"Early hearing tomorrow," he explained, flicking his cigar into the gutter. "Do try to keep out of trouble, gentlemen. Without my adult guidance, you're at serious risk."

Bidding goodbye to Douglas, the three men continued down the street, turning when they came to E Street. The streets were less crowded now and they walked three abreast.

"Sam, you ever been to a phrenologist?" Smith asked.

Houston shot his friend a look to see if Smith was joking.

"Can't say I have, though I know it's all the rage. It's amazin' what catches on."

The whole east coast was caught up in anything to do with the mystical. No one knew how, when, or why it started, but mesmerism, clairvoyance, palmistry, and anything loosely grouped under the category of "the mystic arts" swept like wildfire from city to city. Séances were all the rage. Participants swore they spoke with the dead, which might be anyone from lately departed relatives to Julius Caesar. Tarot cards were popular, too. Fortune tellers and palm readers lurked on every corner, waiting to pounce.

Phrenology was the latest madness. Houston was vague on the details, something to do with assessing a man's personality and mental development by the lumps and bumps on his head. Some claimed it was a legitimate science, not one of the so-called mystical arts. Houston didn't care either way. If you got close enough to see or feel the bumps on a man's head, you might as well talk to him and figure things out for yourself.

"What do you say we give it a try?" asked Smith. "I saw a shingle on the other side of the street in the last block. Who knows, you two might learn somethin' about yourselves?"

Houston looked at Johnson, who shrugged his assent.

"I already have a fair acquaintance with myself," Houston

said. "But if you want a stranger to fondle your head, then lead on, Doctor Smith."

They crossed the muddy street, dodging the mud splatter from a fast-moving carriage, and turned back the way they'd come. The phrenologist's office was down a flight of stairs below the street. Separated from the living quarters by a threadbare curtain, it was a shabby place with a dank and moldy scent.

"It always strikes me as odd," Johnson said, whispering so not to offend the phrenologist, who'd disappeared behind the curtain to get some "equipment" for the "charting." "If these people can predict the future and arrange conversations with the dead, why do they always live so poor?"

"Perhaps like the saints of old they have forsworn material comfort," said Houston, who felt ridiculous now that they were committed to this nonsense.

The phrenologist was a little wisp of a man as dusty and worn as his furniture. He emerged from behind the curtain with a large pad of paper, several pencils, a rendering of a skull with points of reference printed on it, and two sets of something resembling smaller and more delicate versions of fireplace tongs, one larger than the other, and an easel.

"And what brings you gentlemen here?" he asked. "Some extraordinary need?"

"We *do* have extraordinary needs, especially this gentleman," Houston replied, motioning to Smith. "But they'll soon be satisfied. We were just passin' by when we saw your shingle."

"In that case, what brought you to Washington? You see, the more information I have, the more accurate my charting, although I don't want you to be too specific because it might influence my conclusions."

Before Houston could explain, Smith jumped in.

"We have business with Senator Houston of Texas," he

said. "I don't suppose you know anything about him. We hear so many stories it's hard to tell what to believe. Perhaps you have even, ah, charted him?"

Fumbling to open the easel, the phrenologist didn't see Houston glare at Smith.

"What I know is more than sufficient," he replied. "The man is one of the most perfect reprobates ever to walk the earth."

Smirking behind the old man's back, Smith said, "I can well believe it. How is it that you know this?"

The phrenologist's aged face wrinkled even more at the thought of all that evil bubbling in one man.

"My cousin, my wife's cousin, was at San Jacinto. Well, he was *headed* that way. He has it on the best authority that after the battle Houston got away to New Orleans with Santa Anna's fortune. Wagonloads of gold and silver were secretly loaded on a waiting ship. He put out the story he was wounded, but it was all a plot to abscond with Mexico's wealth."

"Abscond, you say! Why the man *must* be a scoundrel," Johnson happily agreed. "Your story fits much of what we've heard. In fact, it's more kind than many. Perhaps you've let Christian charity sway you into giving this anti-Christ Houston the benefit of the doubt."

Encouraged by Johnson's praise, the phrenologist agreed, "Maybe that's true. I try to be a good Christian. But there is no doubt about that man's character. They say he lives in a palace somewhere out in the Texas wasteland, surrounded by half-naked Mexican and Indian women waiting on him like a debauched potentate."

"A debauched absconder!" With the effort to keep from laughing, Smith appeared to be strangling. "The man is reprehensible!"

"If you do meet with him, remain vigilant," the phrenologist warned. "Evil is always charming."

Johnson and Smith pledged their vigilance while the old man concluded his preparations by placing a chair in the middle of the floor.

"Well, now," he asked, "who'll be first?"

Smith pushed Houston toward the chair.

"Why don't you go ahead, uh...uh...Randolph?" Smith suggested. "The gentleman's expertise might help your shyness with strangers."

"Let me assure you, it won't be long before I'll express myself at length," said Houston acidly, reluctantly taking his place in the chair.

Muttering and scribbling notes, the hold man walked a circle around his client. He ran his fingers across Houston's head, front to back, back to front, and side-to-side, ruffling his thinning hair.

"Uh, Randolph, with your hair in that condition, you resemble a rooster caught in a high wind," Johnson snickered.

The phrenologist jotted down a last observation and set his notebook aside. He picked up one of the tongs and measured Houston's head from front to back, side to side, and diagonally, pausing to write down measurements. He used the other tong to measure specific spots on Houston's head. Finally, he transferred his measurements and observations to the chart, stopping every so often to consult a book with a cracked leather cover.

"There," he said, "I have it now."

"Have *what* now?" Houston asked, smoothing his hair in place.

"Let me say that it's rarely my privilege to examine such a finely formed head." The phrenologist's tone achieved the perfect compromise between toadying and pomposity. "You not only possess high intelligence and high moral points, you're a perfect model of constancy. I haven't examined such a noble head since the noted journalist Horace Greeley came in for a charting. You, sir, have all the attributes of a great and noble man. That'll be two dollars."

As they left the phrenologist's grubby parlor and walked up the steps to the street, Smith asked, "Learn anything new, Sam?"

"For one thing, I need to choose my friends more carefully," replied Houston, who'd recovered from his pique and laughed along with Johnson and Smith. "If that old man is any indication, then I improve upon acquaintance. As I always suspected, to know me is to love me, as long as I have two dollars to pay for it. "

23

TOM BENTON WAS A LUCKY MAN. During an over-heated speech on the Senate floor, Mississippi Senator Henry Foote called Benton a coward. When the outraged Benton confronted Foote, the Mississippi Senator pulled a pistol and stuck it in Benton's belly. Benton coolly stepped back, opened his coat and cried, "Let him fire! Let the assassin fire!" Fortunately Foote was disarmed before he could do just that. Now, everyone, including the senators themselves, had to be searched by the sergeant at arms before they were allowed on the floor.

Benton's bravado was the talk of Washington, but, waiting with Houston for the day's session to begin, the Missouri senator admitted, "I don't remember *what* I said, to tell you the truth. All I know is that damn pistol looked as big as a ham. Sam, I can't believe we've been reduced to this."

"You're right," Houston agreed, pushing a pile of wood shavings under his desk with his foot. Not even whittling gave him pleasure these days. "But how do we stop it?"

It was as if the country was its own worst enemy. The growing abolitionist movement demanded the end of slavery in the capitol, arguing that Brazil, the South, and Washington were the only places in the civilized world where slavery was still legal, and Washington was nothing if not symbolic. At the same time, California and New Mexico, which weren't even territories yet, clamored for immediate statehood. A handful of revolutionaries in Santa Fe even formed an illegal state government, complete with a constitution banning slavery. When Congress rebuffed their representatives, it led to abolitionist riots in the North. Calhoun and his supporters then pushed for a constitutional amendment guaranteeing a permanent political balance between free and slave states, meaning there either would be an expansion of the area in which slavery was allowed, or that no new states would be added to the Union for years to come. At the same time, a meeting of Southern congressmen in Jackson, Mississippi, called for a convention of slave-holding states next year, with an eye toward leaving the Union. Fanatic abolitionists, pro-union Whigs, anti-union Whigs, Free Soilers, pro-union Democrats, and secessionist Democrats clawed and scratched each other to a standstill. It took three weeks just to select a new Speaker of the House.

The nation desperately needed reasonable leadership. As a southerner and military hero, Zachary Taylor was in the perfect position to provide it. But instead of moderation, he astonished the South by calling for the immediate admission of California as a free state. In response, South Carolina, Mississippi, Georgia, and Alabama threatened to seize control of federal property in those states. The nation was on the brink of war. The smallest spark might set it off.

Cooler heads tried to find a middle ground, but Taylor refused to compromise and announced not only would he personally take charge of the army and invade the South, he looked forward to it.

―――

"You heard how the old dunce died, didn't you."

Houston never liked Taylor, but Houston winced at hearing the late-President called "the old dunce." It was especially offensive coming from Charles Sumner, a bombastic abolitionist with a handsome fleshy profile and masses of wavy hair. That Sumner was the favorite in Massachusetts' upcoming Senatorial election did not raise Houston's esteem for Massachusetts.

"You've heard about the man who didn't have sense enough to come in out of the rain?" asked Sumner.

Houston didn't answer. Most of Sumner's questions were rhetorical.

"It seems that our late President didn't have sense enough to come in out of the sun."

While Sumner honked like a goose at what he thought was a fabulously clever joke. Houston scanned the crowd looking for escape. Sumner's behavior was particularly distasteful considering they'd come to see Millard Fillmore, Taylor's Vice President, sworn in as President.

The ceremony in front of the capital building would be brief. Out of respect to his predecessor, Fillmore announced that he wouldn't give a speech, welcome news on another sweltering Washington day.

According to Sumner, Taylor spent several hours in the baking sun as guest of honor at a Fourth of July celebration. To refresh himself afterward, the parched President downed enormous amounts of what turned out to be tainted milk, along with raw fruit and vegetables.

"It wasn't long before the Presidential guts erupted," brayed Sumner. "He was confined to his bed, fed ice and quinine, and bled in copious amounts. Thus did the forces of modern medicine conspire to make him weaker by the hour. Taylor rallied to take his own pulse and announced he would be dead within two days. It turned out to be the most accurate prediction he ever made."

Houston saw the familiar faces of Douglas and New York Senator William Seward headed his way. Reverdy Johnson, Taylor's Attorney General, stepped up, too, all of them drawn by the sound of Sumner's voice and his way of speaking with authority even when he didn't know what he was talking about, a characteristic all too common in Washington, Houston noted sourly.

"Does anyone know Fillmore's politics?" asked Douglas, giving voice to the question everyone in Washington was asking.

"How the devil can a man become President and we know so little about him?" asked Houston.

Taylor selected Fillmore as his running mate only because Fillmore, a New Yorker, balanced the ticket with Taylor, a Southerner. They never even met until they took office. It *was* known that Fillmore's wife, Abigal, hated Washington so much that she moved back to Buffalo, leaving the unhappy Vice President living alone at Willard's Hotel. Beyond that, the man was a mystery.

Seward, a small man whose prominent nose and quick gestures gave him the look of an intelligent rat, offered a few scraps of information.

"I can tell you that he was a good party man when we worked together in New York," Seward said. "He's not brilliant, but he'll listen. As to his personal beliefs, I have no idea. I can't even say for a certainty that he has any."

"He's got to be easier that Taylor to get along with," Douglas said. "Dealing with that man was like talking to a stone wall."

"I just hope his health holds up and nothing happens to him," Houston said, wiping the sweat from his forehead with his sleeve. "Since General Jackson we've had nothing but one-term Presidents and two of those died in office."

"Difficult times, gentlemen," Douglas said, shaking his head. "Difficult times, indeed."

24

THE RAMBLING TWO-STORY farmhouse on Chesapeake Bay was badly in need of paint. As Houston rode up, chickens squawked and scattered across the yard. He dismounted and tied his horse to the hitching post in front of the house.

Henry Clay walked out of the door to the rickety front porch overlooking the dirt, grass, and trees that led down to the shore. Moving slowly and carefully, as if every step was a trial, he extended his hand.

"I can't tell you how pleased I am that you came." Clay's voice was a raspy croak, and the withered hand like a dry leaf that might crumble in Houston's grip.

"Your mysterious note was irresistible," Houston said.

The Kentuckian coughed into a handkerchief and Houston glimpsed splotches of blood on the white cloth. Houston knew that Clay was sick, but he didn't know it was this bad.

After directing his guest to a chair on the porch, Clay carefully lowered himself into the rocker beside it and pulled a thick blanket up to his chest.

"This farm belongs to an old friend," he explained. "I like being on the water and stay here whenever I can. I thought it best to keep our meeting secret and the only way to do that was to meet where no prying eyes can see us."

This was, Houston thought, a peculiar meeting. There was a time when he loathed Henry Clay, especially back during the '24 election when Clay's infamous deal with John Quincy Adams helped elevate Adams in the presidency at Jackson's expense, and Adams named Clay his Secretary of State in return.

But Houston didn't hate so easily anymore. Even when they disagreed, he had learned to admire Clay for his ability to work through the thorniest problems. It was Clay who crafted the Missouri Compromise, the agreement that kept the uneasy balance between North and South for thirty years. But for the life of him Houston couldn't figure out why the man wanted him here, let alone the need for such secrecy.

Clay rested his head against the chair and closed his eyes.

"Sam, I need your help, along with a few other key people. I've put together a series of bills that may get us out of the fix we're in and keep the country from splitting in two. The problem is that getting them through Congress intact will be tricky."

"Another compromise?" Houston asked.

"Something like that," Clay said.

"Why me?" Houston asked. "I've made myself so unpopular at home that my re-election is anything but sure. I'm afraid that I've not much to offer, not if my own people won't support me."

Clay flashed a smile that revealed something of the handsome man he was in his prime.

"You're being modest," he said. "You offer a great deal; a Southerner, a military hero, and man known for his independence. Your long association with Jackson means that when people see you they think of a time when there was strength in the presidency."

"You may be the first man ever to call me modest," Houston grinned.

Clay's charm was irresistible. It had served him well over forty years in public life. Hearing the cries of sea birds over Chesapeake Bay, where the sunlight glistened off the water in the distance, and feeling the cool breeze wafting through the big old trees shading the porch, Houston thought that there was something poignant in the moment, too.

"This will be my last great effort. I just hope that I live long enough to see it through," Clay said, giving voice to what Houston felt.

Clay called out and an aide came out of the farmhouse with a brown leather portfolio, weathered with age. Clay withdrew a sheaf of papers, pausing when a spasm of coughing brought tears to his eyes.

Dabbing the white handkerchief at his lips, he explained, "You may, of course, take copies with you as long as you promise to show them to no one else for the time being, but allow me to describe it."

It was an extraordinary array of legislation. No one got everything but everyone got something. The first bill provided that California be admitted to the Union as a free state. A second bill provided that the slave trade, but not slavery itself, be prohibited in the District of Columbia. A third bill set up a territorial government for New Mexico. Also, Deseret, the controversial and virtually autonomous Mormon empire in the Rockies, would become the territory of Utah, with New Mexico and Utah territories joining the Union when they were sufficiently populated, probably as more than two states. In both cases, the issue of slavery was deferred, to be decided later by the states themselves. Another bill strengthened the Fugitive Slave Act and gave it teeth for the first time. A federal commission would be empowered to issue warrants, summon posses, and force civilians to help capture escaped slaves, even in the North. If a slave owner presented a proper affidavit of ownership, the captured slave would be returned, with harsh penalties for anyone who harbored a runaway. A final bill provided that Texas be awarded ten million dollars in exchange for settling its northern and western boundaries, a point of controversy since the days of the Texas Republic.

Intrigued, Houston sat knee to knee with Clay, suggesting a few changes in wording. Some Clay accepted, some he did not.

"What about the President?" Houston asked. "Will Fillmore sign it all? Even four out of five won't do. The balance is so perfect it's all or nothing."

"We've had conversations," replied Clay. "If the package is presented in this way, with minimal changes, he will sign. Calhoun and his cohorts will oppose us with everything they have, of course, but Calhoun's resources are much diminished. He's dying even faster than I am. Webster is with us, by the way, although he'll support us from within the administration, not from the Senate. He's to be Fillmore's Secretary of State."

"Can we ask him to help get this through and *then* join the cabinet?" Houston suggested. "One in the senate vote might make a difference."

"Good idea," Clay agreed. "I'm sure Dan will agree. I should have thought of that myself. Sometimes I feel even more feeble than I am."

With most of the work done, Clay relaxed. He seemed to collapse in on himself as he let his mind roam.

"There was a time when Webster wanted to be President so badly that losing seemed to unhinge him. I've always suspected the disappointment had something to do with his drinking. Somehow being one of the greatest men of his time and Secretary of State under three Presidents wasn't enough.

Of course, no one had the Presidential fever worse than I did. I tried three times and lost every one. The last campaign against your man Polk hurt the most. I was so close it was if I could reach out and touch it."

Clay lowered his head and raised his hand, the tips of his long bony fingers lightly touching his face.

"My son, Henry, died in the war, killed at Buena Vista. Ambition seemed a small thing after that. I would give anything to have him back with me. Anything."

The sun had set while they worked. The aide brought out a lantern and it illuminated one side of Clay's face, leaving the other in shadow. He shivered against the night chill and pulled the blanket up higher.

"What about you?" Clay asked. "When the disease gets hold of a man it's a terrible thing. It dominated my every thought and breath for half my life."

Usually Houston deflected the question with a quip or an answer that revealed nothing, but the something about the moment demanded honesty.

"I don't know, though no one believes me when I say that," he replied. "Sometimes I want it. But other times I don't think it's worth the candle. I've seen men broken by it. I'm not sure I could get it if I tried, and if I can't get it then I won't try. Call it vanity."

"There's nothing wrong with vanity," Clay said. "A man who denies his own worth doesn't have much worth to deny. But what you suspect is true, you couldn't win."

Clay raised his wrinkled hand in apology.

"Forgive me if I'm too candid, but a slave-owner who apparently dislikes slavery? A southerner *and* a Union man? A Texas senator who's more popular in the North than in his own state? A man of two wars some still call a coward? A teetotaler whose drunkenness is legendary? A white man who lived with the Indians? A family man who's away more than he's at home?"

Clay shook his head. "There are too many Houstons; too many contrasts. It makes people...uncertain."

Houston smiled to show that he did not take offense. "I'm supposed to be a liar and schemer, too."

Clay shrugged with an almost imperceptible motion. "We're all liars and schemers. It's a matter of motive and degree. At least that's what I've always told myself."

He coughed into his handkerchief again, the dry and awful sound of a man as his life slowly emptied out of his body.

"Perhaps the only thing worse than wanting the Presidency and not getting it is getting it," Clay said. "As you say, it's killed more than one man."

"The general is the only man I've seen truly happy there," Houston said. "It wore him down, too, but by God, he loved it."

"I can understand that," Clay said. "I think would have loved it, too."

25

AND SO THE old lions who governed the country for most of the century rose for one last battle.

Clay offered the details of his extraordinary compromise in a remarkable speech that begged Congress to put away its differences and pursue a reasonable course. The effort left him so weakened he needed support when he returned to his desk.

Benton's unexpected opposition was a hard blow. The Missouri Senator believed that the compromise gave too much comfort to the South. After a public quarrel on the capitol steps, Houston and Benton, whose friendship went back more than thirty years, stopped speaking to each other. They were not alone. It seemed as if half of Washington wasn't speaking to the other half.

In Texas, Houston's old foes, David Burnet and Maribeau Lamar, nipped savagely at his heels. They'd been rivals for so long that Burnet didn't need a good reason anymore, while Lamar wanted to position himself as Houston's successor when the state legislature finally had the good sense to turn him out of the senate. Houston was not surprised by either man. What *did* surprise him were old friends like Anson Jones, Pickney Henderson, Memucan Hunt, and others who denounced him as a traitor. In the past they could all disagree and move on, but that time was gone. The issues cut too deep for the raw wounds to heal.

———

THERE WAS a feeling of urgency in the air, as if you should have arrived an hour earlier, or if not an hour earlier, then a day, or, better still, a week. People hurried down the Washington streets, their pace seeming to quicken with every step. Important things were happening and everyone wanted to be a part of it. The mood was tense, but more curious than hostile.

As usual, the newspapermen flocked together in the gallery, eyeing the senators almost as cynically as they eyed each other. There were more spectators than usual; mostly men, with a few women scattered here and there like flowers in a field of weeds.

The bustling came to a sudden stop while Calhoun slowly made his way to his desk near the center of the great chamber. Emaciated and feeble, the South Carolinian's sallow cheeks were sunken like craters and his long hair was brittle and white. Only his deep-set eyes flamed with life, dark and angry above prominent cheekbones. With his body failing, John Calhoun had come to hurl his spirit at his foes. It was all he had left.

Too ill to speak, he remained seated with a great black cloak drawn around him while his speech was read aloud by Senator James Mason of Virginia. The words were defiant as ever, but without Calhoun's commanding presence they lost much of their impact. Nothing would satisfy him except the restoration of the exact balance of power between slave and free states by constitutional amendment, along with a promise that the North would cease its opposition to slavery. If that was not possible, "Then let the states we represent agree to separate and part in peace."

When the speech ended, most of the senators from the South and a substantial portion of the gallery exploded in cries of praise and applause. The newspapermen noted that a majority of the senate applauded just long enough for courtesy.

No one knew it at the time, but it was John Calhoun's last public appearance. He would be dead in a few weeks.

After a long and bitter debate, Congress passed the package of bills known as the Compromise of 1850 so that President Millard Fillmore could sign it into law.

Sam Houston of Texas was the only southerner to vote in favor of all five bills.

26

Huntsville, Texas, April 15, 1852
My darling Victoria,

I know that it has been too long since I've written. I can only throw myself on your mercy while blaming my hectic schedule and the primitive traveling conditions here.

Disembarking in Galveston after a pleasant voyage from New Orleans, I discovered that Texas has no railroads to speak of, less than two hundred miles of track in the entire state, I am told. Meanwhile, the roads are quagmires thanks to the torrential spring rains. Wagons bogged down to the axles are a common sigh and everyone carries stout poles to help pry the wheels out of the mud. I am told that once the rains end the roads will revert to their usual state when they will be thick with choking dust. After wallowing in this awful mud for many weeks, I would consider that an improvement.

Despite this poor first impression, I am more optimistic than ever, confident that this is the place in which to invest a substantial portion of my inheritance from father's estate. With that in mind, I arranged a meeting with father's old friend, the

*famous, or infamous, Senator Sam Houston, who appears to
know everyone in Texas.*

*After meeting the Senator, and after observing him on other
occasions, I would describe him as one of the most colorful men
in a state of colorful men, some of whom are only slightly, if at
all, tempered by civilization.*

*He appears to be somewhere in his fifties. His hair, what I
saw of it (I have never seen him without a hat of some kind), is
thick and graying as it cascades over his ears. As you know, at
almost six feet I am considered tall, yet when we met the Senator
looked down on me as his hand engulfed my own. There is no
hint of softness about him. His gray eyes sparkle with vitality.
His face is weathered from the sun, his voice is a commanding
rumble, and his back is straight as a plumb line, although he
walks with a limp as a result of his wounds in various wars. As
well known as he is, there is a sense of mystery and unpredictability about him, as if no one knows what he might do next.*

*The Senator's eccentric tastes stand out even in a place
where the inhabitants are renowned for their eccentricity. I saw
him twice before we were formally introduced. The first time, at
a formal reception in Austin, the rather drab state capital, he
wore a military cap of European origin (I think!) and a short
military cloak of fine blue broadcloth with blood-red lining. The
second time, at the opening of a racetrack in Nacogdoches, he
wore a sombrero with a colorful Mexican blanket thrown over
one shoulder. At our meeting in his primitive office at his
pleasant home here in Huntsville, he wore a tattered straw
planter's hat, a patched shirt, buckskin trousers, shabby
moccasins, and reading spectacles with delicate gold rims, which
he put away as soon as I entered the cabin.*

*When I mentioned father's name, the Senator threw back his
head and laughed. 'How is the old fox?' he asked. 'Does he still
have that Midas touch? That man could turn goat piss into gold.'
When I explained that father died last summer and I inherited*

our mills in Massachusetts and Rhode Island, plus considerable property elsewhere, a great sadness came over him. 'Another good man gone,' he said. 'If I can be of any help to you, don't hesitate to ask.'

After I apprised him of our intention to invest in Texas cotton, he agreed to do what he could, although he asked for time to think it over. We made an appointment to meet again. I also have thoughts of expanding into other areas. Indeed, I have already taken steps in that direction. Once I explain I am sure you will approve.

Unfortunately, all is not well for the Senator. As a result of his labor on behalf of Clay's great compromise and his support of a ban on slavery in Oregon territory, he faces fierce opposition and constant criticism in his home state, some of it shockingly confrontational. It did not escape my notice that he goes armed with a knife in a leather sheath at the small of his back. Even his supporters seem puzzled, if not dismayed, by his actions in Washington.

I found Mrs. Houston to be charming. She is small, dark-haired and a beauty, considering the rigors of the life here, which tends to age women prematurely. There is a popular saying that 'Texas is hell on women and horses.' Although she is much younger than the Senator, it is obvious that they are madly in love and behave like newlyweds. Their active brood of children creates chaos wherever they go. Mrs. Houston - her name is Margaret, although I was never so bold as to call her that - made sure that I was properly introduced to all of them. I knew that you would want details, and I made notes after our meeting. There's Sam, Jr., a husky boy who appears to be nine or ten; Nannie, age five or six; Maggie, a year or two younger; the oddly named Mary Willie, who I am told is two years of age and kept her thumb planted firmly in her mouth the entire time; and their new baby, Nettie, only three months old.

Please understand that the ages are mere guesses on my part.

As you know, I lack experience with children. After my exposure to the ferocious Houston offspring, I would prefer to remain in that happy state, but only if that is also your wish, my dear.

I later learned the rotund older woman glowering in the background was the Senator's mother in law, a frequent guest at his home. With his active children, his law practice, the constant call of politics, a stream of visitors high and low, and the activity involved in running a farm, the Senator's only sanctuary is a small office set away from the main house. No one is allowed to enter except the Senator, his guests, and an impressive nigger named Joshua, who behaves more like overseer than slave. Although he owns a dozen slaves, as I understand it the Senator is in the awkward position of being a slave owner who doesn't agree with slavery. As a result, he rarely, if ever, discusses the issue. I have the feeling it embarrasses him.

Immigration continues on a grand scale here. There are Europeans in large numbers and more coming in, English, Dutch, French, Germans and Poles, most of them artisans of one sort or another. New Braunfels, between Austin and San Antonio, is a full-fledged German town with its own newspaper, the New Braunfels Zeitung. The state is full of enterprising newcomers with more on the way. Even the Mexicans have overcome their natural indolence. Many of them are active in local and state affairs. Such is the diversity of Texas' population the state government issues its proclamations in English, Spanish and German.

When I learned that good unimproved farmland can still be had for less than one dollar an acre, I bought an option on a thousand acres. There is no sense waiting when there's profit to be made. Cotton continues to boom. Last year the cotton crop exceeded three hundred thousand bales, an extraordinary output considering only five years ago the crop was less than fifty thousand bales.

The well-known story of a fabulously wealthy gentleman

named Robert Mills is a fine example for us, or anyone, to follow.

Twenty years ago Mills established himself as a general merchant in Brazoria, which allowed him to deal throughout the fertile Colorado and Brazos river valleys. He also sent merchandise to Mexico on burro trains. His profits were secretly brought back in silver bars, escorted by a dozen heavily armed guards.

Eventually Mills transferred his operation to Galveston, entering into what is known as the 'commissions' business. He started a company that builds wharves to handle the swelling volume of sea and river traffic. He collects commissions for transferring cargo, primarily cotton, cane sugar, hides, and tallow, from the riverboats to his wharves and then to seagoing export vessels. He also earns commissions for shipping to up-river storekeepers imports loaded onto his wharves and warehouses, items such as lumber, clothing, soap, tobacco, wine, farm implements, and medicines. Most of his profit goes into cotton and sugar. With cotton and sugar plantations of well over one hundred thousand acres, they say he is the largest slave owner in the state, with more than six hundred niggers. The gruff and mostly toothless old boy is known as the Duke of Brazoria, a kind of Texas royalty, if you will.

Of course, Mills is too far along for us to hitch our wagon to his star. However, Senator Houston promised to write a letter of introduction to a young man who might serve our purpose. His name is Richard King, a former steamboat pilot poised to enter the cattle business on a large scale. He is currently buying vast tracts of land in Nueces County, with long-range plans to improve the native stock, an ill tempered but tough animal called the longhorn, by importing blooded bulls for breeding. With more ambition than money, there is no doubt King would welcome a loan. Another possibility is that we might become a partner.

Believe me when I tell you that cattle are profit on the hoof.

Once you assemble the land and the animals, expenses are minimal. The beef is consumed locally and the hides exported at great profit. There are few parts of the animal that aren't used in some way. Come that happy day when the Texas railroads approach adequacy, I foresee a time when cattle will be shipped east so the beef can be sold there. A few ambitious men have already driven herds to New Orleans, and they say one small herd was driven all the way to Chicago. I am sure that more will try, but I see no future in that dubious endeavor. You risk having half your assets along the way. To my mind, there is no purpose in driving cattle when one day the railroads will transport them for you.

My dear, I don't mean to give the impression life in Texas is all sunshine and fortune. There are sporadic outbreaks of yellow fever and cholera. With vast distances between communities, life can be lonely, especially for women. Aside from the larger cities such as San Antonio, Galveston, Houston, Nacogdoches and Austin, what social life there is seems to revolve around horse racing, barn raisings, dances, and religious revivals. I've seen wagers as large as three thousand dollars on one race. Senator Houston enjoys the races and has been known to wager from time to time, too, although I have the feeling Mrs. Houston disapproves even if she looks the other way.

The fierce Comanche are as feared as ever, although their butchery is mostly confined to the north and west, away from the main population centers. If you heard as many horrible stories as I have, you would give up your romantic notions about the noble savage as chronicled by Mister Fenimore Cooper.

When the Comanche attack, whenever possible they carry off the women and children after murdering the men in the most gruesome ways. I met one man named Wilbarger who was surprised by a Comanche raiding party while on a surveying trip. Shot by arrows through both legs and scalped while he lay helpless, somehow he survived, although the poor man is a grotesque creature. You can still see the white bone of his exposed skull. He charges for a viewing, which is a lesson that there is money to be made in anything, even misfortune. Wilbarger removes his hat and unties the bandanna he wears over his head. He allows spectators to marvel at and sometimes even touch his gleaming white brain pan, then collects his money and goes on his way as if it was nothing out of the ordinary.

Violence is common and the legal system is primitive. In Brownsville, I saw a man cut to pieces by a Bowie knife wielded by a great hairy creature who called himself 'Rip-Roaring' Jim Forsythe. I have no idea what caused the fight. I am not sure the survivor does either, not that he seemed to care. Judges have such great distances to cover, and it takes so long for them to travel from town to town, that lawful citizens often decide appropriate punishments themselves, anything from a fine to tar and feathers or a hanging.

The guilt of Mister Rip-Roaring Forsythe couldn't be clearly established because the only other witness was dead. Therefore the case was thrown out. The trial was only just concluded when a terrifying Texas Ranger named Henry Karnes ordered Forsythe to get out of Brownsville and never return. Forsythe, who, despite his bluster, was clearly cowed by the formidable Ranger, meekly obeyed.

Now I fear I painted too dark a picture. San Antonio has a thriving theater. Elegant public buildings have mostly replaced the original log structures. I intend to have my portrait painted by a talented young artist named Carl von Iwonski, a German who is the equal of any artist we have in Philadelphia, and whose work can be purchased at a fraction of the cost. The people are friendly and the land is fertile. Education is valued and the government sets aside generous sums for public school-

*ing. Our future and our fortune are to be found here. I am
convinced of it.*

*In conclusion, I leave it to Senator Houston to describe this
remarkable state. 'Young man,' he said, 'Texas can be anything
you want, if you have the cojones for it.'*

*My dear, I'll explain the colorful meaning of that foreign
word in private when we meet again.*

*Your devoted slave,
William
P. S.
A hurried note written after a second meeting with Senator
Houston...after providing much valuable information and
advice, plus several letters of introduction, I make a loan of one
thousand dollars to the Senator, payable in two years. I wrote a
draft against our account in New Orleans. It seems even legends
have financial difficulties. It seemed the least I could do in
father's memory. I'm sure he would approve.*

27

THERE WAS something Houston loved about tearing through a mountain of paperwork, even here in the borrowed office that he sometimes used in Austin.

As usual, he was behind on his correspondence. Tossing away the usual crank letters, as he read the rest he either scribbled a quick reply or wrote a note specifying what action to take or where it should go next. Anything that required a lengthy reply went to a separate pile.

Houston often enjoyed working late and alone, especially when he was away from home. The rest of the two-story building was dark and quiet. Only the flickering oil lamp on the desk illuminated the office. In the silence, the feel of the paper taking the pen felt like a reaffirmation of his station in life. It was serious work and doing it gave him pleasure.

He munched his way to the bottom of the pile, toward the end of a satisfying day. Judging by the rumbling of his stomach, it was time for dinner. He'd agreed to meet Sam Maverick and Gabriel Ledbetter and listen to some irrigation scheme of theirs. From what he'd heard, the plan had merit. Most of Maverick's schemes did. He didn't know Ledbetter, a bachelor from North Carolina, but he'd known Maverick for years, a little rooster of a man who was too convinced of his own righteousness. Houston knew that Maverick didn't particularly like him either. Even so, they worked together when something worthwhile needed doing. That's what politics was all about. And once you had Sam Maverick's word, you had it forever. There was comfort in that. Better a reliable foe than an unreliable friend.

Thinking back on it later, he realized that something must have alerted him. Some disturbance in the air? A footstep more felt than heard? Or was it instinct? All men had it. It was just closer to the surface for some.

Whatever it was, it saved his life.

Houston swiveled in the chair just as the silver flash of the ax slashed through the air, so close that he felt the violent rush of air on his cheek. With a crash, the ax embedded itself in the desk. He instinctively stayed with the turning motion and rolled out of the chair to the floor. Rising to one knee, he saw a wild-eyed, black-bearded man with a ragged shirt and baggy pants tucked into mud-covered boots frantically tugging at a small ax that was buried in the desk halfway up the shining blade. If Houston hadn't turned when he did, his brains would be all over the room.

He desperately glanced around for something to use as a weapon. The Bowie knife he usually carried in a leather sheath at the small of his back was in the desk drawer. He took it off when he sat down because the ivory handle jabbed into his back.

With a grunt, the man tugged the ax out of the desk, staggering backward when he lost his balance for an instant. Houston took advantage of the opening and caught the assassin in a bear hug that pinned his arms to his sides. The man responded by trying to bite Houston's nose with rotten black teeth.

Holding the bear hug, Houston lifted the man off his feet and slammed him to the floor, falling on top as he held tight. The man's breath exploded out of his body with a loud "Huhh!" Houston worked his arms free and grabbed his adversary's wrist with both hands to keep the ax at a distance while the man clawed at Houston's eyes with his other hand. Fighting all the way, the two men rolled along the floor until they wedged against the wall. Houston felt a series of blows on his thigh as the man tried to knee him in the groin. With his greater weight pinning the assailant between wall and floor, Houston smashed his forehead into the bridge of the man's nose until he felt cartilage shatter.

Feeling his opponent weaken, keeping his left hand tight around the wrist holding the axe, Houston clawed his other hand under the black beard to the man's throat, squeezing with all his strength, feeling strong legs flopping and kicking beneath his own. After a series of juicy gurgles, the man finally went limp just as the building's night watchman, Reuben Hogstead, burst into the room, his face red from the effort of running up the stairs. Hogstead pulled his Colt from the belt around his big hard belly, cocked it with both hands, and jammed the barrel into the unconscious man's bloody face.

28

HANS EHRENGARD, a grim-faced German shaped like a potato, finished his examination.

"Hoos-ton, you deal in goot luck!" he barked. "I t'ink maybe Gott watches out for fools like you!"

Ash Smith raised his eyebrows, but Houston shook his head.

"That's just his way," he explained, buttoning what was left of his torn shirt. "He can say 'howdy' and make it sound like an insult. He doesn't mean anything by it. Isn't that right, doc?"

Washing his hands in a basin, Ehrengard nodded. "Yah! What you say is goot."

Houston, Smith, Ehrengard, Maverick, Ledbetter, and Ranger Captain Rip Ford were all crowded into the doctor's office. Word of the assassination attempt spread fast. Houston was hustled into the office only a few minutes ago and there was already a crowd outside, where one of Ford's Rangers stood guard at the door. A scrawny boy with the beginning of a wispy mustache, he had a shotgun cradled in his arms and a

Walker Colt in his belt. It looked like his pants might fall down from the weight.

Houston had to agree with the doctor. If his assailant had a pistol, he'd be dead. As it was, there were deep scratches around his eyes, a big yellow and brown bruise on the inside of his thigh, and a bone-deep soreness down his right side, probably from when they hit the floor.

Smith offered his flask. For the first time in years, Houston took a deep swallow of brandy, choking as it burned a tunnel his throat. He was out of practice. It had been a while since he'd eaten, too. Probably best not to have another.

"Rip, are you sure little fella out there knows what he's doin'?" Houston asked, his voice rough from the brandy. "He doesn't look strong enough to lift that shotgun, much aim and fire it. When did the Rangers start employin' children?"

"Don't worry, Sam, Heldenfels may be a youngster, but he's the nastiest character in my company and that's a fact."

Ford spit a glistening glob of tobacco juice toward the spittoon in the corner of the office, missing by a foot.

"He's already killed seven of Juan Cortina's people down on the Nueces. 'sides that, he thinks you're the greatest man since Jesus. Somebody'd have to kill him at least twice before they got through the door. With a double-loaded shotgun aim don't matter much anyhow. Point it in the right direction and it'll pretty much do the job."

Satisfied about the guard, Houston asked, "Anyone know who the man was? That might be good information to have, especially if he's not alone."

"The way you almost choked him to death, he can't talk even he was inclined to," Ford replied, declining Smith's offer of the flask. "In the future, try not to be so hard on your assassins."

The lanky Ranger walked over to the spittoon and unloaded another glob of tobacco juice, this time hitting the mark. He nodded at Ehrengard, who acknowledged the courtesy with a nod of his own.

"All he does is lie on the floor of the calaboose and whimper," Ford continued, readjusting his chew between cheek and teeth. "From what I've seen, my calculation is that he's just a soft brain who convinced himself the world'd be better off without you. Probably followin' you for a while and workin' alone. We found a journal over at the Gomez boarding house."

Nodding at Smith, Maverick added, "Ash here recognized him. He saw him walk out of there a couple of days back, talkin' to himself. In the journal, he calls you a 'nigger loving tyrant,' among other tender endearments. There's a fair amount of detail; where you went, what you did. Like Rip said, he's been trackin' you. The doctor's right. You were lucky."

Smith offered Houston another drink. When Houston refused, Smith screwed the cap on and slid the flask inside his coat pocket.

"Since he can't talk yet, we don't know if it was his idea, or somebody put him up to it," Smith said. "I tend to agree with Rip. He was on his own. Nobody with sense would recruit him to do anything more complicated than take a piss."

Although no one said it aloud, they were all shaken by what happened. Without giving voice to it, they felt that if they joked about it and made it seem small, it would be as if it never happened.

Turning to Maverick and Ledbetter, Houston said, "I need to change shirts and then say somethin' to the folks outside to show 'em their senator isn't too damaged, but why don't we carry on with our plan and go to dinner?"

To Ford, he added, "Rip, you'll let me know if you find out anything?"

The Ranger nodded. "Bet on it, Sam."

"Doctor, with your permission?" Houston asked.

Ehrengard muttered something in German. Taking it as a yes, Houston slid off the examination table, but pulled up when pain shot through his side.

"You sure you're up to it?" Maverick asked. "That water we're gonna talk about will be around for a while. We can always talk another time."

"Nonsense, I'm right as the mail," replied Houston, knowing that no one in the room believed him.

Smith held his coat and Houston gingerly eased into the sleeves.

"Gettin' out'll do me good. If I don't occupy myself I'd just brood. I might even have another drink. Even Margaret would understand the need."

Seeing Smith's doubtful look, Houston admitted, "Well, maybe not."

As they left the room, Ledbetter shook his head.

"Ain't this just a hell of a thing?"

29

EVEN NOW, Washington wasn't much of a city. It was built on a swamp and never got over it. Surrounded by noxious flats and a stinking canal, at night residents were serenaded by the constant din of frogs. Rain turned the streets into avenues of mud. Pennsylvania Avenue was partially cobble stoned, but even that was broken up by faulty drainage. Flocks of fat geese waddled down the streets and hogs wandered across Capitol Hill. Small, socially cozy, and bloated with self-importance, Washington existed only for politics and sometimes it didn't even do that very well.

There *were* some splendid buildings now; the Capitol, the General Post Office, the Patent Office, the Executive Mansion, the Treasury. But they were so far apart that one of the more irritating foreign ambassadors dismissed Washington as "a city of distances." Houston had complained about Washington for more than thirty years, but he didn't like it when foreigners did it.

"Why would Douglas do such a thing?"

"Because he wants to be President," Houston replied, side-stepping a pile of steaming horse flop as they crossed the street. "If you knew him better, you'd know inside that stout little body is ambition that never sleeps. Stephen Douglas used to be one of the most likable men I've ever known, but he's turned into a demagogue."

"Really, Senator, aren't you being a little hard on him?" asked William Byron James, hurrying to keep up with Houston's long limping strides.

James often dropped by Houston's office at the end of the day to share a smoke. Houston knew the recently elected Rhode Island Senator to be lazy and not very bright, a man who couldn't hold up his end of a conversation if it came with handles. He decided to take a walk in the unlikely hope the air might clear the younger man's muddled head. Houston always thought better on his feet, too. God knows there was enough to think about.

Douglas' Kansas-Nebraska Bill was an outrage. There was no other way to put it. On the surface, it seemed benign enough...except that it would virtually repeal the Missouri Compromise *and* re-open the festering slavery issue that was more or less settled with the Clay's hard-won Compromise of 1850. Try as he might, Houston couldn't make James, or most anyone else, see it. His power of persuasion wasn't very powerful lately.

Douglas leveraged a series of bills through Congress where the North, including Douglas' home state of Illinois, got the long-anticipated and infinitely lucrative route for the transcontinental railroad, ending Houston's dream of a southern route through California, New Mexico territory, and Texas. To get the necessary votes, Douglas used his position as chairman of the Senate Committee on Territories to push a bill creating two new territories, Kansas and Nebraska, where the residents would be allowed to vote slave or free, despite both territories being north of the line established by the Missouri Compromise. The cry of "popular sovereignty," allowing territories to make their own decisions, had an irresistible ring. In Houston's opinion, that was what made it so dangerous. Rumors swept the North that *all* of the West might be thrown open to slavery.

Anticipating that the bill would pass, an abolitionist named Eli Thayer founded the Emigrant Aid Society to channel anti-slavery settlers into Kansas, while a crackpot abolitionist preacher named Henry Ward Beecher sent a steady supply of money and Sharps rifles to Kansas from his Massachusetts pulpit. As the territories filled with passionate abolitionists, more than two thousand Missourians were primed to sweep across the border and claim residence in Kansas long enough to vote, fired by a recruiting pamphlet promising they'd get a chance to "kill every damned abolitionist in the territory." With the sparks flying between pro-slavery settlers from Missouri and anti-slavery newcomers from the North, it wouldn't take much to set off a small war, one that might drag the rest of the country into it.

Opposition to Douglas' bill by the Whigs in the North had virtually killed Whig membership in the South. At the same time, the possibility that slavery might spread out of the South split the democrats between northern and southern factions. With the party of Jackson bitterly divided, and the Whigs in their death throes, a new party rose to fill the vacuum, an alliance between northern Whigs and the most vocal anti-slavery Democrats. To Houston' dismay, this new Republican party intended to present that great idiot Fremont as its candidate for President.

Houston saw disaster coming as clear as he could remember yesterday. With President Franklin Pierce, in Houston's view the most worthless human being ever to hold high public office, in Douglas' pocket, the Kansas-Nebraska Bill was sure to be signed into law.

He explained all this as he walked side by side with James down the Washington streets, but as usual none of it penetrated that fog that seemed to perpetually surround the young man.

With a bored yawn, he asked, "What's wrong with letting the people decide?"

"This popular sovereignty nonsense is just a way for a certain senator to get he wants," Houston replied. "If bullshit was music, Douglas would be a brass band."

"What will you do?"

"Go home."

"What do you mean, go home?"

"It's so popular in Texas that when I vote against it my run in the Senate will end."

"They'd turn *you* out?" James asked incredulously.

"In a heartbeat. But Douglas and his kind get what they want, it will lead to a war the South must not fight and cannot win."

The South *would* fight, too. Houston was sure of it. And it wasn't just about slavery, a point the radicals in the North refused to acknowledge.

"Eventually slavery will die a natural death," Houston explained, although he doubted that James was listening anymore. It taxed the young oaf to pay attention to any voice but his own for more than a few minutes.

"I own slaves, but it's a pernicious system. That makes me king of the hypocrites, I suppose, but killin' it prematurely will bring the storm. We need time to make the conversion. Otherwise the cotton economy'll collapse. Most Southerners don't even own slaves, but draw the line at lettin' the North dictate what they will and will not do. They already feel squeezed enough."

"There's a fundamental question about the nature of the country at play, too. There's always been a strong secessionist movement, North *and* South. In Jackson's day, South Carolina nearly walked away over tariffs. New York City and New Jersey threatened secession, too. The position even has legal merit, however much I disagree with it. Jefferson and Madison wrote that the states could legally nullify acts of Congress. Most southerners feel allegiance to their state and will follow where it leads them."

A glance showed that James looked bored. No wonder he got along with Pierce, Houston thought. They must idle away the time exchanging blank stares. Still, he kept at it, talking to himself as much as to James, his way of working things out.

"So the question is this: Are we one nation? Or are we fragments? Are we 'us', many states only vaguely connected? Or are we 'it', one nation undivided. With time and reason, maybe it can be peacefully resolved, but not if we continue as we are."

Suddenly aware that the lecture had ended, James coughed into one hand to cover his lapse.

"Sir, I believe that you're...uh, well...I...Oh, the devil take it!" he blurted out. "It can't be as bad as all that. Douglas seems like a decent fellow and the President is perfectly charming."

Looking around to get his bearings, James perked up and twirled his cane.

"Dobbs Sampling Room is in the next block," he said. "I believe I'll have a toddy. Care to join me?"

Houston shook his head. He couldn't decide if he was angry or amused.

James nodded goodbye, headed toward the tavern, then stopped and turned back.

"I must say, Senator, I find these little conversations of ours awfully, awfully...*educational*."

Pleased he'd found exactly the right word, he strode

toward the tavern as if it was the most important thing he'd do all day.

"Either I'm dead wrong about everything I believe, or that young man is an idiot," Houston muttered. "Of course, I'm the one standing out here on the street talkin' to myself."

30

CHARLES SUMNER WAS PLEASED with himself, as usual.

Despite a scratchy voice as a result of what everyone agreed was another brilliant speech, life couldn't be better. The future bubbled with prospects, all of them grand. For one full day he'd blistered that great nitwit, South Carolina Senator Andrew Butler, his miserable, backward, fever-infested state, and anyone else of note sympathizing with the South.

It was past time someone put that Southern trash in its place. The rabble had to be crushed, not coddled. Sumner's speech used the stick, not the carrot, and he was proud of it.

Despite Sumner's painful throat, there was much to consider; the presidency, for one thing. It was time for a strong man to step forward. After the pathetic series of nonentities these last twenty years, a man of brilliance towered over the political landscape. There certainly wouldn't be much opposition. The shameful weakling Pierce wouldn't run again. That left Fremont with his new Republican party, old granny Buchanan, and perhaps the aged Lou Cass. He'd brush them aside like annoying insects.

Sumner unconsciously combed his fingers through his thick wavy hair and carefully patted it in place. He placed his cup of tea on his desk and settled in. The day's session wouldn't start for thirty minutes and there were only a few senators n the chamber. There was time to read the newspapers and gauge the ways his speech was praised or damned, depending on the intelligence or ignorance of the editor.

It was a bit of a squeeze behind the desk. The desk and chair were too small for a man of his size and Sumner liked to stretch out. In a world of men both small and small-minded, he saw himself as a towering figure in every way.

As Sumner sipped his tea and read his newspapers, Preston Smith Brooks, a member of the House of Representatives from South Carolina who also happened to be Senator Butler's nephew, approached Sumner's desk, a heavy walking stick under his arm.

He stopped beside Sumner, who was absorbed in his reading.

"Senator Sumner. I bring you greetings from South Carolina."

Sumner cried out as the walking stick lashed his head. Furiously, Brooks flailed away, bludgeoning Sumner again and again. Trapped behind the desk, Sumner rocked backed and forth, crying out with every blow as he writhed in his seat to escape the horrible cane.

Breathing heavily and almost light-headed with pleasure, Foote threw the cane to the floor and waited for the Sergeant at Arms. Sumner, his face bloody and his fingers mangled from trying to block the blows, managed to stand up, but reeled down the aisle before falling face down on the floor.

The next day a pro-slavery mob sacked Lawrence, Kansas, burning the headquarters of the New England Emigrant Aid Company and destroying the offices of both anti-slavery newspapers.

Three days later the abolitionist fanatic John Brown and his gang hacked to death five pro-slavery settlers at Kansas' Pottawatomie Creek.

An attempt to expel Preston Smith Brooks from Congress failed for lack of the necessary two-thirds vote. He resigned only to be re-elected to fill his own vacancy.

Due to injuries suffered in the attack, Sumner did not return to the Senate for three years.

31

Margaret Houston hacked at a stubborn weed with her hoe. She worked it loose, eased the edge of the hoe beneath the clump of weed and dirt, and expertly flipped it over to a small pile just beyond the edge of her garden.

Pleased with her small triumph, she leaned against the hoe and dabbed the sweat from her forehead with a handkerchief she kept tucked inside one sleeve.

"I swear that right now I'm looking at the prettiest picture in Texas."

She jumped at the familiar voice, dropped the hoe and ran into her husband's arms.

After a few minutes, Margaret looked up at her husband's smiling face.

"Sam, how on earth did you get here? Where's the coach? Where are your trunks?"

Houston raised her hand to his lips and gently kissed her dirty fingers.

"I was s'posed to change coaches in Utopia but the driver refused to take me."

"What!"

With their arms around each other, Houston guided Margaret toward the house. The older children were in school, the young ones asleep, and no one else was in sight, not even any of the slaves. The only sound was the distant buzzing of summer flies.

"I was about to load my trunks when the driver walked out of the coach line office. He glared at me and said, 'You're Sam Houston, ain't you?' I said, 'Guilty,' and he said, 'Damn right you're guilty. You ain't riding on my stage, you by God rascal.' He put the lash to the team, and off he went, leavin' me standin there with my trunks at my feet and a stupefied look on my face."

Margaret's face turned crimson. "I'll see that man out of a job if it's the last thing I do."

Houston chuckled and held her close.

"Easy now, old girl. If you get rid of everyone who disagrees with me pretty soon there won't be many workin' people left. The line manager felt bad enough. I made him promise not to punish the driver, though I 'spect he will anyhow. At least he looked me in the eye when he called me names."

They sat on the porch steps, still holding each other, as if they couldn't believe they were together after so long apart.

"It turned out there wasn't a ridin' horse in the whole town," he said. "All the able men and horses were gone thanks to this latest trouble with the Comanches. I heard there was a four-hour fight. Thank the Lord for Sam Colt. I stored my trunks, changed into moccasins, and started walkin'. All in all, it's not a bad way to get reacquainted with home."

Margaret rested her head against his shoulder.

"You know, Sam, there was a time you would have tried to pull that driver down from that coach," she said. "Does that mean you've mellowed?"

"If I have, it must be your influence," he said. "So tell me the truth, Maggie, is really it as bad as all that?"

Margaret took his big hand and held it to her chest.

"Sometimes," she said.

————

A BRIEF but violent summer storm blew in early that evening. Once the children were put to bed, Margaret and Sam touched lightly and knew they would make love with the windows open and the smell of rain and dripping leaves in the air.

They felt such an urgent need that it might have been their first time. It was always like that with Margaret. He'd known many women in his life. High born, lowborn, black, white, Indian, Spanish, French, Creole and everything in between, but none like his Maggie. Their hunger was the same now as their first day. Sometimes they ripped the clothes off each other and laughed about it later as they crawled around on the floor looking for the buttons. For all her rigid public propriety, Margaret was a ferocious lover. It was a fine thing to be wanted by such a woman.

Afterward they lay naked in the featherbed, the sweat of their lovemaking glistening on their bodies in the night. They kept their voices low so not to disturb the children.

"No one ever threatened me or the children, but there's always this *feeling* out there," she said. "The newspapers feed on it. One calls you 'Sham Houston.' The Independence newspaper said it would have been better you were killed at San Jacinto because now you wouldn't be the Benedict Arnold of Texas. Can you imagine! Rip Ford looks in when he's out this way, and I know they've got a Ranger in Huntsville keeping a lookout. Henderson Yoakum comes around. Ben McCulloch's been here a few times, too. Sam is the only one of the children who knows something's wrong, but except for one fight at school it hasn't amounted to anything."

Margaret cradled her head in one hand and ran the fingers of her other hand along the side of his face.

"What will you do now?"

"There's not much I can do," he admitted. "The state legislature made it clear I'm no longer welcome in the Senate. They already picked my successor. When they censured me, I only had three supporters out of eighty votes. They're about to pass a resolution repudiatin' my vote on the Kansas-Nebraska Bill and the Texas convention of counties called for my resignation. I'll leave the Senate right enough, but at least I'll serve out my time."

He didn't know how Margaret would take what he was about to tell her.

"There is one other possibility," he said.

"What is it?" she asked, her heart swelling with the hope that he might quit politics altogether.

Houston was nervous. This was new ground, the first time he'd given voice to it.

"The general used to say the best time to attack is when the enemy thinks you're beaten. If I can get the people behind me maybe I can help avoid what's comin', at least the worst of it. But I can only do that if I'm here *in* Texas. Margaret, this may seem sudden, but I just might run for Governor."

She fell on her pillow and closed her eyes. It would never end. She knew it now. She should have known it all along. Her great fool of a husband thought he could fix everything.

32

HE'D JUST FINISHED WALKING the farm when his trunks arrived. Although the weather was hotter than hell's pavement after last night's rain, the place was even more beautiful than he remembered.

With Joshua's help, Margaret had the farm running like a machine. She'd planted jasmine, iris, phlox, clover, and the ivy he'd shipped home from Washington's tomb at Mount Vernon last year, all that in addition to the lilacs, carnations, narcissus, jonquils and Easter lilies that already covered the farm like a scented blanket. The circle in the front yard exploded in color. There were more trees in the back, too, at least a half-dozen more quince, apple, peach and fig. The vegetable garden was bigger. So was the potato patch. And there were climbing roses on a trellis near the kitchen.

It was too bad Margaret couldn't grow money. They'd be rich by now.

He'd lived in many places but this was the only home he ever loved. If he ever lost Woodland he'd mourn the loss as he might mourn a death of a loved one, but he would never try to recreate it because that would be impossible. The best he could do was treasure the memory.

He distributed his presents amid the usual turmoil. Everyone got a new pair of shoes. They weren't any better than shoes in Texas, but they thrilled the children because they came from faraway Washington. He brought drawing paper, ink, and pens for little Sam, too. Margaret wasn't exaggerating when she said that the boy showed talent. It must come from her. Margaret was a promising artist as a young woman, although she hadn't done any drawing in years. The boy certainly didn't get it from him. Houston couldn't draw a straight line without laboring over it.

When she opened her new music box, Mary Willie insisted on dancing with her father. While it played a waltz, the little girl wrapped herself around his leg with her tiny feet on his boot, showing pleasure that seemed to start at her toes and creep up her body. When they saw how much fun Mary Willie had, all the girls insisted on a dance. After Mary Willie came Nannie, then Maggie, and finally Nettie. Houston felt drunk from sheer joy.

After a while, the happy parents stood at the doorway with their arms around each other while the smaller children played outside. Little Sam found a comfortable spot under a tree where he attempted to sketch the scene.

"Six children, Margaret," he said, marveling at the number. "Who'd have thought we'd produce such a brood?"

"Not me, that's for certain," she teased. "It's shameful the way you took advantage of an innocent girl from Alabama. I had no idea what I was getting into."

"Would it have changed anything?" he asked.

"What do you think?" she asked.

They watched the children for a while before Margaret spoke up again.

"If you can bring yourself to do it, I think it's time to stop calling him 'little Sam,'" she said. "It embarrasses him. In case you hadn't noticed, he's not so little anymore."

Houston felt tears streaming down his face. They surprised him, but he made no effort to hide them.

"Well, that he is, Margaret. From now on, there are two Sams in this house. If I ever slip, please tell me."

Margaret gently wiped the tears away from her husband's face with one finger and gave him a kiss on the cheek.

"Aren't you the sentimental one," she said. "If they could only see you now, 'Sham Houston,' indeed!"

More treasured minutes of silence passed while they watched the children play.

"It's hard when they grow up, isn't it?" she said. "I'm afraid we have a lot of that ahead of us. Young Sam will be quite a handsome man, too. Just like his father. He has the same disinclination for farming you had at his age, too."

They walked into the parlor and continued to unpack. Margaret squealed with delight when she discovered the dozen books he'd brought home.

"Uncle Tom's Cabin!" She held the slim volume at arm's length as though it might bite her. "I wanted to read it but you can't find it anywhere."

"I have no doubt of that," he said. "I'm surprised they didn't ban it. It has half the country up in arms."

"How is it?" she asked.

Houston shrugged. "There's just enough truth to convince people who don't know better that it's all true. I met the author, Harriet Stowe. She showed up at a party for Nat Banks, the new Speaker of the House.

"What's she like?"

"Easier to take in print than in person. She's got a face like the north end of a south bound mule."

She examined another volume, so heavy she used both hands to lift it.

"What on earth is this?"

"It's about a whale," he said. "It's about a mad captain, too, although it goes off in too many directions. Charles Sumner recommended it a few days before that fool from South Carolina nearly beat him to death. I don't like Sumner, but he didn't deserve that. It only confirmed what too many people already think about the South."

"And yet you..."

He knew what she was thinking. Others made the same comparison. It nettled him every time.

"I faced Stanbery man to man, I didn't sneak up on him. He was armed, too."

He'd spoken more sharply than he intended. To make up for it, he handed Margaret a package wrapped in brown paper and twine. Several weeks before leaving Washington, he received his decades-overdue pension for his service during the Creek War, paid in silver dollars. Deciding to turn it into a special gift, he sent the silver to Gault Jewelers in New York City with instructions to melt it down and shape it into silver cups, one for Margaret and one each for the children, with their names inscribed.

"I know we already have a tea service, but this seemed to be the highest and best use of the silver," he said.

Margaret's eyes glistened with tears. She caressed each cup and ran her index finger across the inscriptions.

"Oh, Sam, it's the most thoughtful present anyone's ever given me," she said. "When I think about what it represents, all the pain, I don't know what to say."

"All of that was a long time ago," he said. "No one even remembers it anymore."

33

ALL BUT ONE of the goats were dead, which didn't say much for his future as a goat farmer.

"What do we do, suh," Joshua asked.

Standing in the mud of the goat pen with his hands on his hips, Houston poked at one of the carcasses with his boot.

"Let it run wild for all I care," he grumbled.

"I mean about the dead 'uns," Joshua said.

"What does it matter?" Houston said bitterly.

He'd made a good bargain with Raimundo Landeros. After Landeros bought a parcel of land out in Big Bend country, Houston acquired his goats at a sweet price. They were too much trouble for Landeros to take with him, but to Houston they looked like easy money, the way the little scutters reproduced.

Now the tantalizing profit that seemed almost within his grasp was another loss he couldn't afford, the latest in a long line.

"Joshua, you don't suppose Raimundo knew something was wrong with 'em, do you?" he asked.

"Sam, Raimundo's an honest man and you know it," said

Margaret as she walked up from the stable, holding her skirts high to keep them out of the mud.

They stood around the latest dead goat and stared as if they expected it to spring back to life.

"Something happened," Margaret said. "Bad feed, disease, I don't know. But don't blame Raimundo. It just happens sometimes."

"But why does it always happen to *me?*" Houston asked, sinking into self-pity. "I plant corn and it burns up in the heat. I plant peas and they rot from too much rain. I buy two milk cows and they stop giving milk. The only thing's workin' out are the sheep. I hate the beasts, but at least the wool brings in good money. The way it's going, they'll probably get hit by lightnin'."

He kicked angrily at the mud.

"Let's face it, as a farmer I'm bad luck."

"Oh, stop it!" Margaret scolded. "You aren't bad luck. You've just *had* bad luck. Farmin' comes in cycles. Things just aren't workin' you right now."

"I've noticed." Houston flapped his arms at his sides. "When exactly does my cycle go up? What am I doin' wrong?"

Margaret and Joshua exchanged glances. Houston knew the look.

"Well, what is it? Speak up."

Margaret looked at Joshua.

"You first," she said.

Joshua stuffed his big rough hands in his back pockets.

"Well, suh, you're too impatient. You rush things too much. Farmin's not like that. There's a rhythm to it, a soothiness. Sometimes you come up short in that particular department."

Margaret rolled her eyes.

"I'd say it's a bit more than sometimes."

Taking a seat on a stump outside the gate, Houston said, "Go ahead, Margaret, kick me when I'm down."

"It's the same way you treat the children when they're sick," she said. "We laugh about it. You're always trying to push things before they're ready or at the wrong time. Remember when Nannie was sick and you woke her up to ask if she wanted anything to help her sleep? Sam, she was *already sleeping!*"

"All right, Joshua, your turn," he said, waving at the slave. "Go ahead, both barrels."

"Do you know the story about the farmer who pulled up his crops to see how they were growin'?"

Houston nodded. He'd heard that joke since he was a boy.

"That's you," Joshua said.

The blood-curdling scream split the air like a lightning strike.

Joshua was running toward the house before Houston got off the stump. Margaret followed closely behind, her skirts hitched up and running like a deer. As they drew closer to the house, Houston saw a fat hand frantically wave from inside Nancy Lea's coffin.

For as long as Houston had known her, Nancy Lea worried that she wouldn't be properly cared for when she died. She even ordered two heavy metal coffins from New Orleans. One she kept at her place in Independence, where she had a plaster and limestone tomb built behind her house. To Houston's disgust, she kept the other one at Woodland, propped up on two sawhorses on the back porch. From time to time, she liked to climb in to try it on for size.

Joshua got there first to find Nancy Lea wedged inside, screaming her fool head off. She'd worked one fat arm free from the elbow down and furiously waved her hand it in the air.

"Get me out of here! Get me out! Get me out!"

It wasn't easy. Wedged in tight, Nancy Lea weighed three hundred pounds if she weighed an ounce. As her shrill screams shattered the air, Joshua finally managed to work one shoulder loose. That gave them enough purchase to hoist her to a sitting position, her enormous hips still wedged tightly in place. Houston got behind and reached under her arms while Joshua bent her legs and worked his powerful arms underneath her knees. Rocking from one side to the other, they worked her out inch by inch. By now, her screams were reduced to nonsensical bawling. Houston never wanted to smack a person as much as he wanted to smack his mother in law.

Gasping from the effort, they finally got her out of the coffin and on the ground, only to be rewarded by a clout across the head for Houston and a hard jab on the shoulder for Joshua.

"Let me go this instant!" Spittle flew from her blubbery lips. "I'll not have you pawing at me!"

"Mother, what on earth happened," Margaret asked, eyes wide with alarm.

At great length and even greater volume, Nancy Lea told her story. When she got stuck, she cried out for help. Two of the girls - Nannie and Maggie - came running. Unfortunately, they starting giggling at the sight of their fat old grandmother stuck tight in her own coffin, and once they started laughing they couldn't stop. When her cries for help became the world-shattering screams they heard down at the goat pen, the girls panicked and ran away. They were probably hiding in the woods right now.

Nancy Lea gave Houston another angry clout.

"They're animals! That's what they are! They're wild animals!

Moving in from behind so she couldn't hit him, too, Joshua helped her to her feet. As he exchanged glances with Houston, it was all they could do to keep from laughing like the girls.

Finally standing upright, Nancy Lea jerked her arms away.

"See what happens when you let children run wild? Haven't I warned you? Haven't I?"

Unfortunately for the girls, Margaret was genuinely angry. She could always be counted on to take her mother's side. By the time the switching ended and the tears ran dry, the girls stood facing different corners of the parlor, where they were to remain until released by their mother.

If Houston interpreted their furtive glances correctly, the punishment was a small price to pay for the comical sight of their fat grandmother wedged in her own coffin and screaming bloody murder. Their apologies seemed less than heartfelt. As an experienced politician, he knew deceit when he saw it.

A few minutes later, after Margaret left the room, Houston slipped each of the girls a piece of rock candy from a cache he kept in his office.

"Don't tell your mother," he whispered, "but if I'd been with you we'd *all* be standin' in the corner."

That night, he told Joshua, "It's time to get back to politics. I'd rather tangle with Stephen Douglas than Nancy Lea any day."

34

THE CARRIAGE ROLLED to a stop in front of the house and Houston slowly climbed down, aching in every joint. It was as if even his bones were sore. Good thing no one was here to see him move like an old man. Young Sam was away at Colonel Allen's military academy in Bastrop while Margaret, Joshua, and the rest of the children were at the Cedar Point house on Galveston Bay for most of the summer.

As Houston waited for the throbbing in his bad leg to subside, young Jeff came running out of the carriage house to tend to the horses. Houston waved him off. He wanted to do it himself. They'd earned it these last hard weeks.

Besides, Jeff wasn't ready for responsibility, no matter how much he wanted it. As best they knew, he was about thirteen. Small for his age, too. Houston bought him at an auction in Huntsville, paying three hundred dollars he didn't have for another slave he didn't need. He didn't intend to buy that day. But as the skinny youngster stood weeping and frightened on the block, Houston impulsively made a bid. Now he couldn't take two steps without the grateful boy getting underfoot.

Seeing Jeff's disappointment that he couldn't help with the horses, Houston gave him something to do.

"Get out the big copper tub and draw me a bath in the bedroom?" he said. "Boil the water. Make it as hot you can. Once you get the tub filled, get more goin'. I'll be in there a while."

Houston unhitched the horses and led them to the stable, carefully giving each one a good feed and rub. Damn, his leg hurt! A bath would feel good. Make the air seem cooler afterward, too.

As he limped to the house, he peeled off his sweat-soaked clothes like he was shedding skin, knowing Jeff would gather them up.

Standing naked in the bedroom, he lit a cigar, put it on a chair beside the tub, and winced when he tried the water with his foot. After a few minutes, he eased one leg in, then sat on the chair and used both hands to hoist his bad leg over the side of the tub and into the water.

Sighing with pleasure, he slid into the tub until he was sitting on the copper bottom. Water sloshed over the edge to the floor, but without Margaret to scold him he didn't care. He slid down and dunked his head under the water. Resurfacing, he grabbed a towel, dried his face, smoothed his hair, put the cigar back in his mouth, and relaxed, letting the hot water do its work as he leaned back with his arms on the sides of the tub so that only his head, shoulders and arms were out of the steaming water.

And so ends another campaign, he thought, and a poor one it was, too.

After ten weeks and sixty-seven speeches in fifty cities and towns, Sam Houston was a beaten and exhausted man. The heat had something to do with it. It was the hottest summer that anyone remembered. Heat like that took the enthusiasm right out of a crowd and every day seemed worse than the last. Maybe if it wasn't for the weather…

He sniffed at the self-deception. Be honest with yourself, Houston, he thought. The heat had nothing to do with it. You could have run for president of Sweden and given speeches on top of glaciers and it wouldn't have made any difference. You should have known better. You *do* know better. You just didn't act like it. You were whipped and whipped good.

With no party to back him, most of his speeches were at informal barbecues and picnics sponsored by friends and supporters. While the meat roasted on the spit and the voters roasted from the heat, he usually spoke from the back of a wagon or on a front porch. The crowds were good, at least at first. Early on, he joked that his opponent, Harden Runnels, a square-headed secessionist with no visible qualifications to be governor, or anything else, possessed "all the attributes of a dog save one - fidelity!" The joke played so well that he used it over and over.

But a good joke did not make a good campaign. Texas had changed. Houston had been away so much that the width and breadth of the changes surprised him. The population had tripled in seven years and the newcomers knew only prosperity. Where he saw the threatening thunderclouds of a looming crisis, they saw blue sky. He didn't say what they wanted to hear so they didn't listen. Or was it that he didn't say it very well? That was more likely.

He encountered indifference everywhere he went. The truth is that most voters don't care if Texas is in the union or out of it. Except for the postal service, they don't have much contact with the federal government. The idea of union was an abstraction to most people. What did it matter as long as the rest of the world needed cotton? Union or not, the South would be well and Texas even better. He never found a way to put a dent in that attitude.

Runnels wisely refused to debate. With no opponent to face, Houston never got his teeth into the campaign. In town after town, he lashed out at everything that moved for no purpose, never making a case for himself, or his cause. As the election slipped away, he turned desperate and bitter. He felt it happening, but couldn't do anything about it. What did the Austin Gazette call him, "A melancholy picture of imbecility, vindictiveness and hate in old age?" He never felt so inconsequential before. It was hard to keep going. There were more than a few times when he wanted to give up.

The results wouldn't be official for a while, but Houston knew that he'd lost by at least ten thousand votes. His friends would expect him to be devastated and praise his bravery in defeat. Let them think what they wanted. He'd learned a lesson.

"I won't make the same mistake twice." His voice echoed off the water as he blew a cloud of cigar smoke into the air. "They'll learn soon enough that Runnels isn't the man for the job, not now. Two years isn't so long to wait. I'll do it right next time."

With a strong hand in the White House, there might be no need for him to run. But his narrow victory over Fremont and his upstart Republicans had scared Buchanan to death. Now he drifted like a shipwreck on the ocean. The tide carried him this way and that without going anywhere in particular.

The troubles ranged from the general to the particular. Not the least of it was the death of poor Tom Rusk. He was never the same after his wife died. Houston hadn't spoken to Rusk in two years, driven apart by the same hard feelings dividing the country. But when he heard that Rusk's wife had passed, he wrote expressing his sorrow. Rusk wrote back and they started talking again. During the campaign, he spent two nights at Rusk's home and saw right away that the man spent too much time brooding. Being a fair brooder himself,

Houston knew the signs. Not long afterward Rusk put a Colt in his mouth and pulled the trigger.

What would he do if anything happened to Margaret? The idea made him shudder. He couldn't imagine life without her.

Margaret and Joshua were right all along. Sometimes he was too impatient. He made his move too soon and then waged a poor campaign. It was best to let events come to him. Sooner or later they always did. Just like at San Jacinto, when he fell back and back and back until Santa Anna made a mistake. People always assumed he had a plan and he let them believe it, when most of the time he didn't know what the hell he was doing.

35

"Despite what everyone thinks, bein' a lame duck isn't bad. After thirteen years, I find it liberatin'."

Houston's leg felt better today and the youngster hustled to keep up. He was one of Horace Greeley's boys, down from New York to write about Sam Houston's last days in Washington. In an uncharacteristically generous gesture, Greeley's newspaper was paying for dinner and Houston didn't intend to let it off lightly.

The restaurant was on the ground floor of a three-story brownstone. The cobblestone street was crowded with the carriages of customers coming and going, a new place everyone wanted to try. They nodded to the doorman and walked into the large foyer. Houston shrugged out of his wool cape and checked it with an attractive young woman dressed in a black high-necked dress and white lacy apron. The young scribbler had no winter coat to check. Like most of them, he looked as poor as a church mouse. The elbows of his jacket were threadbare and his shirt collar frayed. Apparently Greeley's generosity did not extend to his employees.

They passed through a richly carpeted waiting room and

then through the oyster bar, mirrored and lighted with crystal chandeliers and smelling of the seashore and horseradish.

At the entrance to the main dining room, the preening *maitre d'* checked his list and found Houston's name. He led them to a table against the wall at the rear of the room. The restaurant was filled with well-dressed people. Expensive jewelry from diamond stick pins to emerald necklaces twinkled in the lamplight. Many of the women wore daring gowns cut low across their breasts. Houston tried to imagine Margaret wearing such a dress. The image made him smile. When the waiter brought the menu, it was twelve pages long.

A waiter passed with a flaming desert on the way to another table. While the diners oohed and aahed, the young man whose name Houston couldn't remember pulled several sheets of paper out of his coat pocket. He smoothed them out on the table and reached into another pocket for a stubby pencil.

"Senator, with all the vital questions facing the country, isn't it frustrating to be forced out now?"

If the question was supposed to be provocative, it failed. These last few weeks a calm had settled over Houston that was impossible to ruffle.

Using a fork to cut a moist piece of Salmon a la Lucullus, whatever that meant, he popped it into his mouth.

"Forced out now as opposed to being forced out at some other time? Maybe I should have left a long time ago. I've lived through all fifteen administrations and I've known twelve Presidents. But I was only home for the birth of two of my children. We just had another baby, our seventh. I missed that, too. I know that answer won't help sell newspapers, but Greeley can always make it up, as usual."

Houston smiled to show that he was joking, but the youngster still squirmed in his chair. The remark struck too close to home.

Houston was enjoying his last session of Congress. He wasn't exaggerating when he said that he never felt so free. Part of it was all the praise. What was it Seward said? How does a politician become a statesman? He either retires or he dies. Houston indulged himself with an ambitious but impossible resolution to establish a protectorate over Mexico, Nicaragua, Costa Rica, Guatemala, Honduras, and San Salvador. As expected, it was defeated, despite having such unlikely supporters as Jeff Davis and Mirabeau Lamar, who was currently sweating buckets as Buchanan's ambassador to Nicaragua. He doubted that his old rival enjoyed life in the jungle. Lamar was more of a drawing-room man. He faced the thankless assignment of cleaning up the mess left by William Walker, who led an inept filibuster to take over the country. In the end, all Walker got was a volley from a Nicaraguan firing squad.

Down on his luck, Lamar needed a job and begged Buchanan for a post. When the President asked Houston's advice, he jokingly suggested Nicaragua and damned if Buchanan didn't do it. It was one of the worst postings in the diplomatic corps, only a cut above ambassador to hell. The only thing missing to complete Houston's satisfaction is that Lamar didn't know it was his idea.

A young man Houston recognized as one of the senate pages stopped at the table. He hadn't grown into his big feet and hands. Even standing still he looked awkward, as if he might fall down any second.

"Senator Houston, I hope I'm not interrupting, but I just wanted to tell you how sorry I am you're leaving."

The boy's voice cracked with nervousness. This was the first time he'd summoned the courage to speak to a Senator unless spoken to first.

"I think I speak for all of the pages when I say that. We

don't even mind cleanin' up the shavings from your whittling. Well, most of us don't mind. I mean..."

Houston rose out of his chair and took the nervous page's hand in both of his own.

"On the contrary, it has been my privilege to work with you and your associates. Young men like you make me confident I'm leavin' the place in good hands."

Even more self-conscious than before, the page nodded his thanks, extricated his hand, and hurriedly left the restaurant, desperately hoping that he wouldn't stumble on the way out.

"Did you arrange that for my benefit?" demanded the newspaperman, whose name, Houston remembered, was Ned Salisbury.

"A trick like that it isn't beyond me, but it wasn't necessary," replied Houston. "I've received more than three hundred letters expressin' regret at my departure. It's been very gratifyin'"

"But it *is* true that they tried to force you out long before your term expired, and picked your successor months ago?"

"Yes on both counts," Houston said. "But I wouldn't give anyone the satisfaction of leavin' before my time is up."

Salisbury looked up from his writing to accept desert, pears covered with chocolate sauce. It looked so delicious that Houston ordered some for himself.

His mouth full, Salisbury mumbled another question.

"Why do you think Texas politicians have such rotten luck? It's as if you people are cursed."

"What do you mean?"

"Rusk killed himself, blew the top of his head right off. Anson Jones was another suicide. Pinckney Henderson suddenly died in office. You were beaten in the race for governor and now you're forced out of the Senate. There are other examples; suicides, madness, and failure.

"As I said at Pink's funeral, 'Even the paths of glory lead to the grave.' Everyone dies, though most let nature take its course. A man's career ends, too, although it's possible mine isn't over quite yet."

Sensing news, Salisbury perked up. "Are you saying you'll run for Governor again?"

"I'm not sayin' anything, particularly, except I don't intend to turn into dust and blow away."

After a few more questions, Salisbury concluded that he wouldn't get anything controversial. He'd wind up writing another gushing eulogy for the old boy's career. Greeley wouldn't like it, but maybe it wasn't such a bad thing. He decided that he liked this great ruin of a man.

They shook hands out on the street, with the coatless Salisbury already shivering. Still operating on Greeley's money, he splurged and hailed a carriage. Houston refused a ride, preferring to walk back to the hotel. After a heavy meal, a walk would feel good in the cold weather.

Today was his birthday; sixty-six years old. The meal was a fine present. The fact that Greeley paid for it made it even better.

36

THANKS to some bureaucratic fool's shortsighted idea of economy, the El Paso to San Diego mail route was in danger of being shut down. Houston rose to defend it, keeping his remarks brief and to the point. There was no sense dragging out his last speech.

It had been a long session, with most workdays lasting well into the night. The senators were tired and irritable. Someone made a motion to adjourn for the day. Houston was leaving Washington in the morning and only now realized he didn't want it to end. It came on him like a sudden chill. He did not want to go. He did not want to leave this place where he'd spent so much of his life. He thought that he'd prepared himself for it, but now that the moment was here he couldn't bear it. He was anxious and afraid.

He rose to speak against the motion to adjourn, lacing his fingers at his waist to still his shaking hands. Knowing it was a foolish effort made him feel ridiculous, but he couldn't help it.

"Gentlemen, we have been here for many days and nights and I know that the members are exhausted. But it is near the

211

end of the session and we still have business. If we leave now, too many of us will drift away. It is tempting to call an end to the night's work, but once we retire I'm afraid the temptation not to return will be too great."

They didn't see the point. Why should they? They'd be back at it soon enough, most of them. The motion to adjourn passed almost unanimously.

Only the senior senator from Texas voted against it.

37

EARLY AFTERNOON and already steaming hot, Houston estimated the crowd gathered in front of the Nacogdoches courthouse to be about three hundred. Most of the women wore sunbonnets or clutched parasols to protect themselves against the scorching sun. There were dozens of fans in motion, too. Seen from the speaker's platform, the fanning motion was almost hypnotic as it rippled through the crowd. The men wore every kind of hat imaginable; sombreros, battered stove-pipe hats, military caps of many nationalities, floppy hats, planter's hats, and straw hats.

As Houston smoothed out his notes on the podium, the applause was polite, but no more than that. It was too hot to show enthusiasm. He removed his coat and tossed it over his empty chair. He unbuttoned his waistcoat, took it off and laid that on the chair, too. Down to suspenders and shirtsleeves, he loosened his cuffs as he stepped back to the podium.

"Might as well get comfortable," he said, rolling his sleeves up to his elbows. "If any of you ladies would like to part with your parasol, I'd be happy to borrow it. I draw the line at wearin' a sun bonnet."

It got the laugh he expected. Already they were on his side.

"Many of you may be wonderin' why I want to be Governor, especially after I was whipped so badly the last time I tried. After all, why do I want a low-payin' job that forces me to associate with an even lower quality of men, by which I mean the legislature?"

After another wave of laughter, he proceeded to explain. There would be none of the aimless bitterness of his last campaign.

"Let's set aside the obvious for a moment, that bein' the need to replace Hardin Runnels," he said. "As you know, I am a Democrat of the old school, one of the last of my kind. In one way or another, my career is connected to every major event in this country of the last forty-five years. I've probably done many things you consider to be wrong, but I don't apologize for any of them. But I *do* ask your forgiveness for those times when you *thought* I was wrong. In return, I forgive you for the times when I thought *you* were wrong, such as the last time I ran for office and most of you didn't vote for me."

He'd found his rhythm quickly, warning, accusing, cajoling, joking, praising and even threatening. He quoted from the Iliad, the Bible, and the Declaration of Independence. Mostly he talked about the Union and how extremists on both sides threatened to destroy the work of so many great men.

"Texas needs an old dog like me to guard against such a thing. If it does happen, our future will be all that is horrible in war, and no man here knows war better than I. Preserve the Union and you preserve liberty. They are one and the same."

Giving a speech, a good speech, was as much about a sense of the crowd as it was about words and ideas. In this heat, if he spoke for much longer the crowd's attention would drift. He'd already skipped the section establishing his bona fides.

Anyone who didn't know who he was by now might be too stupid to cast a ballot.

"My sand is running out and I know it," he said, offering quiet when they expected thunder. "Allow me to perform one last service. You have it in your power to grant that wish."

He had a feel for it this time, a sense of people, issues, and timing that was badly lacking in his first campaign. It was not his best speech, but it would do.

38

As GOVERNOR-ELECT HOUSTON's carriage rattled to a stop, the sight of the new Menger Hotel towering over the ruins of the Alamo chapel a short distance away was a sharp reminder of how much San Antonio had changed since he first saw it more than twenty five years ago.

With a population approaching ten thousand, San Antonio was the largest city in Texas. It was still mostly Mexican, but the Anglo and German influences were growing. For the most part, Anglos ran the government, Germans worked as mechanics and shopkeepers, and Mexicans hauled freight or worked the surrounding farms and ranches.

For Houston, San Antonio's mix of old and new was part of what gave it its peculiar charm. Most of the Anglos lived near the main plaza that boasted two good hotels and several glass-fronted stores. The clannish Germans lived on the outskirts of town in neat limestone houses. Older adobe houses and mud-plastered *jacales* were scattered here and there, most of them overflowing with Mexican families, or newcomers needing a place to live.

Climbing down from the carriage, Houston spotted Sam

Maverick's old flagstone house facing the plaza from the east, crowned by a giant cypress tree in back. He'd heard that the family recently moved to an even bigger place across the river. One of the richest men in the state, they said that Maverick owned more than a hundred and twenty town lots.

Houston couldn't think of all that wealth without a pang of jealousy. With all the debt accumulated during his two campaigns for governor, it looked like he'd have to do the unthinkable and sell Woodland. The idea made him sick to his stomach. There had to be another way, there just had to be.

On the plaza's south side, a steady stream of foot, horse, burro, wagon, and ox-cart traffic passed by the Lewis & Groesbeck Emporium. The popular adobe-and-stone general store was known for its delicacies, some imported from as far away as New York City. He wondered of the locals still called Nat Lewis *Don Pelon* (Mister Baldhead). He made a mental note to drop in, say hello, and pick up presents for Margaret and the children. Nat should be willing to extend credit to the Governor-elect.

On the west side, behind the rounded dome of San Fernando Cathedral, a big American flag flapped and cracked in the wind. That'd be the new military headquarters. Houston reminded himself to pay a call on Colonel Lee, commander of the Department of Texas. He remembered a prediction years ago by Winfield Scott that someday Lee would have Scott's job. It might yet happen. Lee made a sterling reputation in the Mexican War and acquitted himself well during that business with John Brown and his gang of bloodthirsty lunatics at Harper's Ferry. Houston just wished that he liked Lee better. Years ago, Jeff Davis told him that Lee was the only cadet in the history of West Point never to receive a single demerit. Houston never trusted perfection. It wasn't natural.

And there was Jose Cassiano's dormered house at the

corner of the square. He'd visit Jose, too. He owed the old don that much. Thanks to the influence of the *Tejano* families like the Cassianos, the Seguins, and the Navarros, most of the *Tejanos* either supported the revolution or stayed neutral. If they'd thrown in with Santa Anna, the rebellion might have died in its infancy.

Houston was pleased to see that the low one-story building between the cathedral and the Cassiano place hadn't changed. Madame Bustamante ran the best and bawdiest fandango hall in Texas, even though the old girl must be closing in on ninety. Before he met Margaret, he'd spent many a night there and suffered many a morning for what he'd done the night before.

Houston's reverie was interrupted when Jefferson T. Clancy emerged from the Menger like an animal released from a trap. He bounded down the stairs, seized Houston in a bear hug, and pounded him on the back.

"Damn! It's good to see you, *Governor* Houston," Clancy said. "You were spotted on the way into town. Somebody had the sense to alert the best newspaper in Texas that some genuine news was on the road. " Clancy motioned toward the Menger. "I figured our new palace is the only place where you'd stay. What brings you here?"

"You do," replied Houston. "You're comin' to work for me."

"Oh, God." Clancy deflated so quickly it was like watching a carnival tent collapse. "I was afraid you'd say that."

———

HOUSTON CHECKED into the hotel and found himself in a second-floor room with a window overlooking the plaza. He unpacked, changed clothes, and met Clancy in the spectacular lobby full of sparkling chandeliers, mirrors, and marble.

They made an odd pair as they walked to Clancy's nearby

office at the San Antonio Crusader: one tall and craggy; the other short, pudgy, and bald as a hen's egg. Clancy was the Crusader's owner and editor and, judging by his prosperous waistline, business was good.

During Houston's second term as President of the Republic, Clancy spent two years as his secretary. He wanted Clancy to take the same job, only this time for Governor Houston, and aimed to ruthlessly beat down every argument until Clancy agreed.

"But I'm too old," begged Clancy, whose short legs took two strides to Houston's one. "I'm positively feeble, what with the gout and all."

"I'll have none of that nonsense," snorted Houston. "You're ten years younger than I am. Besides, think of the stories you'll have for your newspaper when it's over."

"If I live that long," groaned Clancy. "I remember what workin' for you was like. I didn't get a decent night's sleep for two years. Besides, this time you might be bitin' off even more than you can chew."

"I'd like your thoughts on that before we go to Austin," Houston said.

"Before *we* go to Austin?" Clancy moaned and ran his small hands over his bald head. "You're killin' me, Sam, you know that? You're just killin' me!"

They argued for the next half hour in the tobacco-scented clutter of Clancy's office. Houston knew that he had his man if he kept the pressure on. His prey had two weaknesses: Like anyone in his line of work, Clancy loved being on the inside, and he enjoyed being wooed and flattered.

In Houston's experience, most newspaper editors didn't know their asses from apple butter, but Clancy was an exception; a clear thinker and an honest man. They hadn't seen each other in a good while, but the Clancy he remembered was steady as a lighthouse and capable of great sacrifice, as long as it didn't last too long.

With Clancy resisting and Houston oozing persuasion, they left the Crusader's office and walked two blocks to Matthew Armbruster's image studio, where Houston was to have his portrait taken.

The small studio smelled of many vile chemicals blended into one awful stench. It was such a wicked odor that Houston demanded all the windows be opened or he wouldn't stay. Eager for the prestige of making the Governor-elect's official portrait, the tall skinny Armbruster and his silent young assistant bustled around the room, straining themselves to open windows that probably hadn't been opened in years.

From his first Daguerreotype as a twenty-nine-year-old Congressman, Houston's image had been taken many times over the years. Not everyone liked having it done. Some were impatient with the laborious process. Others considered it vain and unmanly. Houston not only enjoyed it, he liked being fussed over in the studio. He also enjoyed having his portrait painted, although no artist ever got it exactly right.

Over the years and many images, Houston never looked the same way twice. Today, he wore a linen duster, a tartan cravat, and a rough white shirt with a big floppy collar. He settled into the straight-back chair and patiently waited while the photographer's assistant combed his hair and fitted his neck into a brace to keep his head still during the long exposure.

After some thought about the pose, Houston crossed his arms in front of his chest, a stern expression frozen on his broad face.

"Sam, you are the very picture of a determined governor, or at least an angry teacher about to take a student to the woodshed," Clancy said. "Am I right, Armbruster?"

"Yes, sir," replied the photographer, crouching in back of the camera, his voice muffled by the black cloth draped over his head and shoulders. "He's scarin' me to death. Are you sure that's the look you want, Governor?"

Without moving his lips and ruining the pose, Houston replied, "That's exactly what I want. One day I might have to take the whole state to the woodshed."

After a few noises from beneath the cloth, Armbruster barked, "Now!" and the assistant uncapped the camera lens. When Armbruster said, "Cover," the assistant capped it again.

During the wait before the second image could be taken, Clancy chattered while Armbruster and his assistant fiddled with the large glass plates. Clancy sounded like a nervous man who was about to do something against his better judgment, which meant that Houston had him.

"You still interested in my thoughts?" Clancy asked, interrupting his own inconsequential babbling.

Houston grunted his assent. Clancy tilted his chair against the wall and hitched his ankle over one ample knee, a sign this would take a while. Clancy enjoyed few things more than the sound of his own voice.

"First off, people are fearful. That business with John Brown scared the righteous hell out of 'em. What if he got hold of the federal arsenal and stirred up a slave rebellion like he planned? I say thank God for Bobby Lee."

"If Lee wasn't there someone else would have handled Brown," Houston said, jerking his head toward Armbruster in silent warning. "He's not the only officer in the army."

Clancy dismissed the warning with a smile.

"Don't worry, he doesn't hear a thing, do you Matty?"

"It's bad for business." The photographer carefully inserted a glass plate into the camera's innards. "I'm an artist, not a gossip. If my clients didn't feel comfortable, I'd soon be out of business. Governor, king, or common man, nothing said leaves here, and that's a fact."

Clancy looked at Houston for approval. Getting it, he resumed his chatter.

"Brown was a madman, but that sure didn't stop the North from makin' a saint out of him from the minute he took the drop. Nothing elevates a bad man like a good hangin'. He's more dangerous dead than he was alive. Now every time people see two slaves talking they think it's a conspiracy. They remember what Brown said about drownin' the South in its own blood. In the North he's a martyr. In the South he's a madman. That's the problem. North and South don't see anything the same way. In the North, it's about slavery. In the South, it's about home rule. At the same time, the Democrats are split six ways from Sunday, and that opens it up for the abolitionists. I wouldn't be surprised if your old party ran two tickets in the next election, one from the North – Douglas, I think - and one from the South, maybe John Breckinridge. With the Whigs and Know Nothings all but out of business, that leaves the Republicans - the party of abolition - looking like winners."

Clancy stopped to draw breath.

"By the way, that Lincoln sure surprised a lot of people when he whipped Douglas in those debates up in Illinois," he said.

"It was more of an even thing, the way I heard it," Houston said. "But you're right, Lincoln's a national man now. I never thought it likely when I knew him in Congress, but men change. He might even be the Republican nominee, though he'll have to get by Seward."

"If Lincoln gets the nomination and wins the election at least seven or eight states will leave the Union." Clancy ticked them off on his fingers. "South Carolina, North Carolina, Georgia, Alabama, Mississippi, Virginia, Arkansas and

Louisiana for sure. Probably Florida and Tennessee. Possibly Kentucky, too. Hell, maybe even Maryland."

"I didn't hear Texas on that list," Houston said.

"Well, this state of ours is interestin'," Clancy said. "If the legislature voted today, it'd be easy for secession. But if you took it to the people, it'd be closer, especially with all the Dutchmen in the state. But it'll depend on events and, if I may be so bold, on you. For a lot of people, you *are* Texas. Many don't like it, but it's true. Old fart that you are, you're a link to the men who ran this country for a hell of a long time. Jackson, Calhoun, Webster, Clay, Polk, Benton...they're all gone. Even here, now that Lamar's dead you're one of the last of the founders. Good or bad, you mean somethin' to people. Those same voters who went against you in '57 now think maybe you're the man to see us through this, if anyone can. How much use you'll get out of that and how long it'll last I can't say."

Houston rubbed his chin. Clancy's thoughts generally duplicated his own, but it was good to hear it from a man whose opinion he respected.

"So are you with me?" he asked. "Are we going to Austin?"

Clancy rolled his eyes. "Yes, I guess *we* are, dammit. And a bigger fool you've never met, at least 'til the next time you look in the mirror."

It was time to give Clancy a peek at what he had in mind. He deserved to know something.

"Here's a notion I want you to think about, but keep it to yourself for now," he said. "Even if Texas leaves the Union, there's no law says it's got to join some confederacy of Southern states. We've been on our own before."

One of the things he liked about Clancy was that you could see him take hold of an idea and watch it work across his face.

"You want to take us back to the Republic?" Clancy clearly

enjoyed the audacity of it. "If we vote out of the union, you want to keep us clear of the whole business?"

"It may not come to that, if we're lucky," Houston said.

"It will," Clancy said. "There isn't that much luck in the world, unless it's bad luck. You know, there are times when I think you might be as devious as people think you are."

Armbruster coughed to signal he was ready.

Houston settled his neck into the brace while the assistant fussed with his cravat.

"All right, do your worst," he announced. "Everybody else will."

39

SHE HATED the Governor's Mansion with every fiber of her soul. At first, she prayed that she might learn to at least tolerate it, but she hated it more now than the day they moved in. She missed the familiarity of Woodland and longed for its comfort and security. They built it, they loved it, and they lost it, burdened with debt as a result of Sam's two campaigns for governor.

Sitting in a cane-bottom rocker in one of the few places Margaret enjoyed - the second-floor balcony that looked out over the trees in front of the mansion - she wore one of Sam's coats lined with wolves' pelts to keep warm on a cold but sunny day. She knew that the big coat looked ridiculous on her, but it felt better than a hot fire. She liked to do her sewing here, especially patching the children's clothes. Engaged in such a small and peaceful domestic activity, she could shut out the world and let her mind roam.

The mansion *was* beautiful in its way. A wide porch with six graceful fluted columns extended across the first floor, with the balcony across the second. The exterior walls were buff-colored brick. The grand stairway inside was magnificent, too, although she didn't care for it. Margaret Houston was not a woman of grand entrances.

Their bedroom was the first door at the top of the stairs. Their new bed should arrive any day. Sam discovered it while visiting John Hollister, an old friend who lived north of Austin. He tried to recruit Hollister for his cabinet, but Hollister wanted no part of it. The only good thing to come out of the conversation was the bed. Hollister was almost as big as Sam and owned a special bed to accommodate his size. Sam impulsively ordered one for the Governor's mansion, paying for it himself with money they didn't have.

Until the bed arrived, they slept on a plain mattress stuffed with straw. It looked absurd in the big bedroom. The mattress was so low that with his bad leg it was hard for Sam to get out of bed. He had to roll over on his hands and knees and push himself upright.

To the right of the entry on the first floor was the big parlor for formal occasions. Margaret dreaded when the time would come when they would have to use it. Fortunately, after Temple's difficult birth no one expected it of her for now. She never was much for entertaining and it didn't help that Austin was full of people who flattered you to your face and insulted you behind your back.

She remembered how embarrassed she was at the inaugural; pregnant with Temple, big as a plow horse, and racked by nausea. Sam wanted her to come, of course, but didn't press it. He was touched and pleased when she did. Their eighth and last child, Temple Lea Houston was named for her father. The doctors agreed that she shouldn't have any more babies.

The only other place where Margaret felt comfortable was the small family parlor, large enough to accommodate the family, but small enough to feel cozy. Unfortunately, they rarely got together there, or anywhere. With Sam no longer traveling to Washington, she hoped to spend more time with him. But he worked such long hours that some days she only saw him while he slept.

She didn't even have Joshua to talk to. When they weren't needed at home, the Houstons let their slaves work elsewhere for wages and allowed them keep the money. With a staff for the chores, Joshua's responsibilities were light. With Sam's approval, he set up a smithy outside the city limits because it was against the law for niggers to own a business in Austin. He already had more customers than he could handle, despite the usual grumbling about Sam being too free with his head nigger.

It might not be so bad if she didn't feel hostility everywhere she went. It reminded her of the threatening stillness just before a storm. Governor and legislature were at a stalemate. Not much got done because neither side wanted to seem weak and make the first move. Sometimes it was so petty she wanted to scream. The legislature even refused to release the money budgeted to finish furnishing the mansion. She heard what one of those terrible people said: "A man who lived in a wigwam and has a brood of wild Indians for children is not entitled to luxuries at public expense." They moved their own furniture into the mansion, but their family treasures looked meager and ridiculous scattered across eleven rooms, as if it diminished their lives to inconsequence.

There was tension between Sam and their oldest son, too. They quarreled during young Sam's last visit home from the military academy in Bastrop. Like all young people, young Sam was finding his way. He enrolled in the academy as a naïve boy and came home a firebrand for Southern rights.

Two nights ago, what started as a simple dinnertime conversation turned ugly. Sam always pressed his son too hard, pushing when he should guide, demanding when he should ask, and lecturing when he should listen. Young Sam was a good student and a fine horseman, popular with his peers and highly regarded by the academy. He showed promise as an artist, too. But his father's compliments always seemed grudging, as if offered because they were expected, not deserved.

Sam was patient with the other children, but something about his first born made Sam drive him. And now he refused to be driven. The day after the quarrel, he took a coach back to Bastrop, leaving home a week early. The rift wasn't permanent, but it was painful.

Margaret saw Sam walking over from his office in the capital. With that massive frame and distinctive rolling limp, it couldn't be anyone else. She dropped her sewing in the basket beside the rocker and went downstairs to meet him.

He greeted her as he always did. Swooping her up and twirling her around, he planted a kiss on her lips as he set her down. All the strain, hard work, and long hours were etched on his face, but no man enjoyed it more.

"When I left this mornin' you were sleeping like little Temple," he said. "Feelin' better?"

"Better every day," she said, putting a happy lilt in her voice. By now, she was used to the pretense. He had too many worries for her to add to them. "Who wouldn't feel well on a glorious day like this?"

40

"...AND so, considering the benefits derived from this bill, I would appreciate your support. Call on me at any time, so on and so forth...you know how to end it, don't you, Thomas?"

Thomas Lyle Bickford looked up from his writing, his index finger and thumb stained black with ink.

"Yes, sir, I believe I do."

Having handled the official correspondence since he joined Governor Houston's staff, by now he could do it in his sleep.

It still was something of a mystery to him how he wound up in Austin taking dictation from the Governor. The long and winding road began after his graduation from Harvard College. The family doctor suggested that the air in the West might help his nagging cough. The only people west of the Mississippi his family knew were in Texas. Landing in Galveston, he made the rounds, armed with letters of introduction. Those introductions led to others, and one of those led to Austin and a meeting with Governor Houston.

As luck had it, the Governor was struggling to fill out his staff. Before he knew it, Bickford was the keeper of his correspondence, not exactly the adventurous life he sought when he left home. He certainly didn't plan on working long hours for a man who seemed to thrive on tumult.

Bickford took comfort in the fact that he could always go back to Newport if he felt like it. He had no ties to Texas and nothing to keep him here. Even if the South left the Union and Texas went with it, what did that matter to Rhode Island?

Fortunately, he liked the gruff but kindly Governor, otherwise the job would be impossible. Confronted by a hostile legislature at home and frustrated by the ineffectual government in Washington, the old boy rarely showed the pressure he must feel. Bickford marveled at his stamina.

"Make a clean copy so I can sign it," Houston said. He leaned back in his chair, opened a lower drawer and hiked one leg up on it, a habit that made his leg ache a little less. "Are we close to the bottom of the pile yet?"

"Just a few more items, Governor."

Bickford brushed his blonde hair out of his eyes, coughed into one hand, and shuffled through the neatly stacked papers.

"There's a proclamation to sign, and a request for new postmasters in Greune and Pierce Junction, along with your suggestions to Washington regarding who should be named. After that, we have some items regarding the budget. Finally, there's another petition asking for payment to bounty hunters of escaped slaves..."

"Never!" Houston grumbled. "Those bloodsuckers will not get a penny, not in a thousand years. I'll..."

Jeff Clancy burst into the room, startling Bickford so badly that he almost jumped out of his chair. He never got used to the way anyone could walk in on the governor unbidden, unannounced, and, frequently, unwanted. The common touch was one thing, but, in his opinion, a little isolated majesty would make the days less chaotic.

"Good news!" Clancy's happy smile creased his round face

until he looked like a Halloween pumpkin. "You won't believe..."

He jerked his bald head in Bickford's direction, obviously not wanting to continue with the young man in the room. Houston didn't see why not, but he liked to please the loyal Clancy, so he waved Bickford away.

"Go on, Thomas," he said. "We'll get to the rest later."

Piqued at his dismissal, Bickford stuffed the papers into his leather valise and left the room, glaring at Clancy as he passed. For all the effect it had, he might as well have glared at the furniture.

Houston had no doubt that Bickford lingered outside the door to hear what they said. That's what he'd have done at Bickford's age.

"Sam, you depend on that boy too much," Clancy said. "He doesn't have to know *everything*."

"He doesn't," Houston said. "I'm the only one who knows everything."

He rummaged through his desk until he found a leather tobacco pouch. He stuffed the tobacco into his pipe and looked a question at Clancy, who reached into his waistcoat pocket, found a match and passed it over. Houston never kept a supply of matches. He always forgot where he put them.

He struck the match on the underside of his desk. Once he got the pipe drawing, he blew out the match, ground it on the desk, and swept the remains to the floor. It was amusing to see Clancy's impatience turn into a sulk when he realized that Houston was playing with him by making him wait.

"All right," he said, ending the torture. "Tell me your news before the top of your head blows off."

"Rip Ford whipped Juan Cortina," Clancy announced. "The old bastard's finished. Even better, he's probably dead."

"I'll believe *that* when I see the body," Houston said. "Juan

Cortina's been killed more times than any man I know and here we are still talkin' about him."

He shifted in the chair to get comfortable. Nobody delivered good news like Clancy. He was better than a parade.

For years, Cortina led a gang of Mexican and Texan riffraff in raids on both sides of the Rio Grande. Mexico didn't like it any more than Texas did, but neither side could put him out of business. Under pressure, his so-called army would melt away only to reappear two hundred miles away three weeks later.

The latest episode started with the city law in Brownsville, a hard case named Connell who thumped a drunk Mexican senseless before hauling him to the calaboose while Cortina, who moved in and out of Brownsville with the ease of sunlight, watched from a second-floor whorehouse window. Cortina grabbed his pistol, went downstairs, marched up to Connell and got shot him easy as you please. Supposedly the drunk was an old friend of Cortina's, but Houston doubted it. Sometimes Cortina did things just because he could.

With Connell out of the way, Brownsville was ripe for plucking. Two days later, Cortina and a hundred men rode into town. There was a gala across the river in Matamoras the night before and most of the Brownsville men were sleeping it off. Cortina tore the place apart - three thousand people cowed by a hundred men. The torment finally ended when a detail led by a Mexican officer named Tijerina crossed the river from Matamoras and chased the bandits out of town.

Seeing opportunity in disorder, a gang of border dregs rode into town, bragging that they'd find Cortina, whip him, and expected a suitable reward for their trouble. They started by lynching a Brownsville man named Tomas Carbrera, who may or may not have ridden with Cortina years earlier before arthritis crippled him. Cortina retaliated by shooting three Texans. The gang responded to *that* by attacking Cortina's camp near Santa Rita, which was easily turned back after Cortina's sharpshooters knocked a few of the *gringos* out of their saddles.

To his surprise, these "victories" made Juan Cortina a great man in northern Mexico. In a land plagued by civil war for as long as anyone could remember, at least he struck a blow at somebody beside his own countrymen. While the life of a wealthy bandit chief generally used up all his ambition, for appearances sake Cortina issued several windy proclamations against the *gringos* while secretly sending a message to assure Houston he wanted no part of this hero nonsense, not to mention the trouble was mostly forced on him in the first place.

Fearing the Cortina's return, Brownsville begged Austin for help. Houston sent Rip Ford with orders to recruit as many Rangers as he found along the way. Also, at Houston's request, Colonel Robert E. Lee ordered Major Samuel Heintzelman to the Rio Grande with one hundred and sixty five troops. Heintzelman surprised Cortina on the American side, killing eight of Cortina's men, which was when Rip Ford showed up with fifty-three Rangers. Cortina fell back along the Rio Grande, pressed hard by the combined American forces. It was messy business, with settlements and ranches looted and burned along the way, including the customs house and post office at Edinburgh.

Following Lee's orders, Heintzelman stopped at the Rio Grande while Ford boldly followed Cortina into Mexico; Fifty three men chasing two hundred. The Americans suffered badly under heavy fire until a dozen Rangers worked behind Cortina's line and their unexpected charge demoralized the Mexicans, who assumed the Rangers had been reinforced. Cortina was one of the last to leave the field and the marksman Ford assigned to kill the bandit swore that he *must* have hit him.

"I hope not 'cause I don't want Juan Cortina dead, at least not yet," Houston said thoughtfully. "He's more useful alive."

Puzzled, Clancy started to ask what the hell the Governor was talking about, but Houston cut him off.

"Don't you see? This is our chance."

Waving Clancy into silence, Houston gathered his thoughts at he gazed out the window, fingers drumming on his desk.

"Get Bickford," he ordered. "He's probably got his ears flapping right outside the door. Then the two of you go find Ben McCulloch. I know he's in town somewhere. Bring him here as fast as he can."

Once Clancy left, Houston took the opportunity to think the idea through. Was McCulloch the right man for what he had in mind? If not him, then who?

Middling size, black-bearded, and hard as an anvil, Ben McCulloch was raised in Tennessee. If not for a dose of swamp fever, he likely would have died at the Alamo. When Davy Crockett, an old friend of the McCulloch family, was beaten for re-election to Congress he told voters that they could go to hell and he was going Texas. Young Ben promised to meet him in Nagodoches, but came down with the fever. By the time he recovered, Crockett was dead.

McCullough joined Houston's army in time for San Jacinto. After the Mexican surrender, Texas offered plenty of opportunity for a man of his martial talents. In a raid unmatched for size, Buffalo Hump led a thousand Comanche braves all the way from the *Llano Estacado* to the coast, plundering the town of Lynnville. Uncharacteristically, the Comanches were slow getting away. Refusing to give up their booty, as the main body plodded along McCulloch was among the two hundred men who caught them at Plum Creek, killing ninety and sending the rest running for the *Llano*, discarded loot scattered for miles. He scouted for

Zachary Taylor, but quit when he got fed up with Taylor's habit of ignoring information that didn't fit his notions. When the Mexican war ended, McCulloch joined the California gold rush. Elected sheriff of Sacramento County, he was a better sheriff than prospector. In three years, he didn't find a single nugget. Back in Texas, he served as a U.S. Marshal for a while.

Yes, Houston concluded, Ben McCulloch would do very nicely.

Thirty minutes later, he walked through the door.

"Jesus, Sam, can't a man find some peace?" he groused, reaching out a leathery paw to grip Houston's hand. "That boy of yours rousted me out of a nice *siesta*."

"Happy to see you, too, Ben," Houston said wryly. McCulloch's rumpled clothes *did* look like they'd been slept in. "Spend some time with John Barleycorn last night?"

McCulloch grunted and tossed his hat on Houston's desk.

"Take a seat." Houston motioned to a chair. "You can always sleep when you're old."

"I doubt it," responded McCulloch as he eased into the chair. "You're old and you're not gettin' much sleep these days."

Ignoring the gibe, Houston explained the Cortina situation.

"How many men can you raise in, say, three weeks?" he asked. "Rangers and militia?"

McCulloch stared off into the middle distance.

"I'd say maybe five hundred militia. I'm not sure about the Rangers. They're pretty scattered. If my guess about what you're thinkin' is right, they'd be scouts anyhow so I wouldn't need that many."

"That's about what I thought," Houston reached for his pipe to stoke it up again, assuming he found a match somewhere. "It's not nearly enough. They wouldn't be as well armed and supplied as we need either. I'll get in touch with Lee."

"Lee's too smart to fall for this," McCulloch warned, accepting Houston's offer of a cigar.

"He doesn't have to," Houston said. "It's all show. When I talk to Washington, I'll need to say that I've already been in contact with Lee."

"You really think they'll let you invade Mexico?" McCulloch asked, bringing the subject out into the open in his usual bluff way. "I'm all for it myself. But you know Buchanan. He's no good at gettin' started, but he's got a real talent for puttin' a stop to things."

Houston shrugged off the skepticism. When a long shot is all there is, a long shot is what you take.

"Taylor started a war on less. You know that. American blood's been spilt! Brownsville's sacked! Edinburgh, too! The border's in flames!"

McCulloch raised his bushy eyebrows. He looked like a curious bear.

"Sacked?"

"By the time I'm through sacked it will be. Lives are in danger! Innocent people slaughtered!"

Houston stopped his tirade, tamping more tobacco into his pipe.

"How does that sound?"

"Like a lot of damn nonsense." McCulloch ruffled his coarse beard as he thought it over. "You want me to help invade Mexico, but we need the federals to make it official. You want to do it because if you get a unified Texas behind you on this that might make it easier to go independent. Besides, you've wanted Mexico since about ten minutes after San Jacinto. That about right?"

"How many governments since they drove the Spanish out?" Houston asked. "Twenty? Thirty? Most of 'em would welcome us and you know it. We could take Chihuahua, Coahuila, Nueva Leon, and Tamaulipas easy."

McCulloch threw up his hands in mock surrender.

"You don't have to convince me. But it won't help. If Lincoln wins the election, the South leaves the union. If the North doesn't let us go, then we fight, Texas along with the rest. It's comin' and you can't stop it."

Houston stopped opening and closing drawers in his search for a match.

"Delayin' catastrophe is never a bad idea," he said. "Lincoln's not my candidate, but he's not what you think he is. He doesn't have horns, a tail, and cloven feet. The way it's goin', you're givin' him no choice but to fight."

McCulloch wasn't interested. He had his dander up like everybody else.

"Lincoln's just another abolitionist," McCulloch said. "Besides, it's time we admitted North and South are two different countries and stop hidin' behind the idea of a Union that never worked in the first place."

It was as if they found themselves on the edge of a precipice and backed away. The gulf was unbridgeable and they knew it. Best to let it pass and leave their differences mostly unspoken.

"Like I said, I'll be happy to oblige in this little scheme of yours," McCulloch said. "But why not you?"

"The Governor of Texas can't lead an invasion of Mexico. It'd look like a land grab."

"It *is* a land grab, and that's the least of it."

"I know that, but it can't look like it."

"So you want to start one war to avoid another. I swear, there are times when you're as devious as people say you are."

Houston smiled. "Such a thing *has* been mentioned before, from time to time."

They were interrupted by the sound of running feet as the

small figure of Andrew Jackson Houston shot past the open door.

McCulloch looked a question at Houston, but didn't react. Ben was one of the few people who weren't appalled by how Houston let the children run wild. Houston didn't care what people thought. He wanted to give his children the childhood he never had. They'd grow up soon enough.

A few minutes later, Amadeo Montoya, who worked for Delwood Horan, the Senate's sergeant at arms, stuck his head through the doorway.

"Governor?" he asked, embarrassed at having to barge in.

Never asked to do very much, Montoya clearly was uneasy that he was doing something now.

"What is it, Amadeo?"

"Governor, they can't get out."

"Who are *they* and what can't they get out of?"

"The Senate, Governor. They can't get out."

"Why in hell not?"

"Somebody locked the door and took the key."

In a rush of words, Montoya explained that when the Senate ended its session, the Senators found the door closed and locked. Hearing the pounding, Montoya confirmed from the other side that the key was missing. Until now there was no need for a spare.

Which Houston assumed just might have something to do with the sight of his son dashing past the doorway as if his pants were on fire.

"Just a minute, Amadeo," Houston said, rising to his feet. "I have a feelin' this mystery is about to be solved."

He walked to the doorway.

"Andrew Jackson Houston! Get your narrow fanny in here right now!"

The boy liked to hide in a small closet down the hall under

the stairs. He didn't know his father knew it, and until now his father let him have his secret.

"Boy, don't make me come drag you out of that closet!"

Andy's head reluctantly appeared in the hallway.

Houston held out his hand.

"Give me the key!"

Chin quivering as he left the closet, Andy reached into his pants pocket and pulled out the large brass key.

"Why?"

"They was sayin' bad things about you, Pa. I heard 'em. I hear 'em all the time."

"Bad things?" Houston cleared his throat to hide his grin. "Were they now?"

Hand behind his back, he motioned for McCulloch to stop snickering.

"You go home now. We'll talk about this later. And don't tell your Ma."

Houston passed the key to Montoya.

"You can let 'em out now."

With Montoya out of earshot, Houston and McCulloch laughed until tears rolled down their faces.

"That boy has a future in politics," McCulloch said. "He handles those people better'n you do."

41

"I TELL you he's in there now. He's there every night workin' at his desk in a nice bright room. You can see him through the window clear as day. All you got to do is shoot him."

Stackhouse Kurtz, who everybody called Drooler behind his back, saw how that might be an advantage. He might not be the smartest man in town, but he knew seeing a man through a window clear as day would be a help at getting a clean shot.

"How do you know it's him?"

J.P. Dodinhoffer was getting annoyed.

"'cause it *is* him," he whispered. "Nobody else looks like Sam Houston. He's sure not your Uncle Harry. And keep your voice down. One hell of an assassin you are. You're makin' so much noise we might as well have a parade."

"Well I don't know what he looks like and I'm the one 'sposed to do the shootin'," Kurtz said, hurt creeping into his voice. "'sides, I don't have no Uncle Harry."

If it wasn't for the pressing need for quiet, Dodinhoffer would have smacked this big pea wit upside his empty head. Not that the Drooler would feel it. The moon could fall on his head and he wouldn't know it. But it might make Dodinhoffer feel better.

It seemed so easy in the daylight. Five days ago, a man who claimed to represent an organization called the Secret Knights of the Golden Circle offered Dodinhoffer a proposition: One thousand dollars and all he had to do was sneak up on the capital building late at night and shoot the Governor of Texas through a window. A fast horse would be waiting and he'd get away easy.

The man said his name was Smith, although Dodinhoffer suspected that might be short of the full truth. The mysterious Smith claimed he picked Dodinhoffer to do the deed thanks to his reputation as a shootist, which was gratifying to hear. Another thing in his favor was his recent arrival. No one would miss him when he left town.

The fact that his reputation was entirely due to the lies and exaggerations he told about himself was none of Smith's business, not with one thousand dollars on the table.

Coming to a new place, it seemed reasonable to reconstruct his life for future consumption. Careful to keep the details vague, he presented himself as a man who committed mayhem in Arkansas, an affair of honor, you might say. After heading west to the Indian Nations just ahead of the law, so his story went, he was attacked on the road by evil souls out to avenge what he'd done in Arkansas, which forced him to send two more men to hell.

The fact was that he did shoot a man, but not on purpose, and that man probably didn't die unless he bled to death. The rent on his poor excuse for a cabin outside Little Rock was three months past due. The owner, old man Herd, came to either collect the money or throw him out. Dodinhoffer got his pistol from under the bed, intending to wave it fiercely until the old skinflint went away. In his nervousness, he dropped it, it went off, and shot Herd in the leg just above his bony knee.

Dodinhoffer didn't wait around for what might happen next. He rifled the old man's pockets for money and rode away with old Herd screaming for help and bleeding all over the floor. Hope you have better luck with your next tenant, he thought as he galloped Herd's fat nag down the road and out of Arkansas.

But the mysterious Smith of the Secret Knights of the Golden Circle didn't know that. Giving the man his most dangerous look, he declared that the Secret Knights of the Golden Circle should consider the Governor as good as dead...and by the way where would he most likely find the Governor anyhow?

He got one hundred dollars in advance, with the rest to be paid after the deed was done. Tempted to take his newfound fortune and run, the thought of another nine hundred dollars was too much for him. He felt it in his pocket already. After all, he'd already shot one man without meaning to. If he shot a man by accident, it seemed reasonable that he could shoot a man on purpose.

He met the Drooler in the two-bits-a-day boarding house room he shared with four other men. The Drooler was big, ferociously stupid, farted up a thunderstorm while he slept, and shot like the devil himself. The Drooler used a heavy, old-fashioned, muzzle-loading Kentucky rifle that seemed light as a stick in his outsized hands. Shooting was the only thing the Drooler knew how to do well, or at all, and that included thinking. But he did that one thing better than anybody Dodinhoffer ever saw.

In the face of the Drooler's talent, his own marksman-ship seemed a poor thing. He promised the Drooler seventy-five dollars if he made the shot and the next second they were partners in assassination. As such things go, the

Drooler was perfect. He didn't even know for sure what a Governor was.

As they approached the big building in the dark, they saw light shining out of the window. Trees surrounded that side of the building. If they stayed quiet and moved from tree to tree without being seen, they'd make the shot and get away easy as you please.

He'd never shot anyone famous before - hell, he'd never seen anyone famous before - and felt like he might pee his pants. Technically he wouldn't be doing the shooting, but that didn't have a thing to do with the stories he'd tell about it later. He could grow to like this line of work. Maybe he'd become a full time assassin? Did any other governors need shooting?

"I see him," Dodinhoffer hissed as they edged closer to the window.

"Who?" asked the Drooler, forgetting to whisper.

"The Governor you slack-jawed blockhead! And keep your voice down!"

They hid behind the same tree, with Dodinhoffer looking out from the right and the Drooler the left. The shadows were deep enough and the trees thick enough to keep them from being seen by anyone on the street.

"He's old," the Drooler said, as if he'd never seen anyone over the age of sixty. "He's big, too. I wonder if he's bigger'n me?"

"He's not that old and what the hell does it matter if he's bigger'n you? I want you to shoot him, not measure him."

"Who's that?"

The Governor picked up a little girl and put her on his desk.

"One of his brats, I guess," Dodinhoffer said. "It don't matter. That's an easy shot from here. I could make it myself."

They watched as the Governor whirled the little girl

around as if they were dancing and heard her laughter through the window.

"Aw," said the Drooler.

"What's the matter?" Dodinhoffer asked. "You didn't forget anything, did you?"

Now the Governor had the little girl on his lap. It looked like they were writing something.

"I don't think I should shoot him," the Drooler said, finally remembering to whisper. "That girl'd be awful sad."

"What!"

Dodinhoffer couldn't believe it. The nine hundred dollars - minus seventy-five for the Drooler - was practically in his pocket and this muscle-bound ignoramus goes soft on him.

"Look, you damned dunce!" he snarled, forgetting to whisper himself. "You make that shot and you make it now. I don't care if he's got fifty brats with him. We're assassins. Shooting governors is what we do."

In the light from the window, he saw tears glistening on the Drooler's cheeks.

"You're crying!" Dodinhoffer sneered. "You're bawlin' like a baby! I should have known better. Stand aside!"

Dodinhoffer shoved the Drooler with his left hand. It was like trying to move a building. With his right hand he hauled out his old Colt and brought up his other hand to steady his aim. He sensed a movement from the Drooler but paid no attention. A man needed full concentration at a time like this.

In the office, Houston heard a rustle and a soft thump from somewhere outside.

Mary Willie looked up from her stick figure drawing of her father at work.

"What's that, Pa?" she asked.

He lifted the child off his lap, eased out of the chair, and sat her down in his place.

"I don't know," he said, moving toward the window.

He couldn't see anything in the dark. He waited, but heard no more sounds.

"Probably just a critter."

He turned toward Mary Willie with a reassuring smile.

"Time to go home, darlin'. It wouldn't do to keep your Ma waiting."

He lifted her up so she sat on his shoulders as they walked to the Governor's mansion.

They found J.P. Dodinhoffer's body beside the tree. His neck was broken. Whatever the motive for the murder, it wasn't a robbery because he had a hundred dollars in his pocket.

.

42

It was rare when they were all together, especially with young Sam was away at the academy and Houston working late most days. Sometimes one of the girls stayed overnight at a friend's house, although that happened less and less. Texas was full of wild stories about abolitionists or rebellious slaves poisoning the water supply or setting fires. To hear the talk, every slave had murder on his mind and there was no such thing as a natural fire. People were frightened and ready to believe anything.

But tonight they were all here, even Nancy Lea. Could this be the first time the whole family sat down for dinner since they came to Austin? The thought shocked him.

"Margaret, is that true?"

"Yes, Sam, I'm afraid it is," she replied, speaking softly so that no one else heard.

There was reproach in her voice, as if it was his fault. But nothing could spoil his happy mood. Not tonight. He didn't even mind his dragon of a mother in law.

Ladling gravy on a thick slice of turkey breast, he handed

the plate to Margaret to pass down the table to one of the children.

"You know, there are so many of us here by the time I finished serving dinner it'll be time for breakfast," he joked.

The silly remark got the giggles he wanted. Even Nancy Lea smiled. After serving the last plate, he looked around from one face to the next. Young Sam was seventeen now, strong and handsome and stubborn in a way young men can be. Fourteen-year-old Nannie resembled her mother more every day. Unusually precocious for a twelve year old, Maggie wrote better than most adults he knew. Ten-year-old Mary Willie was a ferocious tomboy, with no tree she wouldn't climb, no race she wouldn't run, and no challenge she wouldn't meet. Nettie was eight, bright-eyed and mischievous. Speaking of mischievous, six-year-old Andy was the devil himself. He no sooner got out of one scrape than he'd fall into the next one. Only two, William Rogers was developing his own personality already. Margaret carried Temple, the baby, into the dining room to be with the rest of the family.

They'd just begun to eat, laughing and chattering, when Bickford entered the room. Houston scowled. He left word they were not to be interrupted, but something in Bickford's manner said this was no ordinary message. He waved him to the table. The children didn't think anything of it. They were used to interruptions, although it never failed to irritate Margaret. She yearned for one tiny corner of her life that wasn't constantly turned upside down.

Bowing to the family, Bickford knelt beside Houston and handed over a sheet of paper.

"Sir, I apologize for the intrusion, but the election results arrived, along with some other important news. I felt sure you'd want to know as soon as it came in."

The noisy table went silent, as if even the youngsters knew what they were about to hear would change their world.

"Thank you, Thomas." Houston nodded. "You made the right decision. Why don't you go on home now?"

Apparently a post rider came in and Bickford copied the election results before relaying them to Houston without the accompanying verbiage. That was their usual routine, a way of boiling things down so the Governor wasn't burdened by meaningless information.

"Well, father, who won?" asked young Sam.

Houston looked across the table at his eldest son, face shining with anticipation. The boy has Margaret's eyes, he thought. He always resembled Margaret more than me.

"Nobody won, exactly," Houston said. "But Abraham Lincoln will be the next President."

A frown wrinkled the young man's forehead. "Then how could nobody...?"

"There's more. The South Carolina legislature called for a special convention to decide whether to leave the Union. That's just a formality, of course. South Carolina is as good as gone."

Bickford's carefully aligned numbers told the story:

Abraham Lincoln (Republican) - 1,886,252

Stephan A. Douglas (Northern Democrat) - 1,357,156

John C. Breckinridge (Southern Democrat) - 849,781

John Bell (National Union Party) - 589,581

He never thought it would be this bad. The country was so divided that Lincoln won the election with less than forty percent of the popular vote. That was what he meant when he said that nobody won. According to Bickford's notes, Lincoln did not receive a single vote in Texas and only a handful in the South. If the Democrats hadn't split between two candidates, they'd have won by more than three hundred thousand votes.

"This means war," said young Sam. "There's no going back now."

"Going back from what?" Houston asked. "The South has nothin' to fear. If Lincoln administers the government in accordance with the Constitution, our rights will be respected. If he does not, the Constitution provides a remedy. Nothin' is inevitable unless we make it so."

"Father, how can you be so blind?" His son's face was taut with excitement. "South Carolina is as good as gone. You said so yourself. Others will follow. Just as the colonies left England, the South will leave the Union. There's no reason why one is right and the other wrong. Even Texas will go, despite your ridiculous attempt to divert us and invade Mexico."

"Boy, my *ridiculous* plan would have worked," Houston replied with more heat than he intended. "Even Buchanan liked it, as much as he likes anything that isn't his idea. We had two thousand men ready to move. But once one or two of those little old ladies in his cabinet started talkin' against it, he lost his nerve. Buchanan's problem is the last voice he hears is the one that matters most."

The rest of the family looked on in shock. Even Margaret seemed stunned by how quickly a peaceful family dinner turned into a confrontation between father and son.

"How can you be opposed to people fighting for what they believe?" Sam asked.

"Because what they believe is wrong," he replied. "Texas will *not* go to war if I have anything to say about it. If the South fights, it will lose and all the valor in the world can't change that."

"You're not one of *us* and you *don't* have anything to say about it," Sam answered, practically growling through clenched teeth. "The almighty Sam Houston isn't as grand as he thinks he is."

"Sam, that is no way to talk to your father," Margaret scolded, coming out of her trance. "I won't have it."

"I'm sorry, mother, but it's true. We won't back down. We'll fight if we have to."

"*We* won't back down? *We'll* fight?" Houston asked.

"Come the time, I'll join. I've already promised."

"You will do no such thing," Houston said, rising to his feet.

"Yes, I will!"

"I forbid it!"

"You can't stop me!"

They glared at each other across the table, the young bull challenging the old.

The young man threw his napkin on his plate and left the room in long angry strides.

43

His name was Edmund Cato Sears and he'd come to Texas as a representative from South Carolina and other like-minded states.

He did not like leaving home. There was too much happening. As the flaming center of the revolution, Charleston held abundant opportunity for an ambitious man. Although not yet thirty years of age, Edmund Cato Sears was an ambitious man.

He expected to command a brigade at least. While it's true he didn't graduate from West Point, his two years there gave him more military experience than most. With one or two successes in what would undoubtedly be a brief war, his future in the new Confederacy was assured.

Despite worries about being away, Sears was flattered to be entrusted with such an important mission. Like everyone else, he expected all of the Deep South to secede. Only border states like Kentucky and Maryland were still in doubt. Even so, it was best to take nothing for granted and Sears was charged to make sure that Texas joined its Southern brethren. With its cotton, its manpower, and the ports of Galveston and

Houston, the state was critical to the cause. Its long border with Mexico would make it easier to bring imports into the Confederacy, too. Yes, the state had much to offer. It had much to offer the Union, too. If Texas did not secede, it could be a staging point to attack the soft underbelly of the Confederacy. New Orleans would be threatened and that meant the Mississippi River would be threatened.

Under normal circumstances, there'd be no doubt about Texas's loyalty, but circumstances were not normal. For reasons Sears never understood, Texas had the poor judgment to elect that wretched Houston as governor. Nothing seemed beyond the man, and no betrayal of kith or kin seemed beneath him.

After meetings in Nacogdoches, San Felipe, San Antonio, Houston and Austin, Sears was in Galveston to meet Senator Louis T. Wigfall. A native of South Carolina and a protégé of the great John Calhoun, it was well known that Wigfall despised Houston as much as he loved the South. Sears was empowered to find out exactly what the obstacles to secession were, offer everything from money to arms to help overcome them, and get a commitment as to when Texas would join the Confederacy. It had already been too long.

After a few minutes in the Senator's waiting room, Sears was shown into his spacious office. A window overlooking the port dominated one wall, with the Senator behind a desk with his back to the window. A small man with a thick shock of white hair, a prominent jaw, and a firm handshake, Wigfall's deep, beautifully modulated voice was beautiful to the ear.

Sears explained his mission, although he suspected that the famously well-informed Wigfall probably knew as much about it as he did.

"How much longer will you be in Texas?" the Senator asked, offering a cigar out of a rich walnut humidor.

"With any luck, just a few more days," replied Sears, who preferred snuff but accepted the cigar.

Too late, Sears remembered that one of his roles was that of the diplomat. He smiled to avoid giving Wigfall the impression he had something against Texas and was eager to get away.

"There's too much happening at home for me to stay away much longer," he explained. "The situation changes daily. I just learned that Beauregard took Fort Sumter in Charleston harbor. The federals tried to supply the garrison, but he drove the ships away and bombarded the fort until it surrendered. You can understand my eagerness to return. I have certain, ah, possibilities to look after."

"I understand completely." Wigfall held his unlit cigar between the first two fingers of his right hand and waved it in such a way as to indicate that they were both men of the world. "What happens in the next few months will open a whole new realm of - how did you put it? - *possibilities* for us all."

With the preliminaries out of the way, they got down to business.

"As you know, Senator, South Carolina, Mississippi, Florida, Alabama, and Louisiana have already voted to leave the Union," Sears said. "Others will follow. Tennessee is certain. So are Arkansas, Georgia, and North Carolina. However, there is some concern about Texas, which lags behind. As we see it, the difficulty is the scoundrel Houston."

The mention of his despised rival shook the Senator out of his repose.

"Young man, there you have it," he agreed. "The Governor does everything he can to delay, obfuscate, and deter. His arrogance is infuriating. He's ignored every request to call a special convention to discuss our, ah, *relationship* with the federal government, a convention that would naturally lead to leaving the union. It isn't that he disagrees with us, at least not publicly. He behaves as if we don't exist."

"That can't go on forever, of course. He will be forced to convene a special session of the legislature. There he will work to thwart, delay, and divide us through various parliamentary shenanigans and other diversions that have nothing to do with the issue. If you ask me, the man should be tarred and feathered. I have it on good authority there was at least one attempt on his life and may be others. I don't exaggerate when I say there would not be many tears shed if one turned out to be successful."

Sears was relieved. Now he could report imminent success, and possibly even take credit for it.

"What do you need from us?" he asked. "We're at your service."

"At this time, I'm afraid there's nothing you can do," admitted Wigfall. "We ask for your patience, but not, I think, for long. A few weeks, a month, and we will be with you."

"Despite Houston?" Sears asked. "He is resilient."

"Damn that man and damn everything he stands for, assuming he stands for anything," Wigfall fumed. "We will bring him down, I promise you that."

———

AT THE SAME MOMENT, in another part of the state, there was another meeting between prominent men.

Colonel Robert E. Lee had finally received his long-expected orders to report to Washington. A man of courtesy, ponderously so, at times, Lee rode to Austin from San Antonio to personally inform Governor Houston of the change in command.

"Do you mind of we walk and talk, Colonel?" Houston

asked. "This gimpy leg of mine is giving me trouble. Strange as it seems, sometimes walking helps."

"I'm entirely at your service, Governor," replied Lee, with his usual formality.

Lee was the younger man, but the Virginian seemed like a relic of a more formal time, a bygone era of knee britches and powdered wigs. At two or three inches short of six feet, he was short-legged, and looked more imposing mounted than on foot.

They strolled among the trees surrounding the capital and governor's mansion nearby. Houston walked with a cane. He hated to use it, but it did help.

"This is quite a pleasant day," Lee said, taking a deep breath. "I never got used to the unpredictable weather here."

"Sometimes a pleasant day hides a coming storm," Houston said.

Lee nodded. "And so we come to the point. I have been ordered to Washington."

"To do what?"

"I don't know. Soldiers rarely know their orders before they get them."

"Sometimes civilians have an advantage there. I hear you're to be offered command of the army under Win Scott. Old Win's so fat and arthritic he probably should have retired by now. He must be seventy, if he's a day."

"There is that rumor," Lee admitted. "But there's so much speculation it's hard to tell what's true and what isn't."

Houston waved his cane to shoo away a mongrel dog. There seemed to be more of them running loose in Austin these days. A sign of the times?

"What will you do?" he asked.

"If war comes, and I pray it doesn't, I must go with Virginia. I still can't believe it's come to this."

"Neither can I."

"And what will you do, Governor?"

"I'll continue to do what I'm doing for as long as I can and hope this state listens to reason."

"They circle grows tighter," Lee said. "I don't envy you."

Houston jabbed the end of his cane into the soft dark dirt, the same gesture Jackson often made when they walked the grounds of the Hermitage. The fertile earth reminded him of Woodland. Losing it was an ache that never went away.

"I still have a card or two to play," he said. "I don't envy you either, being thrown into a war you know you can't win."

Lee's eyes hardened. "We'll see about that." He unconsciously smacked his gloved fist into the palm of his other hand. "If those people invade us…"

For the first time, Houston glimpsed the warrior in Lee. He would not want to oppose this man on a battlefield.

They walked in silence, neither man knowing what to say. In some ways, Lee reminded Houston of Polk, although the aristocratic Virginian had an infinitely greater supply of the social graces.

"How is Mary?" Houston asked.

"Her health is difficult, but she is strong. It's hard being a soldier's wife. I'm eager to get back to Arlington. I've been away too long."

"I know what you mean," Houston said. "I've been away more than I've been home for most of my marriage. It's a wonder our wives put up with us. Did Mary ever tell you I almost proposed to her, long ago when the world was young? I didn't do it because I suspected she'd turn me down."

Lee offered one of his rare smiles. He looked younger when he smiled. Houston thought he should do it more often, instead of rationing them out they way he seemed to.

"Yes, she told me about it years ago," Lee said. "The world is a small place, isn't it?"

"She made the right choice, for both of us."

"I think so, too," Lee said, almost smiling again.

"You know, this reminds me of a walk with Ash Smith a long time years ago in Alabama," Houston said. "We were looking ahead, the way we are now. We were sure of the future then, at least we thought so. It was mostly arrogance. You know Ash, don't you?"

"I have that honor, yes," Lee said.

"One difference is that we drank a good deal on that walk," Houston said.

"I don't imbibe," Lee said.

"I don't either, not anymore," Houston said, amused at the formal word "imbibe." "God knows I've imbibed enough for both of us."

Without planning it, they'd walked in a circle and were back where they started.

Lee held out his hand.

"I wish you well, Governor."

"Thank you, Colonel Lee," Houston said, shaking Lee's hand. "Please say hello to Mary for me."

Lee stepped back, snapped off a perfect salute, turned on his heel and walked away.

As Houston watched him go, once again he found himself wishing that he liked Lee better.

He had to stop all this dwelling in the past, too. First he was reminded of the Hermitage, then Woodland, and finally that time with Ash in Marion. He was getting to be a sentimental old man.

44

I⊤ WAS a struggle to get his boots off. Houston got one off easily enough, but he couldn't bend his bad leg enough to get a good grip on the other boot. After struggling and fuming, he finally hollered for Jeff, who tugged if off.

Sitting on the side of the big four-poster bed, he irritably dismissed the young slave and kicked the boots across the room.

"I hate gettin' old, Maggie," he said.

She looked up from her book, her spectacles square on her nose.

"You still look plenty young to me."

The fire in the bedroom fireplace was down to a red glow deep in the ashes. Margaret was covered in blankets up to her shoulders.

"Love'll do that to you, I hear," he said. "Ruins your eyesight."

Someone knocked on the door. Soft at first, then louder and insistent.

"What could it be this time of night?" Margaret asked. "Even the government's got to sleep."

"Only one way to find out," Houston said.

He shuffled to the door in his stocking feet. Suddenly feeling playful, he increased his speed and slid the last few feet on the polished floor.

Margaret giggled. "See what I mean? You're like one of the children sometimes."

He opened the door a crack. The guard who was supposed to be on duty outside the Governor's Mansion stood at attention in the hallway.

"What is it?" Houston asked.

"There's a messenger, Governor. Says it's important and he can only deliver it to you personally. Says it can't wait 'till tomorrow neither."

"Tell him I'll be down shortly."

Instead of struggling with the boots again, he decided to greet the messenger in an old pair of moccasins. If anyone thought it beneath the dignity of the Governor, that was just too bad.

He leaned over the bed to kiss Margaret.

"Sleep well, my love. I don't know how long I'll be."

"Sam, at least take off your nightcap." She didn't bother to hide her amusement. "I'm surprised that boy in the hall didn't fall down laughing."

He'd forgotten all about it, a gift from the children. Although he wore the red velvet nightcap out of loyalty, he knew that it looked ridiculous, the way the tassel fell down over his ear.

He snatched it off and tugged it over Margaret's head. She squirmed, but, trapped by the covers, she couldn't move.

"There. It looks better you anyway."

He moved the tassel to one side and kissed her on her nose. She stuck out her tongue.

The guard escorted Houston to the parlor where he got a lamp burning. The messenger wore a cheap suit that looked like it might fall apart in the rain, trying not to look like what he obviously was, an army officer wearing civilian clothes he wasn't used to on an assignment that made him nervous. Probably a lieutenant, Houston guessed. He was too young to have made captain in the peacetime army. They all looked so young now!

Taking a letter from the messenger's outstretched hand, he reached into his shirt pocket and found his spectacles. He unfolded the letter, glanced down at the bottom of the page and started at the signature: "A. Lincoln." He sat down at the table and pulled the lamp closer.

The letter was brief. It said that when Lincoln became President one of his first acts would be to make Houston a major general in the United States Army. "As an exemplar of Unionism in the South," Lincoln promised all the federal support Houston needed "to maintain your current position," twenty thousand soldiers to put down the secession move-ment in Texas. All Houston had to do was to tell the messenger "yes" and send him back to Washington.

He read the letter a second time. There were no nuances to misunderstand and no way to mistake the offer.

"Do you know what this is?"

"No, sir. I was instructed not to read it. I am Lieutenant Richard Harrigan, assigned to temporary duty on the staff of the President-elect. If I was detained for any reason on the way here, my orders were to destroy the letter. If I didn't read it, I could not reveal its contents. I was instructed to tell you that the President-elect needs your reply as soon as possible. "Speed is critical" were his exact words.

Houston thought it over, absently rubbing the old shoulder wound from Horseshoe Bend. This is one hell of an offer, he thought. And it's too important to decide right now, no matter what Lincoln wants.

"All right, Lieutenant, here's what we'll do," he said. "I want you to come back tomorrow afternoon, at, say, four o'clock."

Harrigan nodded, considerably less nervous now than when he entered the room.

"Got a place to stay?"

"Not yet, sir. I thought it best to come here first, despite the hour. If you approve, I'll try the little hotel down the street I saw on the way here."

"That should do. They always have rooms."

As Harrigan turned to leave, Houston offered a final thought.

"Son, try to relax," he said. "You're supposed to be a civilian. You look like you're on cadet review."

Seeing the lieutenant out the door, Houston went upstairs. Margaret was still reading. He showed her the message from Lincoln and saw the dread in her eyes. He kissed her and told her to go to sleep, although he doubted that she would. Something like this would ruin anybody's sleep.

Back in the parlor, he read the letter a dozen times, as if looking for something he missed, something to tell him what to do. He needed to talk to someone, but who?

Ash Smith was away in East Texas raising a company of men for the war he regarded as inevitable. He paid for the company out of his own pocket, everything from the arms to the uniforms. Even if Smith was close enough to be summoned, they were on opposite sides now. They were still friends, but Smith would be honor bound to reveal such a vital piece of information.

Jeff Clancy wasn't around to help either. He went back home to San Antonio more than a month ago, suffering from terrible pains in his belly. The doctor ordered him to stop drinking, put him on a bland diet, and ordered him to rest. Clancy wept when they said goodbye, convinced he'd let Houston down just when he was needed the most.

Bickford was gone, too, back to Rhode Island, where he intended to join the army, although he sheepishly admitted his family would insist on a captaincy, at least. When he left, the youngster was almost as teary as Clancy.

Houston decided on four men – James Throckmorton, David Culberson, Benjamin Epperson, and George Paschal. He didn't know them as well as he would like, but they were all he had.

———

THEY MET in the parlor a few minutes before noon. Houston didn't want the four men to be seen entering his office. There were too many prying eyes. It was less conspicuous to meet here. He made sure they didn't all arrive at the same time, too.

Houston passed the letter around the table so everyone could read it.

"What, exactly, does this mean?" asked Throckmorton, the last one to read it. Houston could see it trembling in his hand.

"It means exactly what it says," he replied. "Lincoln wants Texas to remain in the Union and he'll do anything to make it happen. Twenty thousand armed men can be very persuasive."

No one else had any questions.

"Gentlemen, I asked you here because I want to hear your thoughts," Houston said, pushing them to say something. "I promise that nothin' you say will leave this room. I want candor, too, not what you think I want to hear."

Epperson wanted to accept the President-elect's extraordinary offer while the others were against it to varying degrees. It was obvious that the boldness of Lincoln's proposal scared them, even Epperson. Houston realized that he probably shouldn't have called them here. He always preferred to listen to others argue while keeping his own counsel. It helped him work out things in his mind. But he was the Governor, not them. It wasn't their job. He shouldn't have been so weak, but it was hard to face it alone.

Houston went to the window, looking outside at the cold day and the leafless trees.

"If only I were a younger man," he said, speaking so softly the others heard the sound, but not the words.

Something clicked. He didn't know how or why, but he'd made up his mind.

"No, not even then," he murmured. "Damn!"

Houston took a deep breath and let it out in a long sigh so that it fogged the window. He lifted his chin as he turned to face the worried quartet at the table.

"Gentlemen, I cannot accept this offer. No matter what might happen in the rest of the country, we'd have our own war right here, one that'd make what happened in Kansas look like church service. I'd have to order federal troops to shoot people I've known for years and it would thrust us into the maw of the very thing I'm tryin' to avoid."

Houston looked from face to face, giving each man a chance to challenge him. Part of him hoped that someone would. But no one did. He had the feeling if he went the other way no one would have disagreed with that either. He felt the need to boost their spirits and show them that the battle wasn't lost, not yet.

"I'm afraid that it's Texas' fate to leave the Union, though I'll do everything I can to delay it for as long as possible," he said. "But what then?"

They looked puzzled at that. Each one glanced at the others, as if someone else might have some insight they lacked, or see something they didn't. Why couldn't they understand? He'd said it many times before. Why didn't anyone listen?

"Leavin' the Union doesn't mean we must join this dangerous Confederacy," he explained. "One does not necessarily lead to the other. Texas was independent before; it can be independent again. *That* is how we can stay out of trouble. We'll return to the Lone Star Republic, not because we want to, but because it's the safest choice given the choices we have."

Reluctantly, he tossed Lincoln's tempting letter into the fire, watching as the flames turned it to ash.

45

Edmund C. Sears
Heavenly Plantation
Charleston, South Carolina

My good friend,

I hope this letter finds you and your family in excellent
health.

As I promised at our meeting in Galveston, we are making
progress in Texas, although events haven't moved as rapidly as I
hoped. As usual, the scoundrel Houston is to blame. Although
the Governor finally called a special session of the legislature, he
managed to delay for far too long any consideration of the wide-
spread sentiment in favor of secession.

At first, the fiend cleverly sidestepped the real purpose of the
special session with claims about a state budget crisis. While the
state does face budgetary difficulties – when has it not? – that
certainly is not uppermost on the minds of its citizens.

With that nonsense finally put aside, Houston produced
another farce. He claimed the present makeup of the legislature
does not accurately reflect the new legislative boundaries drawn

last year. Therefore, he made the preposterous claim that the legislative session should be rendered null and void until new elections can be held.

Once these ridiculous diversions were put aside, to our surprise Houston conceded what we have said all along - that it was best to deal with the issue of secession at a state convention devoted exclusively to that subject. He pointed out your own state of South Carolina dealt with it in exactly that fashion, as did several others.

Only later did we realize what he was up to. Holding a separate convention required that representatives be selected to attend the convention, which meant yet another delay. The man has no ethical foundation at all. He's as slippery as an eel.

Nevertheless, the convention generally went as we hoped, despite Houston's efforts to disrupt it. He actually had the nerve to attend, despite being surrounded by almost two hundred delegates, most of whom wanted to wring his neck. He defied all sense of decorum by placing himself prominently on the dais where he glared at the delegates like an angry old bull.

Although the Governor did intimidate a cowardly few, we held the line. Only six delegates voted against secession, compared to one hundred and seventy one in favor. When the convention opened, I fully expected the vote to be unanimous. Nevertheless, you will be pleased to hear we elected a slate of delegates in time to attend the upcoming Convention of Southern States.

Just when we thought we had won the day, Houston struck again. Working apart from the convention, the legislature drafted an ordinance of secession, which passed by a vote of one hundred and sixty six to eight. Nevertheless, the Governor convinced the milksops in the legislature that passage of the ordinance was not sufficient. He claimed that "such an extraordinary action" must be submitted to the people via referendum. He rallied a sufficient number of weak hearts to his side

*so that now we are burdened by a statewide referendum. I am
humiliated to admit Texas is the only state thus far to require a
popular vote on secession.*

*Please understand, friend Sears, our cause will win by at
least eight to one in the popular vote. But that doesn't stop
Houston. Although he suffers greatly from old wounds and the
ravages of arthritis, he roams the state speaking to anyone
who'll listen, trying to drum up a few shreds of support for his
dying cause.*

*I understand many of his tirades have been booed down. He
has so infuriated the masses - helped, I confess, by our strategic
placement of provocateurs - that his life is in danger. Under
those circumstances, it is extraordinary that he travels alone in
an old buggy without guards to protect him or friends to support
him. Of course, who would defend the devil?*

*There may be a few misguided souls who listen to his
pathetic bleats, but I assure you it won't be long before Texas
joins South Carolina and other Southern states in our glorious
Confederacy.*

*I have other good news to report. The officer commanding
the Department of Texas, David E. Twiggs, of Georgia, is in
sympathy with our cause. Working with an organization to
which I belong, the Knights of the Golden Circle, Twiggs has
secretly agreed to hand over all Union arms, stores, facilities,
and supplies down to the last bullet. In effect, a coup has been
arranged in advance.*

*As you can see, rather than wait while events take their
course, we have proudly taken the initiative.*

Your obedient servant,
United States Senator Louis T. Wigfall

46

HE SPOTTED THEM RIGHT AWAY; five or six rough characters roughly shoving everyone else out of the way to get up front.

They weren't townspeople. He'd bet salvation on that. Two of them were drunk, or well on their way. He could tell by their flushed faces. Nothing like a belly full of whiskey to make a man feel invincible. They weren't carrying shotguns or rifles, so, if they were armed, it was knives and pistols.

A few others scattered through the crowd had been drinking, too, but it only made them noisy and impatient, like children. They weren't professional toughs, not like the hard cases standing not twenty feet away. Funny how there was always an abundance of liquor to rile up the crowd everywhere he went. Whoever paid the bills to dog him and disrupt his speeches was spending a fortune.

Houston was used to the hostility. Most of the time people at least listened to him, except those who were hired to heckle and taunt. Even if they didn't agree, they let him speak. That was all he asked.

But sometimes it turned ugly. Last week in Brazoria, a rock caught him high on the forehead. It didn't hurt, but the sight of blood trickling down his face got the crowds' attention. He had the good sense not to wipe it off, spoke for another twenty minutes, and finished to an ovation. Maybe he should hire someone to throw rocks at him everywhere he went? It'd be easy to find volunteers.

But today was different. There was a sour feeling in the air. Those boys down front were dangerous.

Anahuac wasn't much of a town and he didn't expect much of a crowd, certainly not the hundred and fifty who showed up. He'd no sooner climbed up on the wagon bed in the little the town square than there was a gang of sneering, liquored-up wet brains at his feet. Any townspeople who tried to get close were roughly pushed back, a few even knocked off their feet.

Houston's response was the same as in all the other towns: He ignored them, which infuriated them even more.

As he opened with the same remarks he made in dozens of other speeches in dozens of other places, he saw their intentions easy enough. Pistols and knives appeared as they worked up the nerve to storm the wagon. He'd always known that assassination was a possibility. Now the moment had come. In another minute or two he'd be dead.

His movement hidden by the makeshift podium hoisted on the wagon, he reached under his coat for the knife he kept in a leather sheath at the small of his back. Continuing his remarks as if nothing was amiss, he drew the knife and held it in his fist at his side.

Responding to some private signal, they surged forward. He hoped Margaret wouldn't be too angry with him for getting killed like this. He knew one thing for sure. Sam Houston wouldn't go down easy.

The leader started to mount the rear of the wagon and Houston shifted his weight, knife poised to thrust up under the man's chin. A gunshot blast at his side jarred his senses and seemed to shatter the world. Blinking and stunned, he turned to see Ben McCulloch beside him, looking ferocious with his bristling black beard and heavy eyebrows. Smoke wafted out of the barrel of his Colt, held barrel up at his shoulder.

Three Rangers exploded out of one of the squat adobe buildings lining the square. The lead Ranger cracked the head of one of the toughs with the butt of his shotgun. The blow put the man on his knees, blood pouring from his scalp. The other two Rangers leveled their shotguns at the rest. The one who started to climb on the wagon froze when McCulloch fired his Colt, one leg still on the ground. It was like looking at a painting.

McCulloch smiled, his teeth white against his dark beard.

"Boys, I'd appreciate it if you'd get this trash out of here."

The crowd watched as the Rangers marched the disarmed men toward the Anahuac *calabozo*.

"Where the hell did you come from?" Houston whispered.

"I heard there might be some trouble, so I asked some friends of mine to attend your little talk," McCulloch said, his hard dark eyes roaming the crowd.

He raised his Colt and fired into the air again. The acrid smell of gunpowder strong in the dirty smoke.

"People! People! People!"

Colt poised at his shoulder, he waited for the murmurs to die.

"My name's Ben McCulloch. I disagree with everything my friend the Governor is about to say, but he has sure as hell earned the right to say it. It'd be a good thing to show some manners and listen."

McCullough turned so his back was to the crowd and spoke softly so that no one else heard.

"You can put that pig sticker away, Sam. Nobody'll give you any trouble."

McCulloch holstered his Colt, jumped off the wagon, and leaned against one wheel as if he just happened to show up in time for the speech.

Looking over the crowd, Houston thought that he'd never seen a more peaceful and attentive group of voters.

"I was goin' to say that my friend Ben McCulloch is a good man with a fine sense of timin', but since he disagrees with everything I say, it's best not to bring it up. I wouldn't want to offend him."

If he reached a few, if he made them listen, really listen, then anything was possible. Maybe they'd reach a few more in turn? There wasn't any other way. It probably didn't matter, but it had to be done.

"Since my opening remarks have been scattered to the wind, I'll get down to business. It may be somethin' you don't want to hear, but it needs to be said. Most of you laugh at the idea of bloodshed as a result of secession, but let me tell you what's comin'. To secede from the Union and join the confederacy will lead to war. And you may, after the sacrifice of millions of dollars and hundreds of thousands of lives, win independence, but I doubt it. The North has the money and the men. If it does not whip you by guns, powder, and steel, it will starve you to death. Given time, with all its advantages the North will overwhelm the South. Your fathers and husbands and sons and brothers will be herded at the point of a bayonet. I know that what I say is not popular, but it has the advantage of being true."

"Here is another truth to consider: Despite what you've been told, only a small minority in the North are hostile to Southern interests. Shall we cut loose from the majority for their sake? Secession is being railroaded through the South by the furors of mad politicians, not the by the logic of rational men."

"In my lifetime I have seen this country extend from the

wilds of Virginia and Tennessee, across the Mississippi and into Texas. It scaled the Rocky Mountains and marched on to the Pacific Ocean. During all this it remained free and independent. Tell me, are your rights invaded with no government to protect you? Is the right of free speech and a free press taken from you? Has your property been taken from you? Has the federal government caused you to suffer in any way? The answer to all these questions is no."

"I was taught to believe that plotting the destruction of the government is treason. But now I am called a traitor because I desire to uphold the constitution. The so-called patriots who make that charge claim to have studied the constitution so profoundly they know it better than the men who made it. They intend to violate it because Abraham Lincoln was elected President. Tell me, do they intend to carry that same principle into their vaunted Confederacy? If they do, how long it will last? What will happen if they don't approve of the next election, and the election after that?"

"You know these are not new sentiments. You heard them from me many years ago and you hear them now. All I ask you to do is think about what you intend to do. That is all I or anyone else can ask."

A few applauded. Most did not.

47

STANDING behind her husband at his desk and looking over his shoulder at the returns, Margaret asked, "There aren't any returns at all from some counties. How can that be?"

"That's what fear and hopelessness do to people," Houston replied. "In a state of almost five hundred thousand, with two hundred thousand people of votin' age, only a little more than sixty thousand voted. The pro-Union voters either didn't expect to win so they didn't bother to vote or they were frightened off."

"What will you do now?" she asked. "Everyone thinks you'll fight it."

"I have nothin' to fight it with," he admitted. "I'll just put out a statement announcin' that secession is accomplished."

He swiveled in his chair and hugged Margaret around the waist.

"Oh, Maggie, I don't have many moves left."

After delaying to avoid making the announcement on his sixty-eighth birthday, on the fourth of March Governor Sam Houston announced that after sixteen years Texas was no

longer a part of the United States. The official tally was
46,129 to 14,697.

———

A SECOND OFFER TO keep Texas in the Union by force came
just a few weeks later.

The War Department had sent Colonel Charles Waite to
Texas to replace the disgraced Twiggs, the Georgian who
handed over the garrison at San Antonio to five hundred
secessionists under Ben McCulloch, before Twiggs could do
any further damage. Winfield Scott ordered Waite to "support
Governor Houston or other state authorities in defense of the
Federal Government if the Governor expresses his wish for
such support." The nation was rife with rumors that Houston
intended to hold Austin with a combination of federal troops,
private citizens loyal to the Union, and a few Rangers personally loyal to him.

Inspired and courageous after drinking all day, more than
a hundred Union supporters made a late-night march on the
Governor's Mansion. Torches and lanterns lighting the way,
they stopped at the mansion steps and refused to leave until
they spoke with Houston.

He met them in his shirtsleeves on the steps above them,
leaning on an old hickory cane.

One man stepped forward with a petition that he declared
was signed by every man who could write and marked by
those who couldn't. Houston knew him, a Dutchman named
Groteberg who owned an Austin mercantile. Most of the
Dutchmen supported the Union. One of the reasons they
came to Texas in the first place was to escape the turmoil in
their own country. As his eyes adjusted to the wavering light
cast by the torches and lanterns, he recognized many others
in the mob. Enrique Estrada served him as a courier at San

Jacinto. Now he managed a prosperous *rancho* outside of Austin. Willie Davis was a hatter whose foot was shot off by Comanches. He saw one of the Zavala cousins, too; Jose, the good-looking one. Old Edwin Cornwell, an Englishman who married a well-off Mexican widow, stood shoulder to shoulder with Jasper Grimes, who ran a mill down on the Guadalupe River...he knew so many of them.

Stinking of beer, Groteberg stepped up and handed Houston the petition. The wording was windy but the intent simple: "Those of us who are stout hearts and loyal to the Union" proposed to keep Houston in power by force, "in accordance with your well-known plans." With other union loyalists across the state, they proposed to hold off the secessionists until Colonel Waite made his move.

Houston didn't know who wrote it, but it sure as hell wasn't Groteberg, not with that language. It was probably young Kendell Windham, the firebrand attorney standing at Groteberg's side. Windham reminded him of Buck Travis, another youngster who let his emotions get the best of him and got killed for it.

The wave of memory crested and suddenly Houston was angrier than he'd been in years. He raised his walking stick and cracked it down on the railing so hard that it sounded like a pistol shot.

"Where were all of you *'stout hearts'* when it was time to vote and be counted?" he shouted, his big voice booming over the crowd. "Where were you when Texas needed more than bluster and mobs in the night? By comin' here you do more harm than good. Word of this will alarm every citizen between here and Galveston. We may have civil war in this country, but it will not start here, not while I'm Governor. If you rabble don't disperse immediately, I'll have every damn one of you thrown in jail!"

Cowed by an angry old man armed with a walking stick,

as the liquor wore off in the night air the mob broke up into muttering smaller groups that slowly scattered into the darkness. How could they have been so wrong? When did Sam Houston lose his nerve?

He waited until the last man disappeared before hobbling back inside.

Ash Smith stood inside the doorway, a drawn pistol hanging at his side.

"Put it away, Ash," growled Houston, limping toward the parlor, where the faithful Jeff had stoked up a fire. "This is the Governor's house. We don't need that here, at least not yet."

"If any of those fools took one more step…"

They hadn't seen each other in almost a year. To Smith's disappointment, Margaret and the children, except for young Sam, who was in Bastrop, were visiting her mother in Independence. With feelings running so high, it seemed best to get the children out of Austin.

They settled into comfortable horsehair wing chairs in front of the fire. Houston hiked his bad leg up on a stool. Jeff came in with coffee for Houston and tea for Smith.

Houston gratefully sipped the steaming coffee.

"My God, Ash, have both sides gone mad?"

"The answer seems to be yes," Smith replied, returning to his old sardonic self.

The two old friends stared into the fire.

"I have a company," Smith said.

"I heard," Houston said.

"Outfitted it myself."

"Heard that, too."

"I'm to be a captain."

"Ash, why do this? I'll never understand why…"

"Sam, we've talked about it endlessly, years before most of the rest of the country. We just don't see it the same way. It's between us, but it's not in our way. Why not leave it at that?"

"You're right," Houston admitted, draining his cup. "It's just that these last few months have been hard."

They were silent as they stared into the crackling fire, the comfortable silence of old friends.

"Where will you go?" Houston asked.

"Don't know yet," Smith said. "Moving the capital from Montgomery to Richmond delayed my orders."

Houston slapped the arm of his chair in agitation.

"Richmond's to be the capital? Are they mad? It's only ninety miles from Washington. They might as well dangle it like an apple on a tree."

Smith shrugged as if he expected insanity from his fellow man and was rarely disappointed.

"I agree. Montgomery or Atlanta are better, anywhere but Richmond. I imagine politics dictated it. That explains most of the stupidity in the world."

"And why is the Confederate government issuing orders directly to a captain in Texas?" Houston asked.

Smith gave one of his silent laughs.

"Government's the same everywhere. Nothin' draws attention like a man with a little money and a few connections. They asked if I'd consent to be one of seven delegates representin' Texas to the first Confederate Congress, too."

"Those people better keep a tight rein on their horses," Houston said. "Texas isn't in their precious Confederacy yet."

"Sam, don't even try," Smith warned. "It's too late."

Houston ignored the warning, just as Smith expected.

"What did you say to the offer to go to congress?"

"I told them any body of men stupid enough to declare Richmond the capital was not a body of men with which I wish to associate," Smith said.

Jeff refilled their cups. Once the young slave left the room, Houston spoke up again.

"Ash, I have a favor to ask."

"Anything I can do."

"Young Sam's goin' to sign up. I don't know when. It could be tomorrow. It could be six months from now. I don't want him to know we've talked, but would you see that he serves with you? I don't mean for you to coddle him and I know you won't. But I'd feel better if..."

Smith reached across the space between them and slapped Houston on the knee.

"Consider it done," he said. "I'd be proud to have him."

48

"ALL I DID WAS ILLUMINATE the obvious so that even Jeff Davis could see it," Houston explained to the agitated George Chilton, who, as chairman of the Committee on Public Safety, had come to the Governor's Mansion on behalf of the state legislature.

"Davis and his lackeys have no authority here. It's true that Texas left the union, but that's all it did. It cannot be annexed into another government without the consent of the people."

"Governor, just what do you think the ordinance of secession and the referendum were all about?" replied Chilton, who only now realized that he'd come on a fool's errand. He felt ridiculous standing in the foyer arguing with the obstinate Governor.

"They were about secession," Houston said amiably. "Nothin' more. Texas agreed to leave the Union and it did. Texas did not agree to join any Confederacy, just as it did not pledge fealty to the Sultan of Morocco. Show me where it says anything else and I will be pleased to agree with you."

"But your insistence that *another* referendum is required to decide whether we join the Confederacy is...is...impractical," fumed Chilton, who felt his face warming uncomfortably. "It's so *inconvenient*! The people won't stand for it."

"Democracy is often inconvenient," observed Houston, who enjoyed running Chilton like a dog. "And how do you know what people won't stand for unless you ask them?"

"I warn you, the legislature is not pleased with your behavior," Chilton fumed. "You, sir, are an infuriating man!"

"I am distressed that the legislature is not pleased," Houston said mildly. "And I must be infuriatin', since so many think it."

Chilton cleared his throat, drew himself up, and withdrew a document from his pocket.

"In that case, you are hereby summoned to appear at noon tomorrow and take the oath of allegiance to the Confederate States of America," he said. "All state officers are required to take the oath at that time. However, as your case is a special circumstance, the legislature requires an immediate answer as to whether you will take the oath."

Houston took the document from Chilton's hand. Without bothering to read it, he ushered Chilton to the door.

"Please inform the legislature this is too serious a decision to make on the spur of the moment," he said. "Since the oath is to be taken tomorrow at noon, I will give my answer tomorrow at noon."

"But, Governor, I was instructed...they require...you can't..."

"Mister Chilton, your instructions are not my concern and what the legislature requires is the legislature's problem. You have my answer. Please convey it to your superiors, who are too many to count."

With his big palm on Chilton's back, Houston opened the door and pushed the man out. As he stumbled through the doorway, Chilton couldn't understand what went wrong. When he arrived with the message from the legislature tucked in his pocket, he was certain that he had the upper hand. But if that was so, then why did he feel so humiliated?

With Chilton safely out the door, Houston opened the document and read it through. When he finished, he read it again. Whatever his faults, he thought, that dimwit accurately summarized the contents.

Margaret came into the foyer carrying little Temple on her hip.

"Did you hear?" he asked.

"I expect most of Austin heard."

"Most of Austin probably knew already," he said. "This has been comin' from the moment I went public with the idea that the referendum did not bind Texas to the Confederacy, only to independence."

He handed the document to Margaret.

"What happens to me doesn't matter," he said. "But I've got to think about you and the children."

Without seeming to move, Margaret hiked Temple higher on her hip, a maneuver she'd perfected through eight children.

With her free hand, she slapped her husband hard across the face.

"Damn you, Sam Houston! Who the hell do you think you are?"

Stunned, Houston could only gape. The slap didn't hurt, but the sight of his wife poised to hit him again had him reeling.

"Margaret, you said 'damn,'" he stammered.

"I know damn well what I said," she snapped. "I'll say anything I damn well please."

"But..."

"Oh, be quiet and listen for once. From the day we married, you did whatever you pleased whenever it pleased you do to it. You were away so much the children forgot what their father looked like. We put up with it because we love you. And now - now! - you babble a lot of self-servin' nonsense about consequences to your family. Don't you think it's *just* a little late for that?"

Instead of slapping him again, Margaret pointed a scolding finger directly at his nose.

"We will *not* be some convenient excuse! Take this oath or not, you will stand up like a man and do what you believe to be the right thing, whatever that might be. Do you understand me, Sam Houston?"

Margaret angrily turned on her heel and walked away, leaving her astonished husband standing in the foyer with his mouth open.

————

ALL NIGHT LONG, she heard his footsteps on the floor below the bedroom. She heard it when he took off his boots so not to disturb the rest of the family, and she heard the boards creak while he paced back and forth in his stocking feet.

She knew how his mind worked. How can he take an oath to support a government opposed to everything he believes? But can he do more good if he takes the oath and stays in office? Is the wording of the oath such that he can somehow take it without compromising himself? Does it really matter if he stays in office or leaves it? What can he do? What *should* he do?

The pacing stopped just before dawn and she heard him limp up the staircase.

He held Margaret close and kissed her.

"Margaret, I won't do it."

"I never thought you would," she said, smoothing what was left of his hair. "I'm sorry I slapped you."

"I probably deserved it," he said.

"Yes, you did," she said.

49

A FEW MINUTES BEFORE NOON, he stepped out of the Governor's Mansion. A large crowd waited outside. As it silently parted to let him pass, he cordially nodded at people he knew and ignored questions about whether he'd take the oath. He did not carry a cane. On this day of all days, he wanted to appear to be all the man he ever was.

Careful not to limp, no matter how much it hurt, he walked up the capital steps and down the hall to his office, closing the door behind him. He picked up a rocking chair and carried it to a window. He sat in the rocker, stretched out his long legs, reached into a pocket, removed a clasp knife and a fist-sized piece of wood, and began to whittle, gently rocking back and forth as the chair squeaked on the floor.

He picked this spot because through some trick of acoustics he could hear everything that went on in the legislature's chambers. At exactly noon, R. T. Brownrigg called the session to order. The first name on the list to swear loyalty to the Confederate States of America was Governor Sam Houston. He heard Brownrigg call his name, the man's voice almost cracking from the tension. It was faint, but he clearly heard his name as he whittled, the point of the knife twisting into the wood.

"Sam Houston!"

It was stronger the second time as Brownrigg put a little more mustard in it.

"Sam Houston!"

Houston flipped the wood over and began working the other side. Perhaps a spindle for Margaret? The wood was the right size, though it might not be hard enough for a good spindle. It had been a while since he made anything for her. It always pleased her when he did.

"Sam Houston!"

He heard the faint rumble of voices as the shavings fell at his feet. This time there was an apprehensive tone, as if they just realized that he really wouldn't take the oath.

"Edward Clark!"

Ed Clark must be the happiest man in Texas. All the contemptible pipsqueak had to do to become governor was take a simple oath. They used to be friends, but Clark crumbled under the pressure and joined the secessionists. Having Clark as governor would be about the same as having no governor at all, exactly what the legislature wanted.

He waited until the list was finished. His Secretary of State, E. W. Cave, was the only other officer who refused to take the oath. Pleased he wasn't alone, at the same time he wished there were more.

Now would come the speeches. Houston decided he didn't want to hear them. There'd been enough talk. He went to his desk, musing that it wasn't really *his* desk anymore, although he wasn't sure about the timing. When did he stop being governor? Clark wasn't sworn in yet. Besides, if his argument was correct, if Texas voted for independence but not for the Confederacy, what did an independent nation need with a Governor these last weeks? Texas was in uncharted territory, that was for sure.

He reached into his pocket, removed a letter, and laid it on the desk. Addressed "To the People of Texas," he'd already arranged for the letter to be picked up and distributed to the newspapers.

He decided to go through the basement and leave the back way. He didn't feel like dealing with the crowd outside. As he walked down the stairs and fumbled through the darkness of the basement, a thought occurred to him: he was the only man in the nation's history to be Governor of two states, and the only man to be forced out as Governor of two states. It made him laugh. *That* was an epitaph to remember. Now if he could only get out of this place without breaking his leg in the darkness.

Finding his way out a back door, he returned to the Governor's Mansion and took a seat on the balcony. From here he'd see when it was over. They'd come streaming out of the capital.

After thirty minutes, people began to pour out of the building. It was a festive crowd, with a lot of jovial slaps on the back, whoops, and hurrahs. Someone started singing "Dixie" and they all joined in.

He sensed Margaret come up from behind. She kissed the top of his head and a tender hand caressed either side of his jaw.

"Well, Maggie," he said, holding her hands in his, "it looks like I'm out of a job."

His letter was published in newspapers all over the state, just as he planned:

My fellow citizens,

In the name of your rights and liberties, which I believe have been trampled, I refused to take the oath.

In the name of Texas, which has been betrayed, I refused to take the oath.

In the name of the constitution of Texas, which has been trampled, I refused to take the oath.

In the name of my own conscience, I refused to take the oath.

The office of Governor has no charm for me if it must be purchased at the loss of my self-respect.

I love Texas too well to bring strife and bloodshed upon her. I resolved to make no effort to maintain my authority as chief executive of the state except by the peaceful exercise of my duties and functions. When I could no longer do this I withdrew, leaving the government in the hands of those who usurped my authority.

Perhaps it is proper my career should close in this way. I have seen the patriots and statesmen of my youth gathered to their fathers one by one and the government they created torn to pieces.

I have often declared my determination to stand by Texas no matter what she does. Her people have declared in favor of a separation from the Union and so I go out of the Union with them. Although I see only gloom before me, I will continue to follow the Lone Star with the same devotion I have offered to it for so much of my life.

I stand as almost the last of my kind. I have been struck down because I would not yield those principles I fought for and struggled to maintain. The severest pang is that the blow comes in the name of the State of Texas.

Sam Houston

50

MELANCHOLY OVERWHELMED HIM. He lacked the strength to fight it even if he wanted to. For the first time in his life, Sam Houston didn't care. When he left Tennessee in disgrace, he went on a drunken binge that lasted the better part of three years and almost ruined his life. But at least he cared; that he cared so much was what made it so terrible. When a dark cloud settled over him after Jackson's death, he knew it would pass.

This was something else. He'd ceased to matter, as if everything he did and everything he believed in simply disappeared. At Houston's worst, he could be morbidly introspective and wholly self-absorbed. But this was neither of those things. Something vital was missing, the essence of who and what he was.

Sick with worry, burdens rained down on Margaret. A vengeful legislature demanded the family immediately move out of the Governor's Mansion. They'd have to live with her mother until they figured out what to do and where to go. They spent so little time in Cedar Point in the last few years that the little house above Galveston Bay was practically a ruin.

Despite his many denials over the course of their marriage, Margaret knew that her husband detested Nancy Lea. She used to intimidate him, but that ended long ago. He put up with his mother-in-law because he loved her daughter.

But when she told him they had to move in with Nancy Lea for a while, she got almost no response at all.

"If you think it's best," he said mildly, rocking back and forth on the balcony, staring out at nothing.

They left Austin in seven overloaded wagons. With the spring rains, the roads were a swamp of mud and water. Six times on the first day, they had to stop in the driving rain while Joshua, Jeff, and young Sam unloaded one of the wagons, broke their backs working it out of the soft yellow mud, and then reloaded it. After the second time, they didn't bother to try to keep dry. Sam either slept in the lead wagon with Temple in his arms, or sat quietly beside Margaret while she drove the team.

The addition of ten Houstons meant that Nancy Lea's little cottage in Independence was filled to bursting. With the miserable weather, no one wanted to go outside, but to stay inside for very long risked madness. At times Margaret wanted to scream and tear at her clothes, but she couldn't afford to lose control.

They were saved by an invitation from Asa Hoxey, an old friend of Sam's. A bearded, pipe-smoking physician whose wife died giving birth to their second child twenty years ago, Hoxey invited the outcast family to stay with him for as long as they wanted. His home was a genuine showplace, one of the finest in the state. On a high ridge two miles out of Independence, the two-story house had more rooms than the Governor's Mansion. Deep porches enclosed with glass, still a rarity in Texas' private homes, surrounded the house. The parlor was so big it required two complete sets of furniture.

Twenty-five years earlier, Houston and his staff spent the night in another house Hoxey owned on the way to San Jacinto. The Hoxey's had a new baby then, and Sam spent most of the night playing with the gurgling infant.

"If this baby smiles at me, we'll win the battle," he said, lowering his head and blowing onto the baby's stomach. When the baby waved his stubby arms and offered a toothless grin, Sam laughed with pleasure. "It looks like Santa Anna is as good as finished."

Despite his good cheer, Margaret knew that Hoxey worried about Sam.

"All I can tell you is to be patient," he said. "He's taken so many blows in his life. Be patient, Margaret, and love him. That's the best medicine I know."

As pleasant as it was, after several weeks they moved on, this time to Cedar Point. Margaret sent young Sam and Joshua ahead to get it ready as best they could. The land was overgrown, the house a wreck, the roof leaked, and it wasn't much bigger than Nancy Lea's cottage, but at least it was theirs. She felt a primal need to establish the family in their own home.

"I hate to see you go, but being in a familiar place might be good for Sam," Hoxey said. "The sea air might help, too. He's not coming around as quickly as I'd hoped. Just be patient. I know it's hard, but don't give up on him."

When she started to weep out of gratitude for the man's kindness he took her in his arms.

"I'll have two of my people go with you," he said, holding her close. "Both of 'em are good shots. Things are a little restless on the road these days. Keep 'em with you as long as you need."

They packed the wagons and the little caravan struck out

again. Mercifully, the rains had stopped. The roads still weren't dry, but no longer were they the dreadful, paralyzing quagmires of a few weeks ago. The younger children treated the journey like an adventure, although they didn't understand why their father, usually the best of playmates, was so quiet.

And so Sam Houston passed the months in a world of his own. He barely reacted to the news that Stephen Douglas died of typhoid in Chicago. When Douglas lost the election, Douglas generously swallowed his pride, promised Lincoln his full support, and backed it up with action. He died while traveling in the Midwest rallying support for the Union cause.

Word of a Southern victory not far from Washington left Houston unmoved, too. The Confederates under Beauregard, the Creole peacock who accepted the surrender of Fort Sumter, routed a Union force commanded by Irwin McDowell. When McDowell's demoralized troops fled into Washington, it set off such a panic that the capital was ripe for the taking. But Beauregard's army was as disorganized by victory as McDowell's by defeat, and the Confederates couldn't seize the advantage.

A week after the battle, Houston rose out of his rocking chair on the bluff overlooking Galveston Bay, where the sea breeze kept the summer flies away. He walked to the front porch of the little house where Margaret was mending clothes and looked at his wife as if seeing her for the first time in years.

"Margaret, have I been sick?" he asked, a light in his face that she hadn't seen in months. "It's the strangest feeling."

With a wild cry, she jumped into his arms and covered his face with kisses. And then she began to cry. He didn't understand what all the fuss was about.

51

LIFE WAS busy at Cedar Point. There was acreage to tend and they needed every bit of it. Citing "the controversial circumstances of his departure," the vengeful legislature refused to pay Houston his back wages as governor. The family was penniless. While he owned parcels of land scattered all over the state, the war made land impossible to sell at any price.

For Houston, this was the summer that his first-born son became a man. Although they lived hand to mouth, they never seemed to lack for anything, thanks mostly to young Sam's hard work. His father did what he could, but arthritis plagued him and his leg was worse than ever. They planted corn and potatoes. They raised livestock, including geese, turkeys, and chickens. They even accumulated a little cash money by selling firewood in Galveston.

Late in the summer, Texas was cheered by Ben McCulloch's victory up in Missouri. Confederate troops led by McCulloch and old "Pap" Price, the rotund former Missouri Governor, routed the federals at Wilson's Creek. As unusual, McCulloch was unorthodox and flamboyant, riding into battle wearing a suit of black velvet without a badge of rank.

He disdained an officer's sword, too, preferring his familiar Colt

"He sounds like you, Pa, wearing the fancy suit, I mean," young Sam said.

The young man knelt to lift six newly cut logs bound by frayed rope into the oldest of their two wagons, a rickety thing that threatened to fall apart with every turn of the wheels. Once the wagon was loaded, Joshua would drive it into Galveston and sell the wood.

"I *did* have my own style," Houston agreed, seizing the other end of the logs. "But I don't know about black velvet on a hot Missouri day."

On the count of three, they hefted the wood onto the wagon. Houston grunted with the effort while his son handled it easily.

They'd come to an accommodation about the young man's need to enlist. At eighteen, he could sign up without his parent's permission, but agreed to wait until they got the farm in shape. Margaret hated the idea of her first born going to war, but gave in when he made it clear that he'd go no matter what. Lately, he'd taken to leaving the farm in the afternoon, headed for the other side of Galveston Bay, where he drilled with the Bayland Guards, Ash Smith's outfit. In time, the company would merge into the Second Texas Volunteers.

Houston wanted to talk about what his son would face in the coming weeks and months. Once Joshua was on his way with the wood, they began working on their hands and knees to rid the yard of cockle burrs. After two hours, they took a break for a cool drink from the well. Houston suspected that his son didn't need the rest, but agreed to it for his father's sake. It was as good a time as any to have that talk.

"Son, you've got to walk your own path no matter what I think, but you face a hard road. I'm afraid the name Houston will never be a favorite in the Confederacy."

He dipped the ladle into the bucket and took a long drink, wiping the dripping water off his chin with the back of his hand.

"Men will judge you by a different standard because you're my son. It won't be easy."

"I know, Pa," young Sam said, taking his turn with the ladle. "I've seen it already. I had to hold myself back once or twice, but I think I've won most of the boys over. I'll just have to do the same thing wherever I wind up."

"I'm sure you will, son. I'm proud of you."

"There's somethin' else, Pa." The young man hiked himself up to sit on the side of the well. "I'm not sure how to ask this exactly. If I get into a real fight, *when* I get into a real fight, how do I...?" He stopped, then rephrased the question. "You always said every man is afraid before the fight starts, but..."

"You want to know how to stand fast. When the enemy comes at you screamin' like demons from hell, when men are fallin' around you, when you feel your guts churnin', and every lick of sense you have tells you to run, you want to know what makes a man stick and how you can find some of that for yourself?"

Young Sam son nodded. Like anyone going to war for the first time, he was worried about how he'd behave. Houston remembered the same feeling before Horseshoe Bend.

"What makes you stand and fight, or charge when you think it's hopeless...it isn't country, or president, or some general you've never met, or the land itself. It's not even your sweetheart or your family. It's the man next to you and your best friend down the line. You'll do what you have to do because you'd rather died than let them down. And you'll do it the next time and the time after that because when you're in the middle of it that's what means the most."

Houston watched his son absorb on the thought. After

another drink of water, the young man nodded his thanks and went back to the cockle burrs.

He didn't really understand. Houston didn't expect him to. It wasn't a thing words could make clear, or the kind of wisdom a father could pass on to his son no matter how much he wanted to. He wouldn't understand until it happened, and then, if he was lucky, it would be clear and simple and pure. But it was a hard lesson. He was sorry that his son had to learn it

---

HOUSTON ENJOYED WATCHING the Bayland Guards drill. It gave him a chance to visit with Ash Smith, too. The doctor seemed to thrive on army life.

Standing outside the open flap of Smith's tent, they watched the unit go through its paces. The warm and salty ocean scent was strong in the breeze with the cry of sea birds all around them. Smith was splendid in a stylishly cut uniform of Confederate gray with gold trim. On a whim, Houston wore his old uniform from San Jacinto. It still showed the deep creases from being packed away for so long.

"Good God! Do you ever throw anything away?" Smith asked in mock horror.

"I'm not rich like you," Houston replied. "I can't afford your profligate ways."

"You're lucky you can still get into that old outfit," Smith said, looking Houston up and down. "Most couldn't, not after, what has it been, twenty five years?"

They'd easily fallen into their old bantering ways. Even Smith's conversations with Margaret were the same. At fifty six, Smith's silver hair was thinning, but he still teased Margaret about being married to an old man, and if ever she wanted a nimble youngster he was available.

Houston watched his son's unit as it marched back and forth across the field, the sergeants bellowing orders.

"I wish the boy asked for a commission instead of joinin' the ranks," he admitted. "There aren't a lot of men in our government who'd do me a favor, but I think I could do that much for him."

"A commission is his any time he wants it," Smith said. "He refused it. It meant staying in Galveston when we march off to join Sidney Johnson up in Mississippi. If makin' officer meant staying behind, he wanted none of it. They could make him a general for all he cared."

"Are you sure about that?"

"I got the orders to join Johnson last week and he was offered the commission the day after. I'm surprised he didn't tell you."

"Didn't want to upset his mother, I 'spect," Houston said.

"Besides, he's not doing anything you didn't do," Smith added.

"How do you mean?"

"You signed up as Private Houston, just like your boy, desperate to escape from the family farm. You were about his age, too. A little older, but not much. He's your son, Sam. Don't be surprised when he acts like it."

Houston knew Albert Sidney Johnson well. A West Point man, Johnson served in Houston's cabinet when Houston was president of the Republic. Some thought he was the best the South had, even better than Lee. He'd hit the enemy and hit him hard the first chance he got. And his first born would be part of it.

"It must be true what they say about a man's past deeds catchin' up to him," he said quietly.

"In that case, we're all in trouble," Smith said.

They watched the drilling a little longer, with less than a half hour of daylight left. A crowd of men from Galveston watched, too, several of them eyeing Houston warily. He knew the government was keeping an eye on him and sometimes questioned friends about his activities. It amused him to be considered such a dangerous man.

"Sam, would you like to run the boys a while?" Smith asked.

Surprised at the offer, he glanced at the townspeople, including one man he knew from the Galveston newspaper. An idea came to him that was too good to pass up.

"I'd be honored," he said.

Smith stepped forward. "Men, I'm turning you over to Texas' greatest military man." Turning to his old friend, he announced, "General Houston, the field is yours."

Houston had a little revenge in mind. Despite their bluster, many of the state's leading lights finagled their way out of the war. Quite a few arranged to keep their sons out of it, too. Those who could afford it sent them out of the country, where they were "studying abroad," no doubt for the duration of the war. He ran down a list in his head. Yes, that would do, he thought.

In his old uniform, with his nicked and battered sword at his side, Houston stepped before the troops and swept off his weather-beaten hat.

"Men, tell me, do you see Louis Wigfall here?"

"No," they replied hesitantly, not sure what Houston was up to.

"Do you see Judge Wiley's son here?" he asked.

"No," they replied, getting into the spirit of the moment, their strong young voices rising over the grassy plateau.

"Did anyone see Ed Clark here?"

"No!" roared the troops, thoroughly enjoying themselves now.

Houston went down the list, each name getting a resounding "No."

"Do you see young Sam Houston here?"

By this time the men answered in a roar.

"Yes!"

"Do you see old Sam Houston here!"

"Yes!"

With that, he put the boys through their paces, surprised at how much of the drill he remembered.

52

HOUSTON SET the wagon brake with his foot and climbed down, tired, sore, and glad to be home.

When he was a young man, a place like Matamoras would have been irresistible. He'd have found a way to turn a day there into week. Now he couldn't get away from it fast enough.

He'd put it off for as long as possible, but finally Houston, Joshua, and Jeff drove three wagons south to the border town to buy supplies they couldn't get anywhere else. With the war, Texas was running short of everything it didn't grow or make itself.

He hadn't been there in years, long before they built the bridge over the Rio Grande linking Brownsville and Matamoras. He remembered it as a miserable hole, the kind of place he'd scrape off his boot. The Matamoras he found was wide open and booming, with money, fancy clothes, good times, and grand vices. If law or government existed, he didn't see it. The place seemed to run itself and no one interfered, or wanted to.

It was the blockade that did it, slowly strangling the South.

They said it was Winfield Scott's idea, almost his last action before he retired. Scott called it the Anaconda Plan; simple but brutally effective. So far, Galveston had escaped a direct blockade, not that it helped much. Except for a few raiders, the Confederacy had no navy to speak of and Union ships controlled the Gulf of Mexico. Regular household items sold for ten times their normal price. It was easier for European goods to land in Mexico, usually Vera Cruz or Tampico, and be transported north by land to Matamoras, which turned into a boom town as it filled with people from a dozen different countries. It didn't matter if business was transacted in Yankee dollars, Mexican pesos, French francs, or English pounds. Money was money, except for Confederate dollars, which nobody took anymore. Life was cheap, money was king, and the only loyalty was to profit.

Houston didn't want to leave Margaret and the children at Cedar Point, but he couldn't send Joshua and Jeff off by themselves. It was too easy for two unattached slaves to be kidnapped and sold. It happened all the time. By the time the owners found out, the trail was cold. The only reason Houston kept the handful of slaves he owned was his fear of what might happen if he set them free, which was illegal in Texas anyway. They were safer with him than anywhere else, even if he couldn't afford them.

Margaret was still in a dark mood after watching young Sam march away with Ash Smith's boys. The Bayland Guards linked up with Johnston's army in Mississippi, getting ready for the Confederate push into Tennessee. She couldn't rid herself of the fear that her son was marching to his death. He'd never seen her like this. Sometimes she talked about him as if he was already dead. Houston wished that he hadn't been so specific about the horrors of war back when he was trying to keep Texas out of it. She wasn't even reassured by a letter from her cousin, Columbus Lea. He was serving with Johnston, too, and made a point to look up young Sam. Lea assured her that her son was in good health:

> *He seems to genuinely enjoy the business of soldiering. He's*
> *a young man to be proud of and the men he serves with think*
> *highly of him.*

Leaving Joshua and Jeff to unhitch the teams, care for the horses, and unload the wagons, he walked into the house only to find it empty for a change. Margaret must have taken the children into Galveston. There were two neat stacks on his desk; one of newspapers, the other letters. Feeling out of touch in the weeks it took to travel to Matamoras, do their business, and get back, Houston shuffled through the newspapers until a headline caught his eye: "Calamity in Arkansas."

His eyes moved to a smaller headline just below: "General McCulloch Killed."

He felt dizzy. Fumbling for his glasses, he sank into his chair and pulled the newspaper up close. The story was unusually detailed, as if whoever wrote it knew what they were talking about, for a change. There was a battle in northern Arkansas, just south of the Missouri border. Earl Van Dorn commanded the Confederates, with Ben McCulloch under him. The Union army, led by General Samuel Curtis, dug in at Pea Ridge, overlooking the main road north.

Van Dorn's flanking movement was late getting started and the Union cavalry spotted it. Although his army was dangerously strung out, with McCulloch's men at the point, Van Dorn was in too deep to back off. Everything went well until the support on McCulloch's right was held up. The delay left McCulloch's forty five hundred men dangerously exposed, with the enemy on three sides.

McCulloch had three options: Dig in and wait for help without knowing how long it would take; fall back; or attack.

Characteristically, he made the bold choice. But when an Illinois outfit rallied behind a snake-rail fence at the far end of an open field and stalled the advance, McCulloch called for an Arkansas regiment, shook out a skirmish line, and led it forward, firing a sharpshooter's rifle he'd grown fond of lately.

Houston groaned. McCulloch wasn't the kind of leader who'd order his men forward and stay back himself. And it finally got him killed.

Protected by the tree-lined fence, the Illinois troops waited until the last moment and then delivered a hard volley that sent the out-numbered and out-gunned Confederates retreating back across the field. Despite the setback, they were Ben McCulloch's boys, and they knew what to do. After a few moments, they charged again and this time didn't stop. The defenders fell back, firing as they retreated. An eighteen-year-old private found his general's body just short of the fence. Hidden by the trees, no one saw him fall in the first charge, shot through the heart at close range. Someone, probably a Union soldier, took his rifle and a gold pocket watch.

When word spread that their beloved general was down, his men fell apart. Stunned with grief, hundreds of Confederate troops dropped their weapons and wandered off the field, to be either killed or captured. A few came to their senses and fought, but too few. The battle was lost.

Houston wasn't surprised. If anyone was certain to get himself killed one day it was Ben McCulloch. But while his mind knew it, his senses refused to accept it. He didn't care about the lost battle. There were enough battles won and lost that one more didn't matter. Today's vital road wouldn't mean anything in a week and men would wonder why they fought for it in the first place.

What mattered was that he'd lost a friend who represented

the best of Texas, even when they disagreed on everything under the sun.

His eyes wet with tears, Houston let the newspaper fall to the desk.

"Rest in peace, old friend," he said softly.

No, he thought, that's not right for the man he knew. Instead he prayed that God might give Ben McCulloch a Colt in his hand and a man's work to do.

53

I shook hands with your son on the morning of the seventh,
but after I was wounded I lost track of him. If you haven't
already heard I'm sorry to be the bearer of such news. I'm afraid
that his name is listed among the missing or dead.

HOUSTON CRUMPLED Ash Smith's letter and took Margaret in
his arms. Too grief-stricken even to cry, he felt her tremble
against his chest.

They heard about the big battle up in Tennessee more than
a week ago, but until now the few scraps of information were
incomplete and contradictory. At first it was thought to be a
Confederate victory. At least that was Beauregard's claim
after the first day. "A complete victory" over Grant, he
bragged.

It might have been, too, Houston thought, if only Sidney
Johnston wasn't killed.

Johnston's savage attack at dawn took Grant by surprise.
The Confederates drove the Union army back everywhere
except at the crest of a small hill, where a general named
Sherman cobbled together a defensive line that saved Grant

from annihilation. By mid-afternoon even that was crumbling. Victory by sundown seemed certain.

But everything changed when Johnston went down. Until then the general seemed to live a charmed life. Although several bullets nicked his uniform and one cut his boot sole in half, he wasn't even scratched. His luck ran out when a ball sliced the artery behind his knee. The wound seemed minor and the general ignored it, unaware that his boot was filling with blood. Without warning he reeled in the saddle. Caught by his staff before he fell, Johnston was dead within minutes.

When Beauregard assumed command, the situation still looked good, although the Union defenses gained precious time when thousands of hungry Confederate soldiers threw aside their weapons and stopped to feast on the plentiful rations they captured. With the confusion in his army, Beauregard refused to press the attack after nightfall, preferring to hit a final killing blow the next day. The over-confident Creole didn't bother to form a defensive line, or even replenish his ammunition. The Confederates had pushed back the reeling Union army two miles. Grant was in trouble and both sides knew it.

The battlefield was a nightmare. According to a letter from Ezekiel Atkins, a neighbor's son serving with Beauregard, flashes of lightning in the dark showed hogs feeding on the dead. Houston destroyed the letter after reading it. He did not want Margaret to see it.

Grant was saved when twenty-five thousand reinforcements under Buell arrived during the night. The next day the refreshed Union army hit Beauregard's weary men like a clenched fist. The Confederates fell back, counterattacked, and fell back again. By late afternoon, Beauregard was back across the border in Mississippi, his men too tired and hungry to fight any longer.

"Sam was conspicuous in all the fighting I saw," Ash Smith

said, writing from a Memphis hospital where he nursed an arm wound. *"He fought with the coolness of a veteran. His conduct and bearing was all his mother and father could desire."*

"Unfortunately at the end of the second day Sam and seven or eight others with him could not be accounted for. No one saw them fall but at the same time no one knew their whereabouts. It is my deepest wish that I could offer you more comfort and information, but all we can do is wait."

The butchery was unimaginable. The country had never seen anything like it. More than twenty thousand men on both sides were killed, wounded or missing, almost as many casualties in this one battle than in the Revolution, the War of 1812, and the Mexican War combined.

Still, there was hope. If young Sam fell on the second day, when the Texans covered the retreat, then the Union advance must have swept over him. Houston simply refused to believe that his son was dead.

"Their medical care is better than ours," he explained to Margaret, who frantically alternated between grieving for her dead son and praying he might still be alive. "I'd rather he was treated by them than us. We don't have enough food to feed our army, let alone prisoners. The North can do both. He's probably gettin' better treatment as a Union prisoner than in his own army."

In a second letter, Smith wrote that he'd been promoted to colonel and named commander of the Second Texas Infantry. As soon as he was well enough to travel, he'd join his command in Mississippi. If they didn't hear anything about young Sam by then he'd continue looking.

As weeks turned into months, Margaret couldn't sleep and rarely ate. They were caught in a private hell where they could only wait for a word that might never come.

In a letter to Nannie, who was attending school in Independence, Houston struggled to explain the depth of Margaret's grief while trying to work out his own:

> *Your poor mother is in a state of terrible anxiety. She has mourned until she has almost forgotten what it is like to feel joy. It has taken a terrible toll and I don't know how much more she can stand. Not knowing if your brother is dead or alive is worse than if he died. If he was dead and we knew it at least there would be certainty. As it is we have nothing. We can't bring ourselves to hope because it would be too much to bear if those hopes were dashed. Yet we cannot grieve for his death because it would be as if we killed him ourselves.*

That summer he saw gray in Margaret's hair for the first time.

THE LETTER WAS TORN, stained and dirty. Somewhere along the way, it had gotten soaked and the ink ran, making some of the words barely legible.

Sam was alive! Badly wounded, but alive in a prisoner of war camp in Illinois!

Too weak to write, he found someone to do it for him. His survival was a miracle. Houston wouldn't believe it if it hadn't happened to his own son. Call it an act of God, which Margaret certainly did, call it luck, the view Houston was inclined to take, or call it both.

Covering the Confederate retreat on the second day, Sam was shot in the groin. After crawling a few yards, he lost consciousness. As Houston suspected, the fast-moving federal advance swept over him. Late that afternoon, the overworked Union doctors moved through the carnage, trying to save the men they could while steeling themselves to ignore those who were certain to die. Sam was conscious enough to know that they passed him by, but too weak to cry for help.

That night, a federal chaplain wandered through the bodies scattered across the field, checking for signs of life. Human scavengers, the plague of both armies, had ripped open Sam's knapsack, looking for anything valuable. What they didn't steal lay scattered around his body. The chaplain saw a Bible near Sam's shoulder and picked it up. Inside was an inscription from his mother, with both their names. Dimly aware of a human presence, but to far gone to speak, Sam could only moan in desperation. The startled chaplain found a medical officer and they carried the badly wounded young man away from the gory field.

The next day the chaplain asked the wounded private if he was related to Sam Houston. When he replied that Sam Houston was his father, the chaplain announced that he would not leave the young soldier's side until he was well.

It turned out the chaplain met Houston years ago; one of the signers of a petition to the Senate protesting the Kansas-Nebraska Act. Although he couldn't do much in the face of overwhelming opposition, Houston was one of the few Senators who treated the petitioners with kindness.

Sam wrote that he did not know when he could come home. It depended on the uncertain rate of prisoner exchange and how soon he'd be strong enough to travel. But he was alive! Nothing else mattered.

———

THE DAY WAS SWELTERING. Sometimes September was the hottest month and it felt like it today. On her hands and knees in the soft dirt of the garden, Margaret was planting bulbs for spring flowers, a task she always enjoyed. Jeff worked a little ahead of her. He'd dig a hole and Margaret followed, placing a bulb at the bottom of the hole and filling it back up.

They'd been at it all morning and her knees ached. She got up to stretch her legs. Running a sleeve across her forehead to wipe off the sweat, she saw a grubby bearded man with his forearms resting on the gate, a Confederate soldier whose uniform was in rags, a common sight these last months. Skinny, pale, filthy, and supported by crutches made of saplings, he didn't say anything. He just stared.

Speaking quietly so the soldier couldn't hear, she said, "Jeff, come with me."

If the man needed help, she'd do what she could. Crippled soldiers begging for handouts weren't unusual. They got at least three or four a week. But with all kinds of people on the road these days it paid to be careful.

As they approached the gate the soldier smiled.

"Why, Ma," he said, "I can't believe you don't know me."

54

WHEN THREE UNION gunboats boldly sailed into Galveston Bay, fired off several rounds, and sailed out unopposed, Houston knew it was time to leave Cedar Point.

The shots did no damage. But sooner or later the Union navy would be back, this time in force. Galveston was too big a plum. With New Orleans fallen, except for Vicksburg the whole length of the Mississippi River was in Union hands, effectively cutting off Texas from the rest of the Confederacy.

At least they didn't have to worry anymore about young Sam. After recuperating at home, he returned to the army, twenty pounds lighter than when he joined. Getting back into the war was much against his mother's wishes and led to an emotional scene at home. For the first time in Houston's memory, mother and son argued, an argument that ended in tears.

Margaret eventually relented. She had to. But it was hard to see her fret again.

With his valor at Shiloh, Young Sam was promoted to lieutenant. But after only a few weeks, it was clear that he no longer had the strength for soldiering. His wound, then lying neglected on the bloody field that awful night, did too much damage to his body, and he reluctantly accepted a medical discharge. Angry at the world and not sure what to do with himself, he enrolled in Baylor University.

The day after his son left for Baylor, Houston learned that Eliza was dead.

The news came in a letter from John McGregor, an old friend in Nashville. Houston had to read it twice before he realized exactly who had died. In his mind's eye, Eliza was ever young, not even twenty years old the last time he saw her. It seemed impossible that she could be a woman in her fifties.

He didn't keep up with his first wife, although he'd heard bits and pieces over the years. She remarried, a doctor, so they said, an older man, too. There were children, but two of them died young. Her parents passed long ago. He remembered threatening to kill her father once, just one of too many ugly scenes at that time of his life.

Now she was dead and in the ground. And Houston felt... nothing. Everything that passed between them happened so long ago it was as if it happened to another person. When Eliza left him it changed his life. Good or bad, maybe she should mean something to him, but she didn't. He didn't even feel sorry. For him, Eliza Allen died a long time ago. He'd outlived two wives, although it seemed strange to put it that way. He did not want to outlive a third.

He didn't mention it to Margaret. Eliza was a stranger to them both.

———

WITHOUT ANY KIND of formal decision, or even talking about

it much, they knew that when they left Cedar Point they'd go back to Huntsville, the place they loved best.

The Woodland house stood empty, waiting for someone to live in it, but the owner refused to rent it to them. It was all about politics. Houston was sure of it. Too many people resented his opposition to the war when he was governor, as if that mattered now. The new governor, Frank Lubbock, still had him watched, too. Houston found it amusing, although it infuriated Margaret.

He decided to go to Huntsville and look around for himself, taking Joshua with him to handle the wagon. His eyesight was getting so bad he didn't trust himself on the road. His reflexes weren't what they used to be either.

Although young Sam was at Baylor and Nannie and Maggie were attending school in Independence, they still needed a house of some size in a place where choices were few. When someone mentioned the Steamboat House, Houston laughed it off. Everyone in the state knew about it, but he'd never seen it for himself. After searching for the better part of a week and finding nothing suitable, he decided that he might as well take a look.

From the moment they rounded the bend and the house came into view, he was both appalled and attracted by it. The eccentric design appealed to the part of him that enjoyed such things, but the eccentric layout was troublesome. It would be a chore to convince Margaret that it was possible to live here. She was a woman of tradition and the Steamboat House was anything but traditional.

Houston slowly walked up the steep wooden stairs, leaning on the railing for support. The front door was so warped that it took a series of hard shoves with his shoulder to get it open. Taking their time to be sure they'd be properly equipped to answer all of Margaret's questions, they carefully inspected both floors before going outside to survey the grounds. It took most of the afternoon. His leg slowed him down more and more these days.

Their inspection finished, with his hands on his hips Houston stood on the road in front of the house to take it all in.

Joshua sat on a nearby stump, dubiously eyeing the house as if it might bite him.

"You've been quiet all day," Houston said. "What do you think?"

"It don't matter what I think," Joshua replied. "What matters is what Miz Houston thinks. Half the time I don't even know what my own wife thinks."

"That's no help."

"Married man learns when to keep his mouth shut," Joshua said.

"You've got me there," Houston admitted.

"No, suh," Joshua replied, eyeing the house again, "you got me here."

The location was perfect. It was closer to town than the Woodland house. Margaret would like that. The grounds were pretty, too. Surrounded by crepe myrtle, fig, and cedar trees that helped soften the hard edges of the place, the house was on a small rise less than a mile from Huntsville. A hard-packed dirt road passed in front, with the Oakwood Cemetery a quarter of a mile west. A huge cedar tree provided shade for the front yard, which offered a panoramic view of green rolling hills. Out of sight in a hollow not far to the south were the squat buildings of the state prison, recently turned into a prisoner of war camp.

Margaret's objection wouldn't be the location. The house itself was the problem. The aptly named Steamboat House resembled a Mississippi River steamboat, as if it had been lifted out of the river and dropped on dry land. Houston doubted there was another house like it in the world.

He mentioned the thought to Joshua, who sniffed with disdain.

"You can put money on that. Why would any soul on this earth want another house like that'n?"

"Josh, I'm startin' to think you don't like it," Houston said.

Joshua rolled his eyes in reply.

According to the stories, Doctor Rufus Bailey of Austin College built it as a wedding present for his son. Wanting something special, he drew up the plans himself. The result was a triumph of flamboyance over sense. To Bailey's dismay, the newlyweds thought it was the ugliest thing they'd ever seen and refused to live in it. Houston sympathized with the doctor. Sometimes children were a lot of trouble.

The rooms of the long narrow house lined up one in back of the other on two floors. Some of the rooms were connected by inside doorways while others were not, so there were times when you had to go outside to get from one room to the other. Both floors had gingerbread galleries on both sides. The wide outdoor stairway in front was the only way to get from one "deck" to the other, and the narrow towers on each side of the stairway were the smokestacks of the "steamboat." The parlor was on the "salon deck" upstairs. In addition to the bedrooms and the parlor, there was a dining room, a detached kitchen, and servants' quarters.

As Houston saw it, other than its mad design, it had two practical problems. One was the steep stairway at the front, the "bow" of the "steamboat." With Houston's bad leg, getting up and down the stairs would be troublesome. He could keep the inconvenience to a minimum by taking the dark bedroom on the ground floor behind the stairs. It would be cooler there, too. The other problem he'd just have to live with; going outside to get from some rooms to others, just as on a steamboat. The galleries were covered, but in a hard rain it would still be wet business. Maybe Margaret wouldn't notice flaw until after they moved in?

"Joshua," he announced, "welcome to our new home."

"Oh, Lord, I was afraid you'd say that," Joshua said.

55

It had been a long time since he was asked him to give a speech. He was surprised that anyone cared what he had to say, and even more surprised at the pleasure he felt that someone did.

The invitation came from the Philosophical Society down in Houston. He knew the type, people who got together in weekly or monthly meetings and solved the world's problems with blab and chatter. The way things were going, it would take a lot of both to do the job. When she saw how much the invitation pleased him, Margaret urged him to accept as long as he didn't go alone.

With Jeff driving their big yellow wagon, they bounced south over the rutted dirt road from Huntsville to Houston. He watched as Jeff eased the wagon around a bend, the leather reins held loosely in his hands. The youngster had a gentle touch and the team trusted him.

Houston was in a good mood. The weather was cool enough to be invigorating, but not so cool that his aches and pains kicked up more than usual. His cough wasn't as bad either. He'd lost a little weight, but he felt good, all things considered, with no sign of the weakness in his arms and legs that plagued him recently. Headed somewhere he hadn't been in a while to do something he hadn't done in a while, he looked forward to it.

"You know, Jeff, when I was younger this road seemed a whole lot smoother," Houston joked. "I don't remember that the trip took as long either."

"I'm goin' fast as I can," Jeff whined, his always tender sensibilities wounded by Houston's harmless joke. "This road's one big ol' rut. I can't go no faster and keep us on it."

Houston sighed. "I know, Jeff. I know. I didn't mean anything by it. There's no one could do better."

He wished Joshua was at his side instead of Jeff, but Margaret needed him at home. He could joke with Joshua, who gave as good as he got. Jeff took everything too seriously. You could fart and hurt the boy's feelings. Sometimes spending time with Jeff was positively depressing.

As far as Houston was concerned, they rattled into town not a moment too soon. Jeff stopped the wagon in front of the hotel and unloaded Houston's carpetbag. From here he'd go on to the livery, where he'd sleep in the wagon or in an empty stall.

At least that's what Jeff said he'd do. For all his depressing ways, it was well known that Jeff was popular with women. They loved his soulful look. He'd already fathered at least three babies that Houston knew about. He'd probably tomcat around the whole time they were here. Houston didn't mind as long as he stayed out of trouble. A young man could do worse things.

He flipped Jeff a dollar. Jeff caught it and smiled for the first time in two days.

"Pay the livery and keep what's left for yourself," Houston instructed. "Be back here tomorrow. About ten in the mornin' should do. You watch yourself. Hear?"

Jeff flipped the coin in the air, caught it, and smiled again. He flicked the reins and the team pulled the big yellow wagon down the wide dusty street.

Houston carried the bag inside the hotel. He was eager for a bath. The hotel advertised a bath in every room.

It amused him to see the hotel clerk – a bespectacled little ferret – gape when he signed the register. It was good to see that his name still meant something, if only to oily hotel clerks. Despite the city being named for him, he was not popular in these parts, especially with the war going so badly, just as he predicted.

It was different back east, but still only a matter of time. Houston didn't see how Lee kept going, much less kept whip every Union general sent against him. The man was a magician. The fact that Houston was right about the war still irritated some people. No telling what kind of reception he'd get tonight, but there was no point worrying about it. They invited him. He didn't ask to come.

His turned his attention to the clerk, who looked like he didn't know whether to give his guest a room or report him to the authorities. As a result, he just stood there, managing to look insulting and uneasy at the same time.

"My key?" asked Houston mildly.

That jarred the little man into action. When in doubt, do what the customers ask. Rare is the business that went bust following that sensible policy.

His room was on the ground floor of the four-story hotel, just as he requested. Stairs were a bother. As advertised, the room came with a private bath. It wasn't as fine as the hotels back east, but it was good enough. The hot bath helped. Especially after a trip on a bad road, old age came with too many aches and pains. Unfortunately, the condition appeared to be permanent. The nap afterward did him good, too.

Refreshed and alert, he took special pains with his appearance. After so long of not having to bother, it felt good to make the effort again.

As a concession to what promised to be a warm night, Houston wore a white linen suit. With his recent weight loss, the suit hung more loosely than he liked, but there wasn't anything to be done about it. He packed beaded moccasins instead of boots or shoes. With a reception after the speech, he'd be on his feet a while. Hard leather hurt his leg too much. He had the beadwork on the moccasins redone for the occasion. It wasn't the quality of the original Cherokee workmanship, but it was still beautiful, especially when the multicolored patterns of the beads caught the light. Carefully brushing what was left of his hair, he unpacked a white, broad-brimmed, flat-crowned hat and took a few minutes in front of the mirror to get the angle right. He hated to see a man plant his hat square on his head. No style to it.

His speech would not be long. In fact, it was short enough to memorize, although he'd take a copy with him. He didn't have the stamina for long speeches anymore and doubted that the audience had an appetite for the kind of windy orations that used to be his specialty. He went over what he planned to say one last time, walking back and forth while he practiced.

As promised, there was a rap on the door forty-five minutes ahead of the time set for this speech. Two representatives from the philosophical society would escort him to the hall a short carriage ride away. At the last second, he decided to leave his cane behind. He did not want the audience to see that he needed one.

They arrived at the hall, which turned out to be the new Freemasons Hall, and entered from the alley. He was introduced to the usual people, a blur of names and faces. A few he knew already. Most he did not. He didn't bother to try to remember the names of those he didn't know. It was a politician's trick, and he was no longer a politician.

The only way to get to the stage was a narrow stairway of a dozen steps that took a sharp turn to the left halfway up. He silently cursed himself. In his enthusiasm, he didn't think it through. Of course, he'd speak from a stage. Of course, there would be stairs. He should have brought his cane, but damned if he would ask to borrow one or lean on a stranger's shoulder. Talk would spread about how Sam Houston had turned into a feeble old man. He might be half-crippled, but, by God, these people wouldn't see it.

If he was by himself, or with family and close friends, he'd take the steps slowly, one at a time. One leg up, followed by the other leg to the same step. Then do it all over again; slow but steady. But his pride wouldn't let him do that now. There was nothing for it but to go up those steps like he was young and nimble. Vanity might be a foolish thing, but he would not give it up.

With a deep breath, he took the first step, using his good leg. Swinging his bad leg up to the second step, he felt a stabbing pain when the leg took all his weight.

Another step, another jolt of pain, worse this time. It felt like his leg was on fire.

At the turn, he pivoted on his good leg to keep his weight on it for as long as possible. One step, then the other. Every time his bad leg held his weight it felt like it might buckle. He held his breath to keep from gasping from the pain.

His insides clenched as he mounted the last step and lurched toward the front of the stage, where a podium faced the hall's empty seats. His face covered with sweat, his big hands clutched the sides of the podium for support. Fortunately, the others came up behind him and didn't see what it cost him to climb a few steps.

"Yes, this is very good," he said, leaning on the podium. "This should do very well indeed."

He stood to his full height, keeping his weight on his good

leg. He asked for a glass of water. The request sent them scurrying as if he'd asked for something it took five men to do. The diversion gave him time to recover, although he knew from experience his leg would throb for most of the night.

The heavy red velvet curtain fell at the command of a disembodied voice somewhere offstage, to be lifted just before the event started. He waited patiently on a chair behind the curtain, one in a row reserved for the dignitaries filing in one by one. As the front doors opened, he heard the hum and rustle of people entering the hall on the other side of the curtain.

The curtain raised with a whooshing sound and the introductions began after a round of applause. After a few brief remarks by three different speakers, it was his turn.

"My fellow citizens," Houston began, "to be asked to speak here is the highest compliment that could be paid to this old citizen, soldier, politician and, dare I say, patriot."

He was pleased to see that the hall was full, with a few standing in the back.

"You have come here to listen to what I have to say, knowing the days draw near when all thoughts of ambition and worldly pride give way to the passing of time. I ask you to bear with me a while as I express a few thoughts that come out of long experience."

He'd offer a positive picture of the war, or as positive as he could make it. God knows Texas was desperate for good news. He'd keep it vague enough to avoid any outright howlers.

The North was weary of the war, he said. That much was true, he thought. What nation wouldn't be weary of the astonishing casualties? With the growing anti-war movement in the North, he added, anything could happen, especially with the election next year.

He told them that the South, especially Texas, might find

an ally now that French troops were in Mexico. Using the pretext of unpaid debts, France had recently installed a puppet dictator in Mexico City, an Austrian archduke named Ferdinand Maximilian. Houston predicted French involvement in Mexico years ago, although almost everyone scoffed at him then.

"Where are those skeptics today?" he asked. "I confess that I cannot predict the result of this war with the same confidence I predicted the presence of the French in Mexico. I can only offer what I have mentioned as possibilities, or perhaps even probabilities. But no matter what, let us go forward and nerve ourselves for nobler deeds and defy the hosts that our enemies bring against us. We can do anything! *Texas* can do anything! In me you see a man buffeted by the waves of time. Once I dreamed of an empire for a united people. That dream is over. But it is not too much to ask for other dreams to replace it."

At the reception afterward, at big crystal punchbowl in the middle of the room, he ran into E. W. Cave, the only member of his cabinet who refused to take the oath of allegiance to the Confederacy. Like Houston, Cave was something of an outcast, although he looked prosperous enough.

They shook hands and a wide smile spread over Cave's narrow face, exposing tobacco-stained teeth.

"Governor, I was surprised to hear certain *assumptions* in your speech," Cave said quietly. "Do you really believe all that about the North giving up and the French coming to our aid?"

Holding Cave's bony hand in his own, Houston put his other hand on Cave's shoulder and drew him close.

"Not a word of it, E.W.," he whispered. "It was just something these poor folks needed to hear."

Cave's smiled even wider than before.

"Still up to your old tricks, aren't you?" he said.

56

HOUSTON ENJOYED SITTING in his old rocker by the road in front of the house. The warm sun felt good. He usually wore a wide-brimmed hat, a pair of worn soft yellow moccasins, and old patched clothes. With his leg propped up on a stool, he'd smoke a bit, usually a pipe, but occasionally a good cigar, whittle toys for the children, and chat with passersby.

He was coughing again, a wet racking that came from deep in his chest. His weight was down, too. He rarely felt strong enough to ride a horse anymore. When he did, he tied a cane to his saddle horn for support when he dismounted.

When Houston felt up to it, he'd go over to the state penitentiary and spend time with the Union prisoners of war. He enjoyed hearing about their homes and campaigns. Some of the townspeople thought his behavior scandalous. He enjoyed that, too. It was fun to be scandalous again.

He used what little influence he had to see the prisoners weren't confined to their cells twenty-four hours a day. He even convinced the prison superintendent, a nervous young man named Tom Carothers, to allow some of the prisoners to go into town in groups of no more than three at a time.

"These men aren't criminals, they're honorable prisoners of war," he argued. "My son was a prisoner of war, and he was well treated. Can we do less?"

Carothers wanted to do the right thing. But running a prisoner of war camp was no job for an uncertain man carrying the added burden of a conscience. He didn't have enough food for his own men, much less the prisoners. He didn't have enough guards either. They were mostly wounded veterans released from service. If the prisoners ever rioted or decided to make a break, there wasn't much Carothers could do about it.

Houston negotiated with the ranking Union prisoner; a colonel from Indiana named Enoch Shrake who was captured in Mississippi by Nathan Bedford Forrest's cavalry. Shrake refused to promise there would be no attempts to escape from the camp itself, but gave his word no one would try to escape if the men were allowed to go into town in small groups.

One hot afternoon riding back from the camp, Houston was caught in an afternoon shower. Back at the Steamboat House, he foolishly took a nap without changing his wet clothes. The next morning, he woke up with chills and a fever.

To catch what little breeze there might be, Joshua and Jeff moved his bed from the wall to the center of the room beneath the stairway in the front of the house. When he had trouble breathing, they used pillows to prop him up to a half sitting position as the days passed in a feverish delirium.

Awakened by the thump of boots on the walkway outside, he saw the bright sunlight through the open door blocked by a figure of a man. Houston weakly raised his hand to shield his eyes.

"An old soldier like you can make a better salute than that."

"Ash!"

Smith picked up a ladder-back chair by the window,

carried it to the side of the bed, and sat down. His gold-trimmed Confederate gray was impeccably tailored. A dark plume decorated his hat, which he hooked over the back of the chair. Gold filigree covered the hilt of his sword and matched the design on his scabbard. His black boots were polished until they gleamed.

Straining with the effort, Houston pushed himself higher in the bed.

"Aren't you a splendid sight. You must plan to show yourself to the federals so they'll lay down their arms at the sight of such magnificence?"

"That's it, exactly," laughed Smith. "I always thought you had a head for strategy. It couldn't have been *all* luck at San Jacinto."

Houston's laughter turned into a spasm of coughing that racked his body and left him weak and trembling. Smith poured a glass of water from a pitcher on the bedside table. Houston gratefully accepted it with both hands, drained the glass, and weakly leaned back against the pillows.

"It's good to see you."

"Sounds like it," Smith said. "How are you?"

Houston ignored the question.

"I see you've been promoted. Things must be desperate if they made you a general."

"After Vicksburg and Gettysburg, desperation would be an improvement," Smith admitted. "I'm headed to Matagorda. They put me in charge of the Gulf Coast defenses."

"What's this about Vicksburg and...what was the other one?"

"You haven't heard about our latest disasters?"

Houston shook his head against the pillows. How long had he been here? He started coughing again and reached for more water. Smith pushed him back and refilled the glass, sitting on the edge of the bed and holding the back of Houston's head while he drank.

"Grant took Vicksburg," he said. "Pemberton did his best but once Grant got his teeth into it there was no chance. The Mississippi belongs to the Union now. At practically the same time, Meade beat Lee in Pennsylvania. A place called Gettysburg. They say there were more than fifty thousand casualties."

"Good God!"

Houston seemed to shrink in on himself as he sank deeper into the pillows. It was impossible to imagine so many killed and wounded.

"Did you see Margaret?"

"Oh, yes. I wasn't sure I should disturb you, but she threatened to have Joshua tie me up and drag me in here if I tried to leave. I always said you married above your station."

"As I recall, you told me not to marry at all."

"I was thinkin' of Margaret's life with a reprobate like you."

Houston sensed that Smith was going to ask about his health again and tried a diversion.

"How long can you stay?"

"This is it, I'm afraid. I've got to get over to the coast. They could hit us any time. I shouldn't have stopped, but I was so close I had to see you. I can't say when I'll get back."

"When you do you can stay longer," Houston said. "I'll be up and around by then."

It was obvious that Smith did not believe him. Why should he? Houston did not believe it himself. But Smith took his old friend's lead and avoided the subject.

"I expect nothin' less," Smith said. "This house is enough to make anyone queasy."

Smith rose out of the chair. He reached out and Houston

took his hand. They held for a moment, neither man saying a word. It wasn't necessary. After all this time, they knew.

"Goodbye, Sam."

"Goodbye, Ash."

Smith took his hat from the back of the chair and walked out the door. The last Houston heard was the thump of his boots.

57

"IT'S PNEUMONIA, Margaret. You should make preparations. I don't know how long he'll last."

Doctor Peter Kittrell glanced at Doctor T. H. Markham, who nodded his agreement.

"It's just a matter of time, and probably not too much time," Markham said. "He might come out of this coma before the end, or he might not. It's impossible to say. I hate to be so blunt, but you should know the truth."

They stood at the foot of the bed in the center of the small bedroom. Propped up by pillows, Houston's face was gaunt, his eyes closed, and his breathing rasping and labored. Despite the warm weather, blankets were up to his chest, with his arms outside the blankets. In a chair beside the bed, Jeff slowly fanned his master's face with an ornate Mexican fan. Every so often the young slave erupted with a loud sniff.

Margaret wanted to run and hide from the bone-deep sorrow that robbed her of feeling and energy. She saw her husband dying, but, with the finality of the doctors' cold pronouncements, for the first time she knew, really knew, that she would lose him.

"Are the children here?" Kittrell asked.

"All but young Sam."

She felt distant from the world around her, as if the voice she heard was not her own.

"He went down to Matamoras with my cousin, Charlie Power. They're on a buying trip for the whole town. I don't imagine they'll be back for at least a week."

———

THEY CAME when word spread that death was near. Tom Carothers, the prison superintendent, was first. The children were in and out of the small room, too. Nannie held her father's hand, staring at his face as if she could somehow will him to live. Hat in hand, Joshua stood at the side of the bed, his black cheeks wet with tears. Others came and went, friends, foes, and some who weren't sure. There was a feeling of disbelief in the room, as if it never occurred to them that Sam Houston was mortal, and they had to see for themselves.

Lying on a pallet on the floor beside her husband, Margaret thought that she might have slept a little that night. She'd slept so little in the last few days that she didn't trust her senses. Stiffly, she rose to her feet to see the faithful Jeff still working the fan.

"You go along now and get some rest," she said. "There's no sense breaking yourself down."

He gently closed the fan, laid it on the bedside table, and walked out the door. She watched him stagger to the big cedar tree, curl up at the base, and immediately fall asleep.

Taking Jeff's place at her husband's side, Margaret opened the family Bible to the fourteenth chapter of John and began to read aloud: "In my Father's house are many mansions; if it were not so I would have told you. I go to prepare a place for you." She spent an hour reading the Bible. Sometimes she read aloud, sometimes to herself, hoping to find comfort that wasn't there.

It was almost sundown. A half-dozen people crowded into the little room, with Margaret sitting at one side of the bed and Maggie on the other, her fingers touching her father's arm.

He moved, a jerk of his head, and mumbled something, but neither Margaret nor Maggie heard it. With his breathing so shallow, it was a moment before Margaret realized that it had stopped. Maggie let out a choking cry and lowered her head.

Calm and unhurried, Margaret kissed him for the last time. She held his big hand to her cheek, and then removed the simple gold band his mother, Elizabeth, gave her son when he went off to war more than fifty years before. Inside the band was a simple inscription: "Honor."

As she rose to her feet, someone, she wasn't sure who, asked, "Did he speak? What did he say?"

Distracted from her grief, she looked around at all the eyes glazed by sorrow.

"What does it matter now," she said.

That night, Margaret wrote an inscription in the family Bible: "Died on the 26th of July, 1963, Genl. Sam Houston, the beloved and affectionate husband, father, devoted patriot, the fearless soldier – the meek and lowly Christian."

58

WHEN THEY WERE TOLD of Houston's death, the prisoners of war asked if they could make his coffin. Margaret gratefully accepted, knowing how much her husband enjoyed his visits with them.

Four prisoners carried the simple pine coffin to the Steamboat House the next morning. Dressed in a dark suit, Houston's body was placed inside. Presbyterian minister Dr. John M. Cochran presided over the funeral service that afternoon in the upstairs parlor.

The summer heat broke with a light rain a few minutes before the funeral procession left the house. With Margaret following, the pallbearers carried the coffin out of the parlor, down the steps, and across the muddy road to the Oakwood Cemetery a quarter of a mile away. When the first part of the procession reached the cemetery, the end had not yet left the house.

With the exception of one item, Houston left everything to Margaret. Regarding that item, his will read: "To my eldest son, Sam Houston, Jr., I bequeath my sword worn in the battle

331

of San Jacinto, never to be drawn, only in defense of the Constitution, the laws, and the liberties of his country."

Carothers walked back to the prisoners' camp with Shrake, the union officer, at his side.

"I liked him, truly," Carothers said. "But if he was as shrewd as they say, why did he fail at most everything he ever did?"

EPILOGUE

NANCY LEA

THE DEATH MARGARET's mother anticipated for so long came a few months later, on February 7, 1864. Her remains were placed in her metal coffin and put away in her vault in Independence. She was eighty-four years old.

JOSHUA

The story goes that not long after Houston's death, knowing of Margaret's financial problems, Joshua asked to speak to her. He poured his life savings on the table, all the money he'd saved from his work outside the Houston home, and offered it to Margaret. The amount was reported as between two and three thousand dollars.

Margaret refused the gift and made Joshua promise to use the money to educate his children.

After the Civil War, Joshua built the first home in the new

Rogersville section of Huntsville, where he had a blacksmith shop. Elected Walker County Commissioner in 1882, he served as a delegate to the National Republican Convention in 1888. He died in 1901 at eighty and is buried in Oakwood Cemetery in Huntsville.

————

ASHBEL SMITH

Smith spent most of the rest of his life in the cause of higher education. He helped establish the University of Texas at Austin and was one of three commissioners appointed to establish an "Agricultural and Mechanical College of Texas, for the benefit of the Colored Youths," now Prairie View A&M University. In 1878, President Rutherford B. Hayes appointed him a commissioner to the Paris International Exposition.

Smith never married and died in 1886 at his plantation near Galveston.

————

MARGARET

With her husband's death, Margaret was impoverished. Friends went over the family accounts and managed to arrange a trade of land for a house not far from her mother's cottage in Independence.

In 1866, three years after her husband's death, the state finally paid Houston's back wages as Governor, which allowed Margaret to pay off most of her creditors.

When a yellow fever epidemic swept through Texas, she worked as a volunteer to nurse the sick. She contracted the disease and died on Dec. 3, 1867. She was forty-eight years old.

Although she asked to be buried next to her husband, public ordinance mandated immediate burial for yellow fever victims. Margaret was buried in the Independence cemetery, without even a minister to perform the funeral service.

THE CHILDREN

Within a month of his father's death, young Sam rejoined the army, sending home drawings, sketches, and poems of war life. He was with the Confederates under General Kirby Smith who surrendered at Alexandria, Louisiana, at the close of the war.

After the war, he attended medical school at the University of Pennsylvania and opened practices in Belton and Waco. He eventually quit medicine and spent the rest of his life writing poetry and short stories. He married in 1875 and died in 1894.

Nannie raised her youngest siblings after her mother's death and died in 1920.

Of all the children, Temple was most like his father. Elected to the State Senate in 1885, the colorful trial lawyer roamed Texas and Oklahoma, defending anyone who needed it, scoundrel or saint. He died in 1905.

Andrew Jackson Houston was the longest lived. Twice an unsuccessful candidate for Governor, from 1924 to 1941 he was superintendent of the San Jacinto Battlefield. On April 12, 1941 he was appointed to fill a vacancy in the U.S. Senate, the oldest man to serve in the Senate to that time. He died on June 26, 1941. He was eighty-seven years old.

A LOOK AT:
AND HELL FOLLOWED WITH HIM

A story that crosses oceans and continents from before the Civil War to the years just before World War II, a uniquely American story.

Ranald MacKenzie can do anything, at least that's how it seems to friend and foe alike. From Bull Run to Appomattox, the tireless and endlessly resourceful MacKenzie marches from one victory to the next, no matter how seemingly impossible the assignment. Promoted to general at only 24, he seems impervious to pain and incapable of failure.

When the Civil War ends, MacKenzie's reputation shines even brighter when he is assigned to the Plains Indian Wars to take on the invincible Comanche led by their great war chief Quanah. But there is a price to be paid for 25 years of almost constant and always brutal warfare...

Based on the real-life story of Ranald MacKenzie, whose eventual illness – possibly PTSD almost a century before anyone knew what that was – and terrible end saw him virtually erased from the pages of history; a bare mention, when he is mentioned at all.

AVAILABLE NOW

ABOUT THE AUTHOR

The author of eight novels, Robert Wisehart was born in Indianapolis, Indiana, and now is fortunate enough to live in Santa Fe, New Mexico.

In between Indianapolis and Santa Fe, he worked for many years as an award-winning reporter and columnist for newspapers in Florida, North Carolina, Louisiana and Northern and Southern California, plus occasional flirtations with radio and television as an on-air commentator. Such is the changing world that three of the four newspapers no longer exist.

Later, as a free-lance writer Wisehart did everything from write speeches to ghost books. He labored as a restaurant critic and for a brief time as a one of the dreaded horde of government consultants, two words that can mean almost anything but usually add up to not much. His work has appeared in more than 200 newspapers and 30 magazines, plus several digital outlets.

Wisehart and his wife, Dana, have been married for a lifetime and intend to make it a very long lifetime indeed. They have moved much, traveled well and Dana easily is the best thing that ever happened to him. Their two sons, Marc and Carl, live in New York City.